The Quiet Dead

BY THE SAME AUTHOR

The Wayward Muse (2005)
The Stones of Camelot (2006)
The New Faust the Tragicomique (2007)
The Shadow of Frankenstein (2008)
Sherlock Holmes and the Vampires of Eternity (2009)
Frankenstein and the Vampire Countess (2009)
Frankenstein in London (2011)
Eurydice's Lament (2015)
The Mirror of Dionysus (2017)
The Pool of Mnemosyne (2018)
The Painter of Spirits (2019)

non-fiction:
The Plurality of Imaginary Worlds (2016)
Tales of Enchantment and Disenchantment (2019)

The Quiet Dead

by
Brian Stableford

A Black Coat Press Book

ISBN 978-1-61227-901-5. First Printing. October 2019. Published by Black Coat Press, an imprint of Hollywood Com-
ics.com, LLC, P.O. Box 17270, Encino, CA 91416.

CHAPTER I

When Paul rang the bell of the apartment, the door was answered by an aged maidservant, whom he recognized, but was unable to greet by name. She had no difficulty in addressing him as "Monsieur Furneret," however, even though she probably did not remember him; his brief return to Paris had been announced in advance by letter, and he was expected.

He was shown into the drawing room, where Jane de La Vaudère was waiting for him, dressed with a casual and simple elegance, carefully posed between two Buddhas, one cast in bronze and the other carved in wood; the space on the wall behind her was occupied by the painting of a siren that she had bought from him four years ago, in 1901; whether that was the location that it occupied permanently or whether it had been hung there especially for the occasion, he had no idea, but he was slightly surprised that she had hung that picture in her drawing-room rather than the portrait of her that he had painted. Where was that, he wondered?

"Paul," she said, advancing to meet him, immediately establishing a comfortable informality with that single syllable and the attitude of her extended arms, "It's wonderful to see you again—at last. It's not good of you to have stayed away for so long, always promising an eventual return in your letters but never keeping the promise."

"It's unforgivable, Jane, I know," he said, taking her hand and kissing it, with only a slight awkwardness. "I'm a wretch—but I've suffered from not seeing you for four years more than you can possibly have suffered from not seeing me." He hesitated as to whether to hand over the parcel he was carrying under his arm immediately, but as his hostess seemed to be deliberately not looking at it, he decided that it would be better to wait until she gave him a signal.

"What a wicked thing to say," she said, inviting him to sit down next to a small table where tea would doubtless be served in matter of minutes. "You're making me out to be light-minded and forgetful, at last by comparison with your grave seriousness, but you have no idea how tedious Parisian society is when one is perpetually on probation, perpetually unforgiven for entirely imaginary sins, and starved of understanding of one's work."

"I read the newspapers, Jane," he said. "Toulouse isn't the edge of the world. They're full of praise for you every time a new a book comes out."

"Diplomatic praise," she said, dismissively, "the professional courtesy of apolitical journalism. Not that I'm ungrateful, mind—I'll take ever crumb of comfort I can get, and I still have a few good literary friends here, even though some of the old crowd seem to spend more time in the Midi or in Normandy than in the capital—but you know what a tyrant I am, jealous of everything, and I can't help seeing your absence as a treason of sorts. Green or brown?"

The tea had arrived, in two large urns, on a wheeled trolley.

"Brown, please."

"Lemon?"

"Yes, please."

Jane passed the request to the maidservant with a flick of the wrist, and waited for her to withdraw before taking up the conversation again. Now, she did look at the package, as if an exchange had become appropriate now that his tea had been poured into a Sèvres porcelain cup.

"It's very small," he said, apologetically, "but I hoped that you might have a corner somewhere that could accommodate it." He glanced round as he spoke. The decoration of the room although some stern observers might have considered it a trifle cluttered with *objets d'art*, seemed a little less flamboyant than the last time he had seen it. His memory was a trifle vague, but he was certain that two of the more garish Hindu statuettes had been removed.

Jane unwrapped the parcel with delicate precision and held up the small painting for inspection. Paul had been understandably apprehensive about this meeting, after such a long absence, but now that he was in Jane's presence he could feel himself relaxing; it seemed to him that the unique bond they had formed during the hectic days of their first acquaintance, never entirely severed by distance, was being spontaneously magnified again by proximity.

Did she feel something similar? he wondered. Was that even possible?

She looked up from the painting, to stare at him in a fashion that she had not so far done. She was not a hypnotist, but the attention of the blue eyes nevertheless had an effect on him, as it had the very first time she had looked at him in that way. Then, being unfamiliar, it had been intimidating; now, recalling a fond memory, it seemed welcome and reassuring.

"A sphinx," she said. "Or, I suppose, to put it more pedantically, a sphinge. Lovely breasts, and the eyes, as usual, are positively magnetic. Is this because I told you that I was working on an Egyptian novel?" Her voice was still light and polite, but it seemed to him that he sensed a genuine warmth in it, as if she too were glad, and slightly surprised, to find that a long-dormant intimacy had not deteriorated in the least.

"Partly because of that," he replied. "It's too late, alas, to provide any inspiration, as the book's imminent publication has already been announced, but it seemed not inappropriate as...a gesture."

"Indeed not—I'm delighted. I shall probably hang it in the dining room—or perhaps in my boudoir, where your painting of me has pride of place. Are you returning to mythological themes, then? The paintings you've sent to your dealer during the last two years have been...different."

"I never gave up entirely," Paul told her, "but the material I send to Paris tends to conform to what people in Paris seem to want to buy. My...more obviously fantastic works obtain a better reception in Toulouse. But I knew that you would appreciate the sphinx, for precisely the reasons that the majority of your contemporaries might not."

"Is that a disguised way of suggesting that I'm perverse?—no, don't answer that, of course I am, and I shall refrain from making any remarks about the tide of fashion, in part, because it's a tide from which I've sometimes benefited, and railing against it makes one seem so old. I am old, of course, but I haven't yet consented to admit that I seem it...and please don't bother to tell me that I haven't changed a bit, because I know what I see in the mirror. I might be what you term psychically blind, but with the aid of spectacles, my ordinary sight is quite sharp."

"Everything changes," Paul said, knowing that she was fishing for the compliment, "but beauty isn't a mere quantity that observes a strict negative proportionality with age. You're as beautiful now as when I painted you, and yours is the kind of beauty that improves with age, like good wine for the connoisseur palate."

"I've heard that one before," she said, smiling—presumably because she had, indeed, heard it before, more that once—"from tongues whose hypocrisy have devalued it somewhat...but from you, I'll accept it as sincere, and hope that you haven't spent the last four years cultivating the cunning that you didn't have when you were last in Paris, and were so charming in your innocence."

"Even if I had become a master of calculated insincerity, my dear Jane," Paul assured her, "I wouldn't employ it with you. I owe you too much to be dishonest with you."

She smiled again. "That's a miscalculation of our account, I fear," she said, "but I'm glad of the error. And I can say with all sincerity that you've becomes significantly more handsome than you were before, time and maturity being on your side, although there is...a certain melancholy about you. I'll admit that I feared that your troubles might have taken a heavy toll, and that the deliberately optimistic tone of your recent letters might be a mask hiding a deeper malaise. Your

.

paintings"—she lifted the sphinx, which she was still holding in both hands—"always tell a slightly different story."

"I could say the same about your books," Paul observed.

"Touché," she conceded, readily, "which is exactly why I have suspicions...excuse me for a moment." She stood up and went to place the painting carefully on an étagère whose Japanese vases were sufficiently widely spaced to leave room for its temporary storage, evidently not wanting to ring for the maidservant for the moment. Paul noted that her movements were slightly stiffer than the feline glide of 1901, but still gave evidence of natural stylishness as well as educated deportment.

When she returned to sit down and pick up her teacup, she restarted the conversation, with an accomplished smoothness, at a different point

"Are you looking for premises in Paris," she asked him, "with a view to moving back here, now that your reputation is established and...there's nothing keeping you away?"

"No," Paul told her. "It's just a brief visit—a matter of a few days. I have other people to see here, to whom I have important questions to pose, but I also have...things to which I need to return."

"Ah!" she said "By things, I presume you mean a woman? You've found a new inamorata?" She seemed to be trying hard to manufacture approval, but it did not quite ring true. In her mind, he suspected, he was still classified as an idolater, not entitled to have any other goddess but her, even though, consciously, at least, she knew that the vanity was inappropriate, and even though she sincerely wished him well and would have liked him to be happy.

"No," he replied, attempting to affect a wry smile. "I don't have a new...inamorata."

"Oh, Paul! It's terrible, I know, to feel a certain gladness when someone dies, but to be honest, when you wrote to tell me that Père Culose had collected Juliette, I simply wasn't able see it as an unalloyed tragedy. I thought that, after a decent interval of mourning, you might take advantage of your freedom to form...well, yes, I'll say it explicitly, and hope you'll forgive my bluntness: a healthier relationship. You don't know how many times I've cursed Antoine, God rest his soul, for telling you that you had to be kind to that girl, knowing full well that you would take it so seriously."

"In all fairness to Antoine," Paul said, judiciously, "he did warn me, even while advising me to be kind, that relationships between young artists and models always end badly, and he also advised Juliette to be kind to me, in a fashion that she took to imply that the kindest thing she could do was to get out of my life completely."

Jane was clearly startled by that, and her brow furrowed, pensively. "He never told me that," she said, "but I suppose he wouldn't—the old rogue delighted in using patient confidentiality as an excuse for covering up his little games. He told you to be kind to me too, obviously, because he gave everybody the same advice—but when he told me to be kind to you he took great care to observe that relationships between relatively well-off women of my age and young men of your age were an infallible recipe for short-term heartache and long-term disaster. Not that I wasn't well aware of that, of course...and there was no way, whatever Antoine Cros might have thought about it, that I was going to allow you to leave Paris without painting me first, no matter what we might have been risking. Nothing, as it turned out...but that's by the by. Juliette didn't take his advice, then?"

The line of questioning was indiscreet, but Paul was already convinced that it was not mere curiosity, and the license he had given Jane for indiscretion for years ago was still fully valid. In fact, he found that he wanted to talk to her about it—to her, specifically, because she was the only person who knew enough about what had happened in Paris to understand what had happened in Toulouse

"She wanted to take it, at first," he told her. "I had to work hard to talk her out of it."

"Is that why you decided to paint that second Jeanne d'Arc and insisted on taking her to Toulouse in order to do it?"

"No, I'd already decided to do that—but I had to press the case hard to stop her refusing. Antoine was a great surgeon, but as a psychologist, I can't help suspecting that he was less than perfect, and not just because he took such pride before he died in being elected king of an imaginary country. He really didn't know me at all, on the basis of an acquaintanceship of a few hours...and he certainly didn't know Juliette."

Paul lowered his eyes as Jane looked at him with what seemed to him to be a little too much speculative intensity, perhaps wondering exactly how many liberties she could take, given that any objective observer would surely opine that she and he hardly knew one another, in spite of the fact that they had been exchanging regular correspondence ever since he had left Paris, apparently without the slightest inclination on either part to let the communication fall into desuetude.

Finally, she said: "Did you love her very much?"

Paul hesitated for some time, but eventually said: "No. I didn't love her. That wasn't part of the arrangement."

If she had been startled before, his hostess now seemed positively aghast. "You lived together for two years without...sleeping together?" she said, incredulously. She had long grown accustomed to playing fast and loose with the boundaries of the conventionally unmentionable, and while he was painting her portrait they had conversed together often enough and long enough to establish a confidentiality that their letters had preserved, but she was well aware that she was now being indelicate as well as intrusive. He did not mind in the least; it was not a matter that he could have discussed with anyone else, but Jane was different.

"We slept together," he told her, "for convenience and comfort—but she had warned me before we even left Paris that she was no longer capable of loving anyone, and that she long since abandoned the belief that it was any longer possible that someone might love her. She was probably right on both counts...although, while we were together, I didn't have any inclination to sleep with anyone else, and to the best of my knowledge neither did she, so if, as is sometimes alleged, fidelity is the sole criterion of true love..." He left it at that.

"It's not," was all that his hostess could say to that, for the moment. Her novels, while ambivalent in many other respects in regard to "the mystery of Kama" never doubted that there was far more to authentic love than mere fidelity.

"I agree," said Paul. "Hence my judgment: no, I didn't love her. Whether I'm actually capable of loving anyone, I don't know. Time will tell...or perhaps not. Doctor Cros seemed to think that I was in more danger of falling in love with you than with Juliette, and he was probably right, which might be why he suggested to you that it wouldn't be a good idea to give me the opportunity, or at least that it would be as well not to encourage me to do so...but that's all speculation, and the poor fellow's dead, so he won't be able to examine us again and offer us an updated diagnosis."

"Of which we have no need," said Jane, thoughtfully. After a slight pause, she sighed and said: "Given that discretion seems to have gone out of the window already, in spite of the good resolutions I made this morning, I might as well let curiosity get the better of me. If you didn't love Juliette, why on earth were you so determined to take her with you to Toulouse?"

"I needed her."

"For the painting? You can't possibly have thought that!"

"No—the painting was just an excuse to keep her with me."

"Then I don't understand."

"That's my fault. I've been writing to you for four years, and never explained...it didn't seem to be a suitable subject for a letter. It's probably not a suitable topic for afternoon tea, either, and I hadn't intended to embark upon such a deep matter so early in our reacquaintance...but I had hoped to find or to manufacture an opportunity to discuss it with you in depth before I return to Toulouse, because you're one of the few people who might be able to understand."

"Well, now that you've whetted my appetite to that extent," she said, "there's no possibility that I can let you leave without hearing a full explanation, even if you have to stay for dinner...which I was intending to invite you to do you anyway if...well, if it didn't seem inappropriate."

"You were afraid that I might have changed so much that you'd be only too glad to get rid of me as soon as possible?"

"Don't be ridiculous Paul. But you might have changed sufficiently to want to reestablish our relationship on...less familiar terms that we seem to be about to contrive. To tell you the truth, I was hoping that we might have an opportunity while you were here to discuss...subjects of intense curiosity...and while I can't honestly say that I'm not one to beat around the bush, I'm versatile enough to crash straight through it when I feel a sense of urgency. So tell me the story—the true story."

Paul took time out to pour his hostess a second cup of tea, and then filled his own cup.

"I'll have to start at the beginning," he said, "or I won't be able to keep it straight in my head. You remember the four sketches I made at Flammarion's séance?"

"Vividly.

"And you remember the journey home on the train from Juvisy to Paris, when Antoine played the skeptic to perfection, striving to convince me that I had not, in fact, drawn the spirits of four dead people, including his brother, but that I had simply drawn material from my unconscious mind, which had been screened there by a process analogous to what Flournoy, in his then-recent book about Hélène Smith's supposed visions of Mars, called cryptomnesia?"

"Of course. The occasion is deeply etched in my conscious memory, for reasons you know.

"I do. By the time I got back to the studio that night, I was at least half-convinced that Antoine was right, and I wanted desperately to be convinced, because I wanted fervently to believe that Martine wasn't dead—but the doubts lingered, if only because I was so acutely aware of my own desperation. The whole business had been so strange, do disturbing and so disorientating that I was...well, I think I was still under the influence of Zosima's suggestion, whether or not that suggestion was aided by any kind of psychic magnetism or psychic gravity. I was still disorientated the next morning, and my uncertainties were complicated and compounded by the series of visitations I received, from Antoine, you, Talia and Zosima. By the time I started painting in the afternoon, my head was in a spin. I hoped that painting would calm me down and absorb me thoroughly, to restore a kind of mental stability...and in a way, it worked...perhaps far too well. It absorbed me very thoroughly indeed, and put me back into what I still call, for want of a better term, a trance state."

"I remember," Jane said. "You told us about it when you reached Antoine's house. You were speaking lightly, but I could tell that you were seriously distressed. I was concerned, and I should have tried to intervene to stop Antoine putting you and Zosima on trial again...but curiosity got the better of me, I fear."

"It had the upper hand on all of us that night, even poor Talia. At any rate, for me, at least, things became seriously weird when I lent myself to Zosima's suggestion for a second time. Again, when I woke up in that bedroom, after losing several hours, I was extremely disorientated, and when you took me to see what I'd drawn, I was immediately petrified, once again, by the idea that I had drawn the dead—that I'd drawn Jeanne d'Arc and Juliette, and that Juliette had been murdered, just as Martine had drowned...of which I was ninety per cent convinced by then. It turned out, almost immediately, that Juliette hadn't been murdered, that she had not only seen a murder but had apparently gone into a trance state herself, if not induced by my painting, at least shaped by it...and the hallucination she'd suffered had caused her to jump into the Seine, where she might easily have drowned.

"Again, Antoine wasn't at a loss to provide an immediate explanation of how I'd come to draw what I'd drawn because of what was in my mind at the moment when I lent myself to Zosima's suggestion, and he could undoubtedly have produced a similar account of why Juliette had jumped in the river and why Talia suffered a fit of hysteria that nearly killed her by provoking a pulmonary crisis. But even though each of those explanations might have seemed to hold up if considered individually, it seemed to me that the coincidence of all three of them happening simultaneously added an extra dimension of implausibility. And it wasn't simply a triple coincidence. You told me that Flammarion had also reported that he had had a vision, albeit a familiar one, and you...well, you admitted yourself the next day that you hadn't been quite yourself."

"Yes," said Jane, in a neutral tone, "I did admit that."

"And you also told me, shortly thereafter, that I really had drawn the dead at the Observatory, and gave me what seemed to you to be conclusive proof of the fact."

"Yes," she agreed, "I did that too."

"Which, as you can surely imagine, renewed and amplified my uncertainty and cast me into utter confusion."

"I'm sorry," Jane said. "I should never have told you...what I told you. I have no idea why I did it, given that I maintained the lie so steadfastly with everyone else. Antoine had confused me as well as you, stirring my feelings...and he knew perfectly well that it was a sore point. He had no right to speak to you the way he did in that railway carriage...but he just couldn't resist showing off...and he allowed his own curiosity to run riot."

"He came to see me the next morning to apologize," Paul said, "and to explain why it was more than a mere matter of curiosity for him. Obviously, it was more than a matter of curiosity for you too—and for me, perhaps most of all, it certainly wasn't. I wanted to know what had happened to me, and what might happen to me in future. I wanted to know exactly what kind of weird phenomenon was contained in the dark recesses of my mind, and I wanted to investigate that as carefully and minutely—and as safely—as possible.

"Zosima, of course, wanted to magnetize me again immediately, in order to feed her own curiosity, but the last thing I wanted was to conduct my own research under the spur of her suggestion, magnetic or otherwise. I wanted to be in control, to the extent that I could be. I wanted, desperately, to know whether the apparent psychic links that had been established between me and other people were real or illusory, and what, if they were real, their implications might be.

"In order to carry out that investigation, I needed the assistance of one of the people with whom I seemed to have been linked. For practical reasons, there was only one available candidate: Juliette. So I knew, before I went to see her in the hospital the last time, that I had to persuade her to come to Toulouse with me. Love had nothing to do with it—on my part, or on hers. I wasn't entirely straight with her about the precise reasons for my wanting her to come with me, but she was absolutely straight with me—she told me in advance that she didn't and couldn't love me, and that it would be purely a matter of practical convenience."

"And you believed her?"

"Yes, I did. There was no reason for her to lie."

"You don't know little girls the way I do," Jane murmured.

"Probably not, in general terms," Paul agreed. "But I think I got to know Juliette as well as anyone could. I don't believe that she was lying, even to herself."

Jane seemed to think about that for a moment or two, and then asked: "Was she happy? During the two years before Père Culose came to collect her, I mean. Was she happy, living with you?"

In his turn, Paul had to think about that for a moment. It wasn't an easy question to answer.

"No," he said, finally. "Not exactly."

"*Not exactly!* What's that supposed to mean."

"In simple terms no, she wasn't happy. She was always anxious, frequently sad, perhaps perpetually feeling guilty that she hadn't done what she thought Antoine had advised her to do, worrying that she was holding me back somehow, preventing me from finding a better relationship with someone else, and not liking herself for the jealousy she felt in wanting to have me all to herself. Nothing I said could convince her that she not only wasn't doing me any harm but was doing me good. But then, when she got seriously sick and was coughing blood almost without remission...her attitude changed, and she gave me a different story."

"What?"

"She said that she was sorry for having been so ungrateful. She said that now she had had a chance to look back over her entire life—which wasn't very long—the last two years had been far and away the best. She said that if she hadn't been able to be happy, that was entirely her fault, because she had had every opportunity not to be unhappy, and every incentive, but simply hadn't been able to do it. But happy or not, she said, they'd been the only two years of her life that she's actually lived rather than simply enduring them, and that they'd made up for the rest—that they'd finally given her a reason to think that it had actually been worth living. She said that encountering me was the only good thing that had ever happened to her, and that she was stupid for not having been able to appreciate it more. So, no, she wasn't happy living with me...not exactly.

"She also said that she was lucky that I hadn't been able to love her, because, if I had fallen in love with her, I'd have been sure to fall out again, and then I would have left or discarded her; but as I was just being kind, she knew that she could rely on that, because no matter how ungrateful she seemed, no matter how unhappy she seemed, and no matter how unlovable the consumption made her, she knew that I'd keep on being kind. So she thanked me for not loving her. Given that it was impossible that anyone could love her, she said, kindness was the best that she could hope for, and she was extremely lucky to have found some, because, in her opinion, there was far less kindness in the word than love, and it did infinitely less harm."

Privately he thought that Jane could certainly understand and agree with that, if her books were anything to go by—and he certainly had no intention of asking her questions as indiscreet as the ones that she was asking him; that was not the way their arrangement worked.

"She said all that, and you think she didn't love you? You really don't know the first thing about little girls, do you? And you did all that, and you think you didn't love her? She doesn't seem to have been able to give you much help in your self-exploration. All that and fidelity too? If you'd lived to be a hundred, you'd have been Baucis and Philemon."

Paul managed to laugh at that, as if it were a joke, but any frivolity that had been in the conversation at the beginning had vanished completely now. He filled his teacup for the third time and renewed the slice of lemon, although the lemon was drying up in the bowl and the tea was no longer hot. Jane took a sip from her own cup and pulled a face, but she did not ring for the maidservant in order the replacement of the urn. She looked at the window; it faced westwards, but the elevation of the houses opposite was already insufficient for the sun still to be visible over the rooftops, even though the afternoon was not far advanced. Dusk was still some way off, but the shadows were already projecting a certain suggestion of gloom into the room. There was no need as yet to employ artificial lighting, but Paul glanced at the chandelier, which had contained candles last time he had been in the drawing room, rendered virtually redundant by the gaslights accommodated in the walls. It had not yet been adapted to carry electric bulbs.

The twentieth century was already a century of rapid progress in Paris, manifest inside houses as well as in the streets, where the memory of Baron Haussmann's transfiguration had not had the opportunity to grow old before everything was being ripped up again for the relentless expansion of the Metropolitain, under the Seine and out into what had once been surrounding villages but were now mere outlying districts of the sprawling City of Light.

Antoine Cros had installed electric lighting four years ago, but Jane had not. She was still living in the nineteenth century, in terms of vulgar residential illumination

After a long pause, during which Paul simply waited for the inevitable question—the question that would mark the crucial watershed in the discussion—Jane de La Vaudère eventually said: "And have you seen Juliette since she died?"

"No," said Paul, and added, pedantically: "I don't *see* the dead; at least, not consciously—you know that. If I actually saw them, the problem of figuring out exactly what kind of freak I am would be much more straightforward than it has proved to be."

"A slip of the tongue," she said, and only hesitated slightly before adding: "I infer, then, that you *have* drawn her—more than once."

"Yes."

"And you haven't sought to avoid the haunting? Quite the reverse, in fact?" She knew him well, and had just proved it.

"I don't think that there's anything I could do to avoid it," Paul admitted. "Or, for that matter, to encourage it. And even if your suspicion that I loved her without being aware of it has no substance to it, I had been living with her for two years and I sat beside her for many long hours while she died, slowly. There's every reason why she should have been present in my mind for a long time thereafter. If Antoine were still alive, and I consulted him about the drawings, he would undoubtedly say that there's absolutely no reason to think that there's anything slightly supernatural about the fact that my peculiar somnambulism has produced numerous sketches of Juliette over the last two years."

"He said exactly that to me to me when your portrait of Talia went on display, a few weeks before he died," Jane said. "It was the last time I saw him—the last serious conversation we had, at any rate. I wasn't with him when he went to see the painting, but once he'd seen it, he was eager to discuss it with me...Camille, I suppose, seemed too far away in Juvisy, and Zosima, although still only a fiacre ride away, was even further away spiritually...and in any case, they hadn't been in that railway carriage. They hadn't been...bound together in the way that the three of us were...which raises the question..."

"Yes," said Paul. "I've sketched Antoine too...and you."

She raised her eyebrows. "I'm not dead," she said.

"Nor was Juliette, on the night I drew her at Antoine's house," Paul reminded her. "Zosima and Camille, you'll remember, both mentioned the book that members of the British Society for Psychical Research had recently published, called *Phantasms of the Living*...and my correspondence with Camille has kept me up to date with their investigations of what he and they call telepathy. Antoine would dismiss all that as nonsense, of course, and say that it's absurd to look for a supernatural reason why I might sketch people who aren't dead...especially people that I think about often and intensely...but there's still a puzzle."

"Antoine wouldn't think so," Jane opened, thoughtfully. "I don't have to be hypnotize to imagine him sitting with us in a third armchair, sipping his green tea, and saying, with ruthless common sense, that you're an artist, so there's no reason at all to wonder that instead of walking in your sleep, like vulgar somnambulists, you draw. And he'd say that since you feel a compulsion to draw when you're in that particular state of unconsciousness, you have to find a subject, and that your mind will automatically pluck something out of the various ideas that had recently crossed your mind, or had been stirred up in the cryptomnesic store-room of forgetfulness, in the minutes before you fell out of consciousness. He'd say that there's no puzzle at all about the fact that you drew Talia after you received news of her death, or him after you received news of his, or that you've drawn Juliette repeatedly...and that you've also drawn me, on occasion, when you've been kind enough to spare me a thought because you'd been reading one of my books, or one of my letters, or planning to write one of your letters to me. He'd say that it was all absolutely natural."

She was right, Paul knew. But she knew as well as he did that there was a puzzle—more than one, in fact—and that she had an interest in its solution as well, if not as urgently, as he did.

"Well," he said, aloud, "perhaps I'm simply irrationally obsessed. But I'm seeing Flammarion tomorrow afternoon, and I suspect that he'll see a puzzle, even if Antoine wouldn't."

"I don't go to Juvisy anymore," Jane said, quietly, "or even to séances in Paris, although I still get invitations. But Antoine might be right, mightn't he, about the fact that you've sometimes drawn me—that that, at least, might simply be an effect of memory, and not a phantasmal visitation at all. It couldn't be, could it? If I'm not mistaken, the idea is that it's only in moments of existential crisis that people like you or I can project phantoms subconsciously in the way that Juliette apparently did on that traumatic night. Fakirs can do it deliberately, but they require years of training and mortification of the flesh before they master the art of astral projection—which is almost lost, in spite of the theosophists' intense attempts to renew it. I haven't witnessed any murders, and I've never learned astral projection. You didn't think to bring me a portrait of myself, then, instead of that sphinx?"

She was speaking calmly, if not lightly, but Paul took note of the slight inconsequentiality that had crept into her discourse, and suspected that she was more disturbed than she seemed, not merely by the fact that he had drawing her in the one of his fits of strange somnambulism, but by the other confessions he had made, and by the situation itself. Their communication in writing had always been measured and disciplined, because the medium of handwriting compelled measure and discipline; it had not been without intimacy, but it had been carefully externalized, scrupulously polite intimacy, the intimacy of friends who were inevitably distanced, and not simply by the kilometers that separated them. Doubtless she had assumed, as he had, that when they met in the flesh again, they would continue in the same vein, which was not conspicuously different from the strangely conspiratorial relationship they had established while he was painting her portrait—when, separately forewarned by Antoine Cros, they had both been conscientiously determined not to fall prey to the temptation to transmute a certain flirtatious flippancy into anything more intense and potentially damaging.

It did not seem to be that simple, Paul, adjudged, wryly, for either of them.

"I haven't tried to turn any of my recent sketches of people I know into portraits," Paul told her, "but I have brought some of them with me to Paris. I didn't bring them with me this afternoon because...like you, apparently...I wasn't sure exactly how this first renewal of our acquaintance was going to work out. If you wish, though, I'll show all of them to you...but I won't show any sketch of you to anyone else without your permission."

Jane hesitated before responding to that, probably because there was more than one issue she wanted to take up. In the end, as the practical and intelligent woman she was, she decided to take them in order.

"I certainly do want to see them," she said. "Not just any you might have made of me, but the others...all of them, at least that you don't need anyone's permission to show me. You didn't say anything when I mentioned the possibility of staying to dinner, but I'm assuming that you will...or, rather, that you'll come back when you've returned to your hotel to collect the sketches. Is that settled?"

"Of course," said Paul. "I'd be..."

"Never mind the formulaic politeness—and don't bother to dress for dinner. We're obviously past that. By 'anyone else' I presume you meant Camille?"

"Yes, I had intended to show him all the sketches I'd made when I see him tomorrow, including those of you, if I could obtain your permission. He and I have been in frequent communication, as you know, and although he's agreed not to publish any account of my 'case' until I give him permission to do so, he's taken an intense interest in it. He's not only familiar with all the published research but can assess it sanely and intelligently. He's already been invaluable, and will doubtless continue to be...but he's not the only person with whom I have an appointment tomorrow."

His interlocutor had no need of the traditional three guesses. "Zosima," she said, without even giving it the inflection of a question.

"Yes; she's agreed to see me tomorrow morning, before I go to Juvisy. I have no intention of showing her all the sketches, but I think that she has a moral entitlement to see some of them...those of Talia, at least."

"At least? Not only those, then?"

"I'll begin with one of those, and decide later what else I might show her. I wasn't sure that she'd agree to see me—I haven't been in regular communication with her, as you can imagine, and all I know about this cult that she's founded is what I've read in the newspapers, but..."

"Oh, don't believe all that rubbish," she said. "Worse than salon gossip, although the professional courtesy of apolitical journalism shouldn't allow me to say so. I don't know much more myself—we don't exactly meet in society, as you can imagine, and I know enough to be suspicious of hearsay, but so far as I can make out, it's not a cult in the same sense as all the quasi-Rosicrucian, neo-Martinist and offshoot theosophical not-so-secret societies that have proliferated over the last twenty years. It's more like a convent with spiritist overtones, which functions primarily as a refuge for women who...need to get away.

"The press and popular gossip represent it as a kind of sapphic sorority in much the same way that they represent Natalie Barney's salon, but there's a word of difference. Natalie's crowd mostly consists of upper-class esthetes devoted to a cult of female beauty and its celebration in flesh-grinding and poetry; Zosima's followers mostly aren't aristocratic, mostly aren't esthetes and aren't poets at all, and I suspect that many of them aren't even ardent lesbians—there are many other good reasons for determined misandry in our world than the mere accident of nature that causes some women to lust after their own sex.

"Antoine would probably judge that what she's actually offering her recruits is a form of psychotherapy, in which her hypnotic revelations of supposed anterior existences merely function as a palliative for present woes, and I'm not unsympathetic to that interpretation, even though I have more open mind than his. I'm astonished, though, that she's agreed to let you into her temple—I thought that rule one of the sorority was that no man would ever set foot there."

"She hasn't. She's given me a rendezvous at a café nearby. She didn't say whether she'd come incognito, but either way, it's not the most convenient location for an exhibition of sketches. In all probability, though, she views it as an exploratory preliminary...much like this meeting."

"As I've already said, you and I are past that. Supernatural or not, the bond we formed four years ago obviously hasn't been broken by a mere four-year interim in physical proximity, so I'll take that as a license to indulge my curiosity to the full. I presume that I'm right in taking it for granted that the portrait of Talia you exhibited more than two years ago, which helped to make your reputation, isn't the only portrait you've painted based on one of your...somnambulistic sketches...is that the right word?"

"Probably not. Some would-be pedants already use somniloquism for what spiritist medium do, who talk instead of walking, but no one, so far as I know, has yet invented a jargon term like somnifabrication or somnartificium. But I'm not sure that you have the question the right way round. Perhaps it's not a matter of whether I've done other paintings based on sketches made wholly or partly in a trance state, but whether I've ever done any that weren't. Even when I'm sketching while fully conscious—as I was, for instance, when I made the sketches for the portrait that's apparently hanging in your boudoir, I wonder whether I slip automatically into a different state of mind. Don't you feel the same while you're writing?"

"Yes, I do," she agreed, without hesitation, obviously having given the matter some thought, probably long before she had met him, "but there are many degrees. Sometimes, when it seems entirely conscious, it's a hard grind, like milling corn by hand; sometimes, when I let go and it almost becomes automatic writing, like the phenomenon Camille's hypnotists used to try to induce in his séances, I seem to have established a direct link between my hand and some kind of well of creativity—the unconscious mind, in Antoine's jargon, although that's really only the prelude to an explanation that still remains elusive. I've never forgotten, though, an observation that I made of your drawing, that it was so much faster than the laborious physical process of writing. Your connection with the well of creativity, whatever it consists of, seemed much more immediate and fluent than mine can ever be. I envied you that...and still do."

"It's not entirely an advantage," Paul told her. "The rapidity, I think, is either a cause or a consequence of the fact that nothing is engraved in my memory. I don't even know whether I see what I draw in my imagination, or whether the visual phase of the process is skipped completely. Four years ago, I suggested to Juliette that it wasn't actually me who had drawn her image as a murder victim—that she had somehow taken possession of my hand, at a distance. She said that it was nonsense, and perhaps it was, but it seemed plausible at the time to me, and it still seems plausible that when I'm deeply entranced, it really isn't me that is making the sketches, that my hand is obedient to another design than mine. Antoine would doubtless dismiss that as mere illusion, and perhaps he'd be right, but...what do you think?"

"I know the feeling you mean," she said, "and I've heard other writers—poets, especially—say the same. It's built into the legendry of literary creation, in the language of inspiration and the idea of the Muse. I know writers who are utterly convinced that all of that is just a way of speaking, and that they're entirely responsible for what they produce...but I also know some who are convinced of the opposite, and not just the mystics and other belated members of the club des hashischins. It's a mystery. I've heard painters talk in exactly the same vein, and not just Symbolists—although I suspect that everyone who used to exhibit in Péladan's Rosicrucian Salon would sympathize with you entirely, and probably envy you your prolific somnifabrication. If you can make a technique of it, you won't be short of students."

"That's not my objective," Paul said. "I want to understand it. I still remember the little lecture that Zosima gave us on the fateful night, when she explained briefly why even sincere mediums felt an enormous pressure to fake the phenomena that their audiences expected of them rather than trying to objectively and methodically to investigate and understand what happens to them. That, I think, rather than Talia's death, might be what made her turn her back on the séance circuit, and whatever good her present organization does in providing a refuge for women in need, I suspect that her own motives are still primarily exploratory, trying to figure out what kinds of phenomena her hypnotic skills can bring out, in a conducive environment."

"You're probably right," Jane agreed, "and I'm certainly in no position to pass judgment on her attempts to use her suppose magnetic powers to help people remember their anterior lives, as I've wondered more than once whether I ought to seek that kind of assistance myself. I probably would if I weren't so scared of finding that I'd been Messalina...or Medusa. Are you going to ask her to magnetize you again...as a means of furthering your research...and hers?"

"Probably," Paul admitted. "I wasn't ready for it four years ago, and I think I was right to run at the time. It wasn't just cowardice...but now, I think I'm ready. I might suggest to Camille that we try again at Juvisy...in private, without an audience."

"But not without me," Jane was quick to say.

"Zosima tried to exclude you last time," he reminded her. "She might not consent..."

"She was just being petty," Jane said, interrupting him. "And I don't care if I'm a distracting presence. I want to be a distracting presence—and I want to be there. If you do decide, I want to be there, if only to look after you if things go wrong again. Promise me that you won't do it without me."

"If that's what you want...," said Paul, but didn't finish the sentence or make the promise requested, which was not entirely his to make. In order to change the subject, he said: "It's rather gloomy in here when the sky's cloudy, isn't it?" he said. "You haven't thought of installing electric lighting?"

Jane looked around, as if surprised by the gloom that had colonized the room even in mid-afternoon. "I'm used to it," she admitted. "In any case, I still inhabit a world, mentally, in which the servants bring in the lamps as the twilight fades, as a kind of vesperal ritual. I never really adapted to the gas jet, let alone the electric bulb. It's a failure of adaptation, not so much to the changing world as my own advancing antiquity— and don't bother with the usual flattery; you and I don't need that. I'll be fifty years old soon and fifty is old even for a man, let alone a woman...especially a vain woman like me. But you'd better to go back to your hotel to fetch those sketches before it really gets dark. I want to see them, and I want to see them before Flammarion, and before Zosima. I'm entitled to that, aren't I? I don't know quite what I am to you—and if you suggest that I'm a second substitute mother, replacing Amélie Lambrunet, I'll never forgive you—but I'm something, and it's more than Camille, and far more than Zosima. So, yes, I'm entitled to make demands of you, however whimsical. That's a kind of vanity to which I can still cling. And thank you, by the way, for coming to see me first, for being willing to show me the products of your...somnifabrication first, for affording me an importance that I might not deserve, but if which I'm certainly prepared to be jealous...but I'm rambling."

As she finished speaking, she stood up, and Paul automatically stood up too. Again, she offered him her hand, but this time, he did not kiss it, by way of a slightly daring social ritual. He clasped it, sincerely, as an improvised symbol of collaboration, or even conspiracy. She understood, and nodded.

She showed him to the door of the apartment herself, and remained on the threshold as he went downstairs in a gloom that was even worse, without the aid of the unactivated gaslight, than the grayness in the drawing room...with the result that when he glanced back at the threshold in which she was still standing, she was surrounded by a vague nimbus of subtle, quasi-supernatural light, as befitted a true idol.

CHAPTER II

In the fiacre that took him back to his hotel, Paul wondered exactly what Jane de La Vaudère's expectations of him were now that they had met face to face again. She had told him once, in what must have been a carefully calculated indiscretion, that when she had she had first seen him, on the way to Juvisy for the séance that had changed his life, that she had thought, albeit not very seriously, about the possibility of seducing him, simply because of his youth rather than any special physical attributes. She had left it unsaid that she had rejected any possibility, not for reasons of conventional morality but for the reasons summarized in Antoine Cros's judgment that any such seduction, on the part of a woman in her position—who already referred to herself, in double-edged jest, as "Scandalous Jane"—of a young man in his situation would be bound to end in heartache and disaster.

In fact, he knew nothing about the history of Jane's sentimental life, and knew well enough that rumor was a direly unreliable source of intelligence, but he also remembered the generalized verbal sketch that Antoine had made him of married women who lived alone in Paris while their husbands remained in their provincial châteaux, with the heirs to their name. Perhaps, Antoine had suggested, such women might be able to find the romantic amour in Paris that they had not been able to find in a marriage arranged for them by their relatives while they were still imprisoned in a convent in compulsory ignorance, if not innocence; but even if they did, what could come of it?

If they were beautiful, as Jane undoubtedly was, they could undoubtedly have their choice of lovers, and in their forties, they could still have their choice of lovers ten or twenty years their junior—but again, what could come of it? Nothing but a temporary passion, sooner or later exhausted as its initial impetus wore off, with no future relationship possible, and the breaking of which might easily cause lasting damage to one or other party. While he had painted her portrait before leaving for Toulouse with Juliette, the model whom he did not love, he and Jane had been two people who were very definitely not going to fall in love with one another, because that refusal was the sane and responsible thing to do—but he suspected that the temptation had been there on her side as well as his, and their meeting this afternoon had left him in no doubt that something was still there, probably augmented rather than diminished, in spite of their advancing ages. It was, however even truer now that the sane and responsible thing to do about it was nothing...except, perhaps, to admit Jane as a witness to any further experiments he might now be ready to undertake in induced somnifabrication

With Juliette, as he had frankly confessed to Jane, it had been perfectly possible to have sex without either of them loving the other. She was a prostitute—or an ex-prostitute—and he was a man; having sex without love was perfectly normal for both of them. But if he or Jane had been so unwise as to make any advances to the other, it would have led to a very different situation, emotionally as well as socially. Of necessity, he knew, Jane must have Platonic friends, men to whom she was close, and affectionate, without the disturbing intrusion of any explicit eroticism. That was the company he could and ought to join, for both their sakes. He had read and understood her novels; he knew that she was fully and poignantly aware that unbridled passion can only lead to torment and destruction, except in the most remarkable of circumstances.

Returning to his constant obsession, the simple fact was that he had no control over the source of his somnambulistic creativity. Poor Talia, a genuinely talented somniloquist, had told him, when she had recognized in him a spirit even more kindred to her than Zosima, that people like them could not choose to see the people and things that they wanted to see when their consciousness surrendered its censorious control, and were far more likely to see precisely what they did not want to see. Talia had seemed to believe, although he had not had the opportunity to discuss it at great length with her, that the contrariety in question was a consequence of some strange rule of cosmic perversity, that it was a kind of punishment for daring to be different from the common run of psychically blind humankind. Paul did not believe that, but he was not sure even so, of the diplomacy of showing Jane the drawings that he had made, without being consciously aware of it, a selection of which he had brought with him for that purpose.

He could not help feeling that the diplomatic problem in question was acute, now that the finale decision had now to be made—two decisions, in fact, in rapid succession. But it was not only a problem in diplomacy, because the nature of the drawings bore upon important questions as to the exact nature of what he did, and what he could do—and those questions would be difficult to settle without some kind of input from the people concerned; it was not a matter that he could productively discuss with Camille Flammarion alone.

He sighed, as the fiacre drew to a halt and he went back into the hotel and climbed the stairs to his room. Jane had demanded to see all the sketches he had brought, and he felt that he ought to meet that demand, if only because it might reduce the possibility that she could help him understand what was going on if he exercised a sterner censorship, but there was a reluctance to be overcome in so doing, an embarrassment if not a shame.

The dead, he thought, were a great deal safer as subjects, for more reasons than one. He had had no hesitation, after making portraits of Talia following her demise, in using the sketches as raw material for a portrait in oils—a portrait in oils that he was not the only person to deem a fine piece of work—and he believed that he could safely have done likewise with any of his posthumous sketches of Juliette, or Antoine Cros...but dealings with phantasms of the living, if that was really what they were, appeared to be very different, at least in his idiosyncratic case; and when it was difficult to tell the difference, the problem became even more complex.

The puzzle had not certainly not originated, but had definitely made itself manifest in a fashion that could not be ignored, on that astonishing evening at Juvisy, when he had drawn four sketches in rapid succession, two of them definitely identifiable and two of them deeply problematic. But even the simplest of the four, the portrait of Charles Cros, still posed awkward puzzles. Charles Cros had been unambiguously dead when he made the sketch, but Antoine Cros had had no difficulty arguing persuasively that Paul might have made the sketch from a portrait of his brother that he had seen, but had not remembered consciously. Even if that were not the case, however, it was not necessarily true that it was the spirit of the dead poet and inventor that had somehow visited Paul's consciousness and prompted the portrait.

Talia had been convinced that a mental link had been forged between her mind and Paul's, as a result of Zosima's suggestion, and that Paul had actually "seen" the image of Charles Cros in her mind, where it had been engraved because she and Zosima, as a matter of routine had investigated some of the people whose presence at the séance they anticipated, and the fact that Antoine Cros had a dead brother—a famous dead brother—had leapt to their attention as potentially significant.

By contrast, there was no way that the second recognizable image among the four sketches—Martine's—could have originated in Talia's consciousness, because Talia could never have seen a picture of her. On the other hand, Talia had claimed, remarkably, that the link forged between their minds had enabled her to perceive Martine in Paul mind, where she had contrived to manifest herself as a phantasm on the very brink of death. Indeed, Talia had told Paul that she had actually been conscious of Martine drowning. Paul had not believed her, because he had not wanted to believe that Martine was dead, and even when he had been forced to accept, reluctantly, that she probably had downed when the lifeboat she was aboard had capsized, it still seemed unlikely in the extreme that she had been drowning at the precise moment when Zosima had hypnotized him.

The third face that he had drawn still remained enigmatic to some degree. A doctor named Roimantel had told Antoine Cros that he thought he recognized her as Madame Scrive, Jane de La Vaudère's mother, and that rumor had run around like wildfire. Jane had initially denied it flatly, and before anyone else who had known Madame Scrive—dead for more than forty years—could be consulted the publicity had already biased their perception. Antoine had suggested that Paul might have synthesized the face unconsciously by extrapolation from Jane's own features, and Talia had complicated that suggestion that the extrapolation might, in fast, have been hers.

The matter had acquired a further twist when Jane had confessed to Paul privately that the face was, in fact, her mother's but that she had lied to Antoine Cros because she did not want to admit to herself or anyone else that her mother might be haunting her. But how reliable could Jane's identification be, on the basis of an old portrait, in view of the confused psychology of her own attitude? That was another factor that he had to take into account in showing Jane the sketches he had made since that fatal evening.

All three of those faces had, however been mere faces, with no trace of a body. He had not thought that significant at the time, although he thought so now. The fourth figure he had drawn had had, at least apparently, a body as well as a face, but a very peculiar body, as well as a very peculiar face. Camille Flammarion, a believer in the possibility of interplanetary reincarnation, had wondered aloud whether it might be an extraterrestrial of some kind—a hesitant conjecture that rumor had rapidly inflated into an assertion that the blurred figure was, in fact, a "Martian." Martians had been prominent in the public consciousness at the time, not merely because of the recent publication of Theodore Flournoy's book, which featured a Martian incarnation, among others, but also because of a lurid thriller translated from the English, which described an invasion of Earth by monstrous Martians.

Antoine Cros, by contrast, had immediately identified the figure as a sketch of a human fetus, and, having accidentally discovered that Paul had had a twin sister who has died in the womb, and whom his mother had subsequently died trying to deliver, he had immediately concocted a psychoanalytical account of why Paul might have drawn an imaginative image of his sister, based on irrational guilt feelings regarding her death. Talia, on the other hand, once she had heard the blur identified as a fetus, had immediately jumped to the conclusion that Paul had read in her mind a secret that she had never confided to anyone, that she had once given birth in secret to a premature stillborn child.

Paul had begun to wonder at the time whether there could be phantom fetuses, of which there did not appear to be any elaborate legendry, perhaps because of the common assumption that the soul did not enter the body until birth, so that stillborn children could not have any afterlife. If that were the case, then a psychoanalytical explanation of some sort had to be constructed for his representation of the fetus, whether it were to be construed as an image of his own sister or a telepathically-transmuted image of Talia's daughter.

When he went to Toulouse, therefore, he had been interested to discover whether he would be able to draw any more somnifabricant pictures of the woman tentatively identified as Jane's mother and, even more importantly, whether he would draw any more fetuses. He now had affirmative answers to both those questions, but what those answers signified, he was far from certain.

Adding in the lurid images he had produced four years ago on the night after the séance at Juvisy, of Juliette as an agonized Jeanne d'Arc on the pyre and Juliette as the victim of a furious stabbing, added a further dimension of complication. Both images had been full length portraits, not mere faces, but neither could have been, as it were, drawn "from life." Juliette had, indeed, hallucinated that she was on fire, and she had seen a friend furiously stabbed to death, but she had been on the Butte de Montmartre, neither burning nor stabbed, until she had run all the way to the Pont Neuf—a distance of three kilometers—in order to throw herself into the water. What he had drawn, therefore was a dual imaginative transfiguration. When he had set forth to Toulouse he had been particularly interested to know whether he would produce any more somnifabricant images of the living Juliette, and whether they, too would be transfigured. Again he now had an answer to that question—but what that answer might signify, he had absolutely no idea, unless it was that he was utterly insane: a possibility that he was exceedingly reluctant to accept.

He hoped that Jane, at least, would try to talk him out of it, and was eager to discover how she might go about it. She was an amateur psychoanalyst of a very different stripe from Antoine Cros, but she was highly intelligent and had a prolific imagination. If anyone could come up with a plausible story, he thought, it was surely her.

Having collected his large portfolio, he did not linger at the hotel any longer. When he went downstairs the clerk at the reception desk, who had not been able to attract his attention as he went in, told him that three visiting cards and two sealed letters had been left there for him, with urgent requests for responses, but he did not collect them. He told the clerk that he would pick them up when he returned later that evening, when he would have time to read them, and perhaps time to write responses if he felt that any were required.

He went outside, and caught another cab immediately. He knew that he would be very early for dinner, according to present social convention, but Jane had assured him that he and she had surpassed social convention, and he suspected that it would be far better to show her the sketches to her before the meal rather than afterwards, lest impatience cause either or both of them an indigestion.

Jane received him in the same drawing room was before. The gaslight was now burning, but the room only seemed moderately illuminated to Paul; the heavy Parisian sky was not visible through the curtained window, but Paul could still feel its presence, which seemed quite alien after four years spent under Provençal skies. He had lived in Paris before, and had grown accustomed to the complex variegations of its light—of which, as a painter, he was acutely aware—but when the weather had been sullen, as it was today he had always felt that the light became oppressive and sinister, and that sensation had been renewed in him as easily as his peculiar affection for Jane de La Vaudère.

"Dinner will be a trifle elementary, I fear," she said. "My new cook is not as versatile as my old one, but she's not unaccomplished, and I'm lucky to have her. Times have changed, alas. Now, the sketches. Will this table be adequate? You can spread them on the floor if you prefer to display them all simultaneously."

"On the contrary," Paul said. "One by one is definitely the more appropriate procedure. They're in thematic rather than chronological order, because that seemed to me to be the best way to convey an impression of their peculiar spectrum."

"As you please," she said. "I can see that you intend to aim for dramatic effect, but I doubt that the suspense will kill me. I'm in your hands."

Paul did not open the portfolio fully, but he began to take out the sketches one by one. He set them down on the table carefully, so that each new one would cover the previous image. The sheets of paper that he employed for his experiments were all the same size, only a fraction larger than folio.

"This is the sketch from which my portrait in oils of Talia was taken," he said, "and this is another posthumous sketch of her."

Jane examined the two pictures, one by one. "You drew both of these in your sleep?" she asked.

"The first one, yes but before drawing the other I hypnotized myself in advance. I can't always induce the state voluntarily, and the result is often incomplete. Both images were produced in a seemingly deep trance, though, even though the second one was deliberately self-induced."

"From which Juliette awoke you be snapping her fingers?"

"No, I didn't think that was either necessary or desirable, although I did instruct her when conducting such experiments that if I hadn't come round after a certain interval, she was to try that, and other methods of restoring consciousness. What do you think of the sketches?"

"I can't say that I remember the girl very well, but they're certainly recognizable, if a trifle flattering. As I remember her, she wore an expression of near-hysteria even when she wasn't having a fit, but I obviously didn't see her at her best. While not exactly serene, she looks considerably less distraught here than I remember her—but that's not at all surprising. I know that you saw her two or three times while you were painting my portrait—she even came to the studio once while I was still there—but I have no idea what kind of relationship you had."

"Nor have I, really. She seemed to think that she could confide in me, because she thought that we were similar and that we had formed a telepathic bond. She told me that she would still be aware of me, even when I was in Toulouse...and she told me that if she were capable of willing anything after she was dead, then she would come into my dreams and make every effort to communicate, to demonstrate to me that I really was in contact with dead souls."

"And did she?"

"I don't know. I did dream about her, for sure, and as you can see, I drew her; but whether her will had anything to do with that, I can't say."

"Of course not," Jane agreed. "Antoine would say that there's nothing more natural than a young man dreaming about a little girl, especially one so expert in playing the helpless little waif...and one who, lesbian or not, would have been only too glad to spread her legs for you, and maybe even go to Toulouse with you instead of Juliette...who, I'm prepared to wager, must have detested her."

"She certainly didn't like her—and didn't even like me drawing her after she was dead, although she admitted herself that it was unreasonable."

37

"Jealousy is inherently unreasonable," Jane observed, "and even if she was telling the truth about not being able to love you, it wouldn't have prevented her from clinging to you like a possessive leech, avid to prevent a single a drop of your bodily fluids, including your spiritual fluids, being sucked by anyone but her."

Paul winced at the calculated double entendres, and passed on hastily.

"The next two are posthumous portraits of Antoine, again, one drawn during sleep, the other in a self-induced trance. Give me your impression."

Again, Jane inspected both portraits carefully. "Again, no significant difference," she said. "It's a good likeness, and although you haven't captured his smug vanity, you have given him the earnest professional concentration that he adopted for consultations. I presume that he didn't make you the same promises as Talia, but we can probably be sure that if he did discover, to his utter surprise, that he was embarked upon some kind of afterlife, you would certainly have been on his visiting list, and that he would also have tried, if trying were a possibility, to make himself known to you, just as we can presume that, if he's here in spirit now, he would be gnashing his insubstantial teeth at the thought that he couldn't prove to you that your having drawn him was perfectly natural and understandable."

"Yes, I think we can safely presume all of that that. Now Juliette—all posthumous, although I also sketched her frequently while conscious, unlike Talia and Antoine. There are three, this time." Paul laid the three pictures down, one by one. Jane inspected them with even more minute care, as if searching for evidence of something.

"I can't say that I remember her very clearly either," Jane said, eventually. "I didn't like her from the very beginning, for some reason, and almost made a point of not looking at her while she was haunting the studio with such conscientious discretion when I was sitting for my portrait, so it might be partly my prejudice that sees them as very flattering...almost angelic, in fact. Considering that she was just a parasitic little whore, I'm sure that she'd have been exceptionally pleased to think that you saw her like this." She paused and waited for a reaction to her provocative description, but he knew that there was no point in supplying one. Then she added: "And how many more of these have you made during the last two years? A lot, I'd wager."

"Quite a lot," Paul admitted.

"Again, natural and understandable—and I can't even say with conviction that they were painted with love, because if I took that inference from their appearance I might have to conclude that you loved Talia too...although I'm not sure that wouldn't be an unreasonable conclusion, given your excessive sentimentality. Can I see the pictures of me now?"

"Not yet, if you don't mind," said Paul, in as neutral tone as he could contrive. He reached for the portfolio again, but Jane stopped him with a gesture. "Did you see her like this when she was alive?" she asked "Quasi-angelically, I mean. I saw your second Jeanne d'Arc when it was exhibited, of course, but nothing that showed her as she actually was—and clad in armor, waving a sword, it seemed to me that she simp-ly looked ridiculous."

"Perhaps I should have brought a sketch made con-sciously, for comparative purposes, but I didn't bring any of those pictures. I never drew her again while I was entranced, after that terrible night at Antoine's, until she had died—not recognizably, at any rate...but that certainly doesn't prove that I only draw the dead, given that...well, we'll get to that." He took out another sketch and set it down. This one depicted two faces.

"Antoine and Charles," Jane observed. "Together—at least on the page. Not looking at one another, though. Perhaps you ought to show this one to Henry, the surviving broth-er...and you might show the others to Laure-Thérèse, heredi-tary Queen of Araucaria and Patagonia...although I doubt that she'll keep up that charade for long. Too sensible by half, and even older than me. Ah! I didn't expect that. That wasn't supposed to happen"

Paul had set down another sketch, this time of a woman's face. It was the same face that he had drawn at Juvisy, detailed more elaborately.

"Why wasn't it supposed to happen?" Paul prompted.

She frowned. "Because I thought you only drew a picture of her at Juvisy because I was present—because it was me that she was haunting. I can make up Antoinesque stories to suggest why my dead mother might have appeared in your unconscious mind, even while you were in Toulouse and I was in Paris, but if it really was a phantasmal visitation...unless her dead soul was aware that you would come to Paris, sit in that chair and show me the picture...in which case this very moment, here and now, is the haunting. I can't believe that the dead are that subtle, though. On the other hand, if the Antoinesque explanation is correct, what is your unconscious mind playing at?"

That, Pau thought, *is the big question.* Aloud, he said: "Flammarion still has the picture I drew at the Observatory, but I made a copy of it when I went to see him before leaving for Toulouse, and I've looked at often in Toulouse...and I think about you frequently, often in connection with your mother and the crucial significance of that identification..."

He paused, warily.

"If you're waiting for me to say that I think about you frequently too, I do...but we have exchanged a lot of letters, and I think about what you write and what I might reply, so it would be surprising if I didn't, wouldn't it?"

"I suppose so," Paul agreed, although that had certainly not been what he was waiting for her to say, and he suspected that it was a deliberate evasion.

That suspicion was confirmed when she said: "No further comment, for the moment. Go on."

Paul hesitated, but made no protest. He laid down another image.

"Martine Lambrunet, I presume?" Jane guessed. "I don't remember the earlier sketch clearly enough to be sure."

"That's correct," said Paul. "Here she is again."

"A true beauty," opined Jane. "I can see why you loved her in your youth...unless, of course, you've flattered her as you've flattered Talia and Juliette. Who's that?"

Paul had set down another picture, of an older woman.

"No one you know," Paul told her. "That's Amélie Lambrunet, as I remember her."

"Well, it's understandable that you might draw her as well as Martine, whether she's dead or simply on your mind."

"Entirely understandable—but the possibility you raised with regard to Martine's picture is also relevant to this one. When I showed them to Gaston, he said—and Victor agreed with him subsequently—that neither picture was a good likeness. Either my memory had betrayed me, they said, or the dead modify their appearance to reflect the prejudices of those they haunt. They were joking...but partly to cover up their unease at the idea that I really might be able to draw the dead. Perhaps my memory had betrayed me...and perhaps dead souls really do modify the aspect they take on for the purposes of haunting, in order to adapt to the prejudices of those to whom they appear."

He set down another sketch.

"I didn't know that one, either," said Jane.

"That's my mother," Paul told her, "again, as I remember her. It looks like a portrait that was made when she was alive...but I suppose it would, since that's the only image of her I have. But that's the first time I've ever drawn her, so if it's a haunting, it's recent, and if it's a memory resurfacing from the unconscious, it's belated."

"Who's that one?" his interlocutor asked, beginning to show slight signs of impatience, as Paul set down another image, this time of a younger woman."

"You don't recognize her?"

"No. Should I?"

"I was rather hoping that you might. I don't recognize her either, although I've got a nagging suspicion that I've definitely seen her before. I've been racking my brains ever since I drew it, but I just can't place her. I have a strong suspicion that, whether it's a haunting or cryptomnesic revelation, there's a memory that could and ought to recall if only I could run across the right cue. You're sure you haven't seen her before?"

"If I have, I've forgotten her even more fully than you have. Why are you hesitating? And blushing?"

"Because...well, you'll see," said Paul, steeling himself. "That's enough dead people, for now—especially dead people that you don't know. Here's one of the ones that's making you clench your hand behind your back with impatience."

He set out a portrait of Jane, which depicted her full length, in the nude. It drew forth the gasp that he had anticipated.

"Damn!" she said, after a slight pause for thought. "You could have imagined me with hair long enough to cover up my breasts and allowed me to place my hands more modestly— but I suppose I ought to be glad that it isn't a good likeness. Perhaps I had breasts like that when I was your age, but I certainly wouldn't have posed for you in the nude four years ago, let alone now. Are they all like that?"

"It depends what they mean 'all' and what you mean by 'like that,'" Paul said. "You didn't make any comment while I was showing you the dead, but you must have become aware of a distinctive feature now.

"They were all just faces," Jane said, immediately leaping to the right conclusion. "When you converted that sketch of Talia into an oil painting you had to add the neck and a suggestion of some kind of bodice, even to give the impression of a real head. The dead have no bodies, at least in your imagination—but it isn't just *your* imagination, I suppose. I've seen other images produced in séances—often they're no more than figures that children might have drawn, but more than once, I've seen heads like yours, heads without bodies, more-

or-less competently drawn. I've seen manifestations at séances too that were just heads, or faces. Do you think it's true, then? Do the dead really have no bodies? Can they only manifest their faces...clearly, at any rate. When I've seen full length manifestations, they've always been extremely vague...except that there are often hands...hands that you can see, as well as hands that can touch. Sometimes, though, they're disembodied too. Whereas the living...tell me that they're not all like that: nudes with pert breasts who look as if they're begging to be taken...surely you don't see me...oh, that's...too much!"

Paul had taken out another image and laid it on top of the full-length nude. This image too had Jane's face, and a full length naked body, but she was not simply standing. She was nailed to a cross, as in religious images of Christ, with two significant exceptions. One was that the arm were passed over the arms of the cross and the hands brought back up again, so that although the nails securing them to the cross were driven through the wrists, the wood of the cross was lending some support to the body beneath the armpits. The other difference was that, whereas in religious depictions Christ's head, wearing a crown of thorns, was usually inclined forwards and his eyes closed, Jane's head was erect, with no crown of thorns and her eyes were open, staring directly at the eyes of a beholder.

After drawing breath, Jane said: "Is that really how you see me?"

"Not consciously," he replied. "Nor is it how I imagine that you might see yourself. I have no idea what it signifies. For obvious reasons I nearly refrained from showing it to you, because I thought it was sure to make you think badly of me, but I decided that if I were to look for help from you to figure out what happens to me when I fall into a trance, then you needed to see...the full range of the phenomenon."

"And there are others...like that?"

"No, that's unique, in detail. There are a few others that might be you, but I couldn't be sure. These are the only two that are definitely representations of you, but why they take

43

the form they do, instead of representing you as I actually remember you, fully clothed and serenely self-confident—at least, certainly not suffering—I don't know."

"Oh, don't be disingenuous," she retorted, sharply. "You read my books, I know you do. You know the kinds of things I sometimes write. You could, if you were being honest, say that it's perfectly understandable that when your unconscious mind pictures me, it not only sees me naked and lubricious but as a victim of torture. Antoine would probably tell you that it would be surprising if you saw me in any other way, once the censorship of consciousness was removed, rejuvenated breasts and all."

"Antoine wasn't always right," Paul said, quietly. "I dare say that Juliette would have said exactly the same, if she hadn't been dead by the time I drew those images, but she certainly wasn't always right. Perhaps they would be right, and, as a man, I'm incapable of thinking of living women, when the censorship of consciousness is ripped away, in any other terms than pornographic ones, but it's not a conclusion to which I want to jump too quickly. For what it's worth, though, you're the only full length nude that I've drawn while entranced with an unambiguously recognizable face...the others are mostly less distinct, and all unrecognizable. What that says about my unconscious, I don't know...but it certainly doesn't chime with what popular legend and the Society for Psychical Research report about the conditions under which phantasms of the living are normally produced. So, it's a part of the puzzle, and at the risk of offending you or diminishing myself in your eyes, I thought I ought to show them to you. I won't show them to anyone else, unless you give me permission to show them to Flammarion."

"Did you bring any of those other nudes?" she asked.

"Only this one," he said, displaying another sketch, which showed a naked woman, seated on what might have been a divan, seen from behind, in a considerably more impressionistic style than the unambiguous images of Jane, The woman's face could not be seen, so she might have been Jane—or, indeed, anyone.

"These images are exceptional in more ways than one," Paul added, feeling that he ought to keep talking lest an ominous silence fall. "If they aren't genuine apparitions, but have simply been drawn from memory, the imagination has evidently played a considerable part. But the most significant fact is surely there aren't any others like them, of other living individuals that I can recognize. I never sketched Juliette again after that night at Antoine's until she was dead, nor did I ever sketch Talia until she was dead, and I've never sketched Zosima or Camille while entranced, either naked or clothed—not recognizably, at any rate. But the situation is even more completed and mysterious than that...and this is where the situation becomes seriously weird."

He turned over another image, of a young woman...except that from the waist down, the body was piscine.

"The wistful siren!" Jane exclaimed. "Is that a new sketch, made since I bought the painting?"

"Yes, it is," Paul confirmed. "Probably drawn from a memory of the picture. And given that the sketch for picture you bought was drawn in a semi-entranced state, as were other mythological paintings, perhaps it isn't really surprising that I've been producing more of them in recent years while asleep or in deliberately-induced traces. But..."

He placed another image on top of the pile: another picture of a partly-human chimera.

"And what's that?" Jane demanded, although Paul was a little surprised that she had not recognized the depiction.

"It's another siren" he said. "The idea of a siren of the singing kind being a mermaid is fairly recent. The most ancient of the Greeks imaged sirens as creatures with beautiful or furious women's faces, but possessed of avian bodies with massive claws—like this one."

"Well," the author adjudged, reverting to studious objectivity, "neither siren is anything that could plausibly be called a phantasm of the living, nor a phantom of the dead. That's definitely pure imagination, although I suppose it could have been based on a picture you've seen in some ancient bestiary. Judging by the number of sheets that you still seem to have in your portfolio, I presume there are more mythological monsters?"

"Yes—I brought a number of them, because they're more varied and more bizarre than the pictures of human faces. The number of samples isn't proportional to the relative infrequency of their production...but it does add a further dimension of mystery to the question of what might be going on in my mind when I draw in a trance. If there were a simple answer, though, I suppose that I'd have figured out some time ago...or at least got closer to it."

While he was speaking, Jane had lifted up the sketch of the avian siren in order to take another look at the mermaid.

"This might be a silly question," she said, "but do you recognize either of these faces? The bodies are obviously fanciful, but the faces might be...based on real human individuals."

"That's an intriguing question," Paul agreed. "I don't recognize either of them. Do you?"

"No," she said, a trifle uneasily. "Next?"

He pulled out a third image, this time of an individual whose upper body was that of a young woman, but whose lower body, beneath the waist, was that of a long snake.

"That's Melusine," Jane said. "It's a familiar story—or rather, a familiar version of the story. In some variants, she's fishy below the waist too, but the snaky lower body has become standard."

"Do you recognize the face?" Paul asked.

"No," she said, again...but even more hesitantly than before. Then she added: "No, I don't, and I don't have the feeling that I might have seen her before without being able to place her, but...there is something familiar about it...almost...do you remember what Antoine said about your picture of my mother...that there was a family resemblance. But it's just a picture of a human face, in which it would be very easy to find a family resemblance with *someone*, wouldn't it?"

"That's probably true," said Paul. "How could my imagination synthesize a hypothetical face without drawing upon my awareness of features that actually exist? I remember when my Mourgue la Faye was exhibited in the Salon five years ago, I got a letter from one young woman claiming that it was a picture of her and threatening a lawsuit."

"How did you answer it?"

"I didn't. I just ignored it. I had crazy letters even then—you can imagine how many more I got after the *Mercaba* publicized me as a painter of spirits. There were dozens even before I went to Toulouse with Victor to see Gaston, and there were hundreds by the time I came back. When I offered Juliette a job as my secretary I thought that it would be a virtual sinecure, but it turned out to be anything but. It eased off once I was out of Paris, obviously, but earlier this afternoon, when I came out of the hotel, five people had already left contact details there me. *Five*—after four years, and even though my return to Paris didn't get any publicity, so far as I know."

"It wasn't just the *Mercaba*, though, was it? You were in all the dailies—only for a day or two, admittedly, but the spiritist community is very swift to invent legends, and some of them last a long time. I know that Madame Pommerat, Henri Lemastur and Baron de Rochemure were all looking for you while you were painting my portrait. I kept them at bay when they wanted me to intercede, and Juliette must have done so too—she was forever having to leave us to go downstairs in response to Madame Cambourg's ring, to tell some reporter to get lost, always frowning at the thought that she'd be leaving us alone—but if La Pommerat has heard through the grapevine that you were returning, I'd be willing to bet that one of the notes left at your hotel today was from her and another from Rochemure. She still hosts her salon, of course, and probably still holds occasional séances there with Lemastur's help, but I don't attend. Go on—the next monster, please?"

Paul displayed a picture of a sphinx—or, to be pedantic, a sphinge.

"Oh, she said. "That's the sketch from which the painting you've just given me was made...or one very like it. Well, I think I got the best of the bunch, so far. Do all your monsters have pretty female faces?"

"Not all of them," he said. He put another picture on top of the pile. This one was a drawing of a tigress with a human head; the tigress had exaggerated, splayed claws.

"Not all pretty, then, even if they're all female so far. Didn't Antoine once compare Zosima to a tigress, while we were in your studio? But that face isn't Zosima's—she was more handsome than pretty, but her features weren't nearly as nasty as those. Are you going to show these pictures to her?"

"Some—perhaps most, in time—but as I said, I won't show anyone the pictures of you, unless you give me explicit permission to consult Camille about them."

She made a dismissive gesture.

"You can show them to anyone you like. The nudity and the nails might give them both a slight thrill. Let me know if they come up with any interesting theories to account for them...although I suppose neither of them will have any difficulty coming up with a plausible story, even if they're too discreet to voice them...*ah!*"

Paul had turned over another sketch. Again, it showed a tigress with a human face, perhaps the same one as the previous image, but this time, she was agonizing: bristling with half a dozen arrows, none of which appeared to have penetrated deeply but which might...must...have been poisoned. The expression on her face was horrific.

The next picture had a strangely androgynous head and the body of a manticore—but this was a much more active figure than the previous ones; the manticore was not simply posed, but was tearing apart a prey with apparent fury. The prey in question looked like some kind of antelope. Like the tigress in the previous image it appeared to be agonized—unsurprisingly, given what was apparently being done to it.

"Are there many more like that?" Jane asked.

"Not here, and mercifully, not very many in the pile back in Toulouse," Paul said "My imagination doesn't seem to go in for horror very frequently, and mostly in the context of imaginary monsters rather than people burning or being stabbed to death.... It distresses me a little, but it's an aspect that I didn't want to censor from the gallery."

She shrugged. "I've written much worse," she said, curtly. "I must have far worse things than that floating in my unconscious in a regular basis. You wouldn't think it to look at me, I know, and what it signifies about me, I have no idea...but, as I said before, you've read the books. It's all on public display. I've no cause to be surprised, but somehow...I didn't think of you in that way. Next?"

Paul added another picture to the pile. Again, it was impossible to attribute a sex to the bloated head, or even to identify it as human. The body, such as it was, mostly consisted of tentacles, like those of the "Martian" than the *Mercaba*'s artist had drawn on the basis of an inaccurate second-hand description of the alleged fetus that he had drawn at Juvisy.

"That's one for Flammarion," Jane observed. "Uglier than the species he usually depicts, though—far more like the monsters with which I populated my alien world in the double star story."

The next sketch was similar with regard to the head, but the body, although indistinct, was obviously that of a seven- or eight-month human fetus—obviously, at any rate, to everyone who had ever seen a drawing of one in a medical text-book.

"Your sister?" Jane queried.

"Perhaps. Or some other child, born premature and dead. Any of hundreds who have died in the womb in the last few years...perhaps even one that was alive at the time of sketching. How would I know? But this one, and others like it, would raise some of the most awkward philosophical questions, if it weren't just a matter of my perverted imagination at work—which, especially given its similarity to the previous image, seems by far the likelier hypothesis, wouldn't you agree?"

"In respect of those, yes," Jane said, warily.

The next picture had nothing human about it at all. It was an insect, pure and simple: a black beetle with horn-like projections on its head."

"Taken from Egyptian mythology?" she asked.

"Perhaps, he said, "but that wasn't the first thing that sprang to mind when I drew it, or to Juliette's. Her surname, if you remember, was Scarran; the other girls used to call her Scarab. On the other hand..."

The next sketch depicted three fanciful moths, vaguely reminiscent of tropical Luna Moths.

"Are they supposed to be alien inhabitants of other worlds?" Jane asked.

"I don't think so," said Paul. "I assume that they're what they seem to be: insects. But I can't imagine why I've sometimes drawn insects, without any evident chimerical aspects. Not birds, not fish, not crabs...just insects. Never any severed insectile heads...only detached human heads, mostly of people I know."

"Only mostly?"

"That's right. You've seen a few of those I don't know already, but these are more peculiar."

Paul pulled out the last two sheets of paper from the portfolio. Each contained the images of three heads and a blurred fetus. Jane peered at the heads for some times, and then shook her head. "I don't recognize any of them. But why three faces and a fetus, twice over?"

"I have no idea," said Paul. "But note that the pattern is the same in each case: two females, one male, and something that might be a fetus."

"Might be? So far as I can remember, they look more like fetuses than the one you drew at Juvisy, but not as much as the one you showed me a few moments ago...and it wouldn't be very difficult to mistake them for the head with

50

tentacles you juxtaposed with that one...or for disembodied heads supplemented by some impressionistic shading"

"I know. Perhaps they look a little more like fetuses because I've taken the trouble to look at medical textbooks since I made the first drawing, but the drawing I showed you just now proves that I can do much better, so the various ambiguities are...enigmatic."

Jane studied the two pictures carefully. "It's a long time since I studied the Juvisy picture at Antoine's house...can I conclude from what you've just said that you're present belief is that that one really was a fetus, a trifle indistinct because you didn't know then how to draw one?"

"I can't be that definite, even though I have a copy of the Juvisy drawing in Toulouse. All I can say is that it was something that might have been a fetus, some later repetitions of which—but not all—resemble a fetus more closely, probably because I now have a better idea if what one looks like. The other might well be an attempt to improve on the *Mercaba* image—again, something only explicable in psychological terms. And let's not forget that there's a measure of interpretation in all these images—*all* of them. Sometimes it seems like flattery, sometimes bizarre transfiguration, sometimes slight inaccuracy...but none of them is photographic; they're all interpretative—even the ones that look like simple portraits of familiar individuals."

"And you expect me to be able to help you figure out what all of this means?" she queried, seeming a trifle overwhelmed.

"It's more hope than expectation," Paul told her, "but I'll be grateful for any suggestions...except, of course, the one that I'm simply insane."

"No, I agree with you about that one. Neither of us is insane, in spite of the inference that idiots sometimes take from what I write, and would probably take from what you draw, when we're dredging material up from the well of creativity in a fashion that's mostly or entirely unconscious. Camille will agree with me, I'm sure...about Zosima, I'm not so sure, alt-

51

hough she can hardly look unkindly on the pictures of her darling Talia. She'll want one of those to hang on her wall, I shouldn't wonder, if she allows herself decorations in her monkish cell. Given her proclivities, she might ask you for one of the images of me, too. Don't give her one—show them to her, by all means, but nothing more. You can turn the first one into an oil painting, if you like, though. I'll hang it in my bedroom...where no one else will see it, alas."

Paul did not challenge the "alas." She would not have had to explain it, in any case, because the maidservant came into the drawing room then, and said, a rather caricaturish fashion: "Madame is served."

Paul put all the sketches back in his portfolio, and they went to dinner.

CHAPTER III

"Enough about strange drawings," Jane said, once they had started on the main course. I want to know about you—especially about any new women in your life, whether they're love interests or not."

Paul hesitated over a simple denial, but in the end, he said: "I have made one good female friend."

"Is she young? Is she pretty? Has she anything to do with Académie des jeux floraux?"

Paul was only slightly started by the accuracy of the guess. As a writer, Jane had to know that the institution she had named was the oldest literary society in the world, and that it awarded annual prizes for poetry, nowadays in French as well as Occitan. She had to figure, too, that as an artist settled in Toulouse, he would have been drawn to the games and the imagery associated with them.

"She's peripherally involved with the games," he said. "She's an artist. She's designed medals for the prizes, and has done paintings for the décor."

"Painting of flowers? Or paintings of the legendary Clémence Isaure?"

"Both. Her paintings are very elaborate, full of floral symbolism, very intriguing...mystical wouldn't be putting it too strongly. The holy grail figures in them frequently."

"Unlike your image of me crucified," Jane observed, "which doesn't even have a wound in the side, let alone some necrophile trying to collect the blood flowing out of it...but it's a connection of sorts. You've never sketched her in your sleep?"

"No...but I have sketched her consciously, and there are, as you say, degrees of entrancement."

"You should have brought one to show me. Does she paint in a trance, self-induced or aided by hypnotism?"

"Strictly self-induced, so far as I know, but not in a methodical or deliberate fashion. It happens spontaneously. I think. She's wary of talking about it, but yes, I think she is something of a medium, if that's what I am, and certainly worthy of interest in that regard."

"Only in that regard? I noticed that you didn't answer either of my first two questions." Jane seemed to have settled into an interrogative mode, perhaps feeling licensed by the fact that she was a hostess in a fuller sense now; the food, as she had promised, was uncomplicated but flavorsome, and the wine excellent. Paul took a long sip from his glass before answering the provocation

"She's older than me, in her thirties, I think. Not conventionally pretty, but she's slender and delicate, and has a certain strange beauty...not as evident as yours, but one might classify it in the same species. Her name is Clémence, but don't read too much into that; it's what her parents christened her, deliberately, after Clémence Isaure. A trifle irreverent, perhaps, but Paris is by no means short of Maries."

"Is she healthy?"

"She doesn't cough blood, if that's what you mean. She gives the impression of being frail, but yes, I think she's healthy."

"Married?"

"Widowed. She was married to a regular competitor in the games, a modern troubadour of sorts. He drowned in the river...accidentally...about two years ago, shortly before Juliette died. I knew them both slightly before then, but I got to know her better afterwards...shared mourning."

"She's unattached, then—but you wouldn't call her a girl-friend, even though her mourning must be over by now?"

"Must it? At any rate, no, I wouldn't call her a girl-friend. I suppose there's a certain...mutual curiosity, but she's very wary, as I say. The marriage doesn't appear to have been very happy, although her grief at the fashion of its ending was certainly real and acute, but the experience seems to have dissuaded her from rushing into a further relationship of a similar sort."

"What a delicately romantic way you have of putting things. Does she know that you draw the dead when you're entranced?"

"She knows what happened at Juvisy, and that I don't know how to interpret it—and no, I haven't drawn her husband, even though I can remember what he looked like and would recognize him if I did."

"So," said Jane, "your story is that you simply see your Clémence as a specimen of investigation, someone who might be able to help you gain some further insight into the phenomenon of what you call somnifabrication, and not as a potential lover?"

"That's an accurate summation of the situation," he agreed, reaching for his wine glass again.

"I'm not sure that you're the best person to judge the accuracy of your own feelings in such situation. Would you be able and willing to reciprocate if she decides that you're a potential lover, once her mourning is far enough behind her?"

"That's a very odd way of putting it."

"Is it? I'll take that as a prevarication, and therefore a perhaps, tending toward a *probably*. Is she the only other artist you've found in Toulouse who goes in for a measure of somnifabrication?"

"No, but she's certainly the most extraordinary and the most interesting, if only because of the sharp differences in our work. If it were possible to work out where her imagery is generated and how it's transmitted, it might cast some light on what happens to me."

"But she doesn't draw dead people?"

"That's a point yet to be clarified."

"A mystery woman dangling lures, then—the most dangerous kind of all. And you didn't bring me a picture of her...consciously sketched, of course. You didn't want to show her to me."

"I didn't think she was relevant to our discussion of my situation."

"Of course you didn't. I'm only a substitute mother, after all, not a Clémence Isaure or a Virgin Mary, in spite of idolization being effortless four years ago. You can think of me now as a statuesque nude or a crucified martyr, with a very uncomfortable pose on my cross, but not as a *femme fatale*. Your unconscious doesn't want to depict me as my Yvaine made flesh—my reincarnate Lilith, my evil Eve—even though you read the story in *Les Sataniques*. Your unconscious can't see me as my lovely Viamalah, or my poor tortured amazon— although, after all, they're all me in a sense, fragments of my personality projected into my work. But neither of the images you showed me that have my face are the selves I discover in my own semi-trances. Is that censorship, Paul, or do you really not see the hidden me in your trances, the version of myself that only peeps out from my unconscious in my exotica, among the black panthers and the dancing girls?"

All that Paul could think of to say in response to that was: "I'm sorry. It's not conscious."

"So you have nothing for which to apologize. And if these are phantasms of the living rather than products of your own busy unconscious, the fault is all mine: it's my unconscious that is presenting myself to you in that guise, my unconscious that wants yours to see me that way. But even if it isn't, you have nothing for which to apologize, so I'm the one who should be saying that I'm sorry."

"Not at all," said Paul. "Everything you said was true, after all, and I have no excuse for being unable to see the selves represented obliquely in your books—which I have, in fact, not merely read but loved. Perhaps we ought to remember what Talia said: that we seers and somnifabricators can't choose, and that we're far more likely to be afflicted by things we don't want to see than things we do."

"*We seers and somnifabricators*," she repeated. "If I were honest with myself—which is perhaps not a wise thing to be nowadays—I'd have to accuse myself of vulgar jealousy, of a rather stupid kind. I'll make you a confession, since I know that you're far too polite to interrogate me in the intrusive way that I've just been interrogating you, even though I have not the slightest vestige of a claim over you, I'm jealous. I was jealous of Juliette because you asked her to go with Toulouse with you, even though I couldn't possibly have gone in her stead. I told myself that I disapproved because I knew that she would be bad for you, that you'd be hurt, and that I felt sorry for you, but that wasn't true; I was just jealous. And what you told me this afternoon about her telling you that she was glad that you didn't love her, because it meant that you'd carry on being kind to her no matter what, made me jealous again, even though I didn't believe a word of it, because I couldn't imagine anyone having that degree of kindness for me...even you.

"And then, when you told me a few minutes ago about your Clémence, about her being a seer of sorts, a kindred spirit, who might be able to help you in your quest to understand yourself, I thought: well, I'm a seer of sorts, a kindred spirit, who might be able to help you with your research, but she's in Toulouse, and I'm here, and in a matter of days you'll go back to her and I won't see you again for another four years, or perhaps never. I wouldn't mind so much if it were just mere lust, any more than I'd have minded if you'd only wanted to screw that little whore, but you say that it isn't, although you won't say that you won't if she wants you to.

"And all of that is absurd, I know, because only this morning I was reminding myself that we hardly know one another—that we've only ever had a dozen real conversations and exchanged a few dozen letters—and that the kind of relationship you had with Juliette and the kind you have and might yet have with Clémence would be quite impossible for us...except that somehow, crazy as it seems, there is some kind of weird bond between us, and when you clasped my hand this afternoon before going back to your hotel, I felt it forcefully. I don't know what it is, and I certainly don't know what to do about it...except that I definitely want to be there if Zosima sends you into the well of souls again...but if there is such a thing as psychic magnetism, the fact that you and I are poles apart only seems to be drawing us together. I'd ask you if any of that made sense, if I weren't already certain that it doesn't."

Paul drained his wine glass, but didn't dare reach for the decanter, because he was certain than it would be a breach of etiquette. Fortunately, the maidservant came back in to that point with a tray carrying desserts. With practiced ease she cleared away the redundant dishes and placed the new ones in position, and then she somehow found the time and the dexterity required to switch the wine-bottles one-handed and to fill new glasses.

When she had gone, Paul said: "I don't suppose it's any consolation to you, but I'm far more confused than you are, and far from optimistic about finding any solution to the puzzles by which I'm confronted. You're much more widely-read than I am, so you know very well how long artists of various sorts have been grappling with the idea of inspiration without ever coming up with the ghost of an answer, and how long metaphysicians have been struggling with the question of what happens to the soul after death, if anything, without ever being able to make up a plausible story, so what chance have I got?

"Most people, I know, just give up; they either settle for putting their faith in some arbitrary set of pretences, or they reconcile themselves to willful blindness by simply not caring. One of the things I admire most about you is that you're not prepared to do that. In your books, you keep on addressing the problems even though you despaired some time ago of being able to find an answer. You keep on drawing material out of the well of inspiration, using it and applying it, even though you know that it can't reach a satisfactory conclusion and that in the eyes of some narrow-minded people it makes you look bad. That's courage, and it's a courage I wish I had, and I hope that knowing you, even at a distance has enabled, and will enable, some of it to rub off on me.

"II also know that what you do is costly, that it sometimes hurts. One of the first things of yours I ever read was the story in which you represent your chimera as a monster that seems benign at first, and then metamorphoses into a woman who plays what you call the little waif act, and then becomes a monster again, which wears human hearts, torn out by cunning rather than brute force, as a decoration. It was a gaudy work of the imagination, but when I read it I thought that it had some truth in it, not only as a general description of the chimera that we seers all pursue, but something of particular relevance to me."

Jane winced slightly at that, but suppressed the reaction and said nothing. Paul took a deep breath and continued.

"The truth is," he said, "that I ran away, and I took Juliette with me not because I loved her, or because Antoine Cros had asked me to be kind to her, but because I wanted, and needed, someone to cling to. She said that that was why she wanted and needed me, and that she was being purely selfish in letting me be kind to her, but she didn't know that it was actually the other way around; because I didn't have your kind of courage, your ability to cope with the clawed heart-collecting chimera. Now, I've come back, but it isn't courage that has brought me back, it's desperation. I know, or at least feel, that allowing Zosima to hypnotize me again will probably be just as dangerous as it would have been four years ago, and it still frightens me, but not as much as going on without knowing—because for me, psychic blindness isn't an option. Even if I can't reach an understanding of where the dead are coming from, or why, I need to find a way of living with them.

"I could think of have a dozen reasons why I ought to have come to you first, before seeing Zosima or Camille, and why I was so glad when you wanted to insist that you want to be present when the experiment is repeated, but the simple truth is that I'm scared, and I need someone to cling to, and you're the most beautiful, the most intelligent, the most imaginative and the most idolizable person I've ever met, and I hoped that you wouldn't refuse, even though you had no motive for agreeing other than simple kindness. That's my confession."

She laughed. "I'm met more refined flatterers," she said, "but flattery is an art in which naivety, and even brutality, have their advantages. All right; if that's the way you want to look at it, or want to convince we that you look at it that way, cling all you want; I'll be glad of it. I'm sorry I'm not Juliette...but you've got by without her for two years, so you can't have needed her as much as you pretend, and you can't need me as much as you pretend, thank God—and thank you, for being prepared to pretend."

"I haven't," said Paul, quietly.

"Haven't what?"

"Haven't got by without Juliette."

Jane frowned. "You mean because she's still haunting you?"

"No...well, yes, she *is* still haunting me, but that doesn't mean that I'm not without her. Talia haunts me too...and so, without even being dead, do you...but I'm still without. Clémence...well, even if she did decide that perhaps I'd be acceptable as a lover...she isn't what I need. What I need, before I can tell myself that I really am *getting by*, if something that's out of reach, perhaps something that doesn't even exist...but I feel now, as I've always felt, that if I don't find it...then I'll lose my mind. I used to think that I had time to search, time to strive, but I don't think that any longer. I dare say you'll tell me that I'm still young, that I have all the time in the world, but I don't so. I live too closely with the chimera, and with the dead. I understand better now, I think, why so many people become obsessed with hearing the dead speak, with courting somniloquists. It's not because the dead are too far away, it's because they're too close at hand...but silent."

After a slight pause, Jane said: "I hear you. You do realize, I suppose, that if you said that to anyone but me, they probably would think that you're verging on insanity—perhaps even Camille Flammarion."

"Perhaps—but I hoped I could rely on you not to jump to that conclusion too swiftly."

"I won't let you down," she assured him. She added: "Quiet they might be, but don't you find that their silence speaks volumes?"

Paul contented himself with saying: "Yes."

"But when all is said and done, they only come intermittently. There are whole days aren't there, when the rule of consciousness in untroubled. There are days when one could almost be...we'll, not happy, but unhaunted. It's only for a while, but the while is precious. That isn't to be underestimated, in my experience. I wouldn't call it courage, but it's something. Perhaps, when we took back, we'll be able to say, like your Juliette, that it was more than we could reasonably have expected, and chide ourselves for not having been sufficiently grateful."

"Perhaps," Paul conceded.

"When I was young," the author mused, "people used to envy me. They still do, I suppose, albeit for different reasons but I took a particular vanity from the envy I had back then— unreasonably, as I couldn't actually claim any credit for being young enough and beautiful enough to attract that special kind of envy. But I took it anyway. One evening, at a ball—there were still balls in those days—a stupid little girl, younger than me and not significantly less pretty, looked at me with eyes filled with envy, and said: 'You could have as many lovers as you want.' It wasn't true, but I could understand the semblance. I can't remember now what I said—probably that standard quip about it being the quality that counts, not the quantity—but I can remember what I thought. And what I thought, as I looked around that glittering society occasion was: 'But how many of them do I want?' And the answer, which is probably obvious, was: 'None of them,' I wanted something else, something more, something impossible. And I've never stopped wanting it. Which probably doesn't seem like the kind of encouragement you wanted—but I did get by, and so can you. And when you do, and you look back, you'll probably be able to say to yourself: *all things considered, it was as much as I had any right to expect*."

"But you haven't reached the end yet," Paul observed. "You have a great many books to write yet, and no matter what you think, when I compliment you, it's not flattery but the simple truth. There's more than one reason why you're still envied and still enviable."

"But we've just established, haven't we, that that's not the point. You're young and handsome. I won't say that you could have any woman you want, but if that were your top priority, you wouldn't be short of choice. You're not rich, by any means, but you're beginning to be successful. Your paintings sell now; you can make a living, and you don't have luxurious tastes or a miserly frame of mind. You're enviable, and I dare say you're envied—but it's not enough, is it? Perhaps your sense of urgency is exaggerated, but even at my most optimistic, I can't say more to encourage you to hang on except that it might not be as bad as you think—which is, I suspect, letting you down somewhat, give that I'm the person you thought you might be able to cling to. Camille Flammarion will do better than that, I'm sure, and Zosima too."

"But they don't know," Paul pointed out. "They aren't like us."

"Don't underestimate Camille. His visions aren't like our visions, but he has them. Perhaps everyone does—even Antoine, who posed as the sanest man in the world, but still died thinking of himself as the King of Araucaria and Patagonia. What differentiates you and me from the others isn't that we tap into the well of souls more readily, or that we dredge things up that we can recognize and appreciate in one another's game—it's something more than that. You didn't believe that little girl, did you, when she said that you and she could look into one another's minds?"

"No," said Paul. "I didn't, but..." He stopped.

"Exactly," said Jane. "But...I could make up a story, you know, in which you and I, without quite being aware of it, can look into one another's minds—unconsciously, at least. Perhaps, if we're haunted by some of the same ghosts and some of the same monsters, it's because we're seeing them in one another's minds. I thought of that four years ago, as the likeliest explanation of how you came to draw my mother. In the train carriage on the way back to Paris, while I was still refusing to admit that it was my mother that you had drawn, while listening to Antoine's fatuous hypotheses, I was thinking to myself: *What if it's true? What if this young fool who can do tricks with charcoal really can pluck images out of my mind, Antoine's mind and God only knows where else?* I didn't know at the time, of course, that Talia had already concluded, beyond her capacity for doubt, that you'd formed a link with hers, but it adds another prop to the story now. Even on what I had, though, I thought: *but it's not a disaster; after all, he can't have seen everything in my mind, he can't read my thoughts, and he seems to like me, to think highly of me, of my work. Perhaps it's something good, something healthy, something to be welcomed.*

"I remembered that a few hours ago, when you showed me the other picture of my mother. I was doubtful, of course. *He can't possibly have taken it out of my mind while he's in Toulouse and I'm in Paris*, I thought—but then I thought: *Unless there's a special bond between us to which distance is irrelevant.* And from then on, I thought about each image: *could he have got that out of my mind?* The mermaid, obviously, could have been the mermaid I bought from you, filtered back to him through my impression of it. The bird-siren, not so obvious. But the ones that really made me wonder were the images of me. And now, looking back, it's easy to make up that particular story, to explain why, when I think of myself, I think of myself naked, devoid of arbitrary accessories, and I rejuvenate myself, nostalgically. But most of all, yes, I do often think of myself as a martyr, just as your Juliette found it so easy to do, and I can think of half a dozen hypotheses to account for my thinking in terms of a cross rather than flames. But the significant thing about that story, that train of thought, isn't that I can make up some sort of narrative, but the fact that I want to...that I'd almost like it to be true."

"Almost?" Paul queried.

"Obviously—because we never quite succeed, do we? There's always a rebound, a reaction. As soon as the thought was formed that the bond might be good and healthy, the antithesis looms up: that it might be harmful and sick. Four years ago, I thought: *of course it would be nice if a linkage of minds could enable us to feel close, could strengthen us, but what are the odds? What if all we can share is our own kinds of sickness: me, the small, frail middle-aged woman who spends so much time imagining all kinds of hideous orgies of lust and torture in pagan temples, and him the handsome ingénu who draws the dead in his sleep and thinks he murdered his twin sister and his mother before he was even born?*"

"I prefer the first version of the story," said Paul, calmly, "I don't think either of us is sick, and I do think that the bond we formed is something good and healthy, at least potentially. What you expel into the pages of your more exotic novels and what I expel into the images in my portfolio isn't a symptom of sickness, nor is it an expression of perverse desires or convictions; it's a consequence of exactly what we both set out to do as soon as we realized that something strange was happening: to explore, to go in quest of explanations."

"The trouble with exploration," she commented, "is that you can't know what you're going to find."

"No," Paul admitted, "but at least you can tell yourself that finding it would be an achievement, no matter what it is, and that at least you've plucked up the courage to look. It seems to me, having read your books, that that's what you've done, and are still doing."

They didn't go to the drawing room in order to have coffee; it was served at the table. When the maidservant had gone again, without offering a cigar that Paul would, in any case, have declined, he looked at Jane expectantly, looking for a response to his cue.

Instead, she said: "I haven't been a very good hostess, I fear. I wanted to be at my best for you, and clearly I haven't been. I've allowed myself to talk far too much, about myself—which is never a good idea—and to be far too confused in what I was trying to say. I don't have any excuse. Can you forgive me?"

"There's nothing to forgive," Paul assured her, "and if there is, the fault is all mine: I'm the one who brought trouble and confusion into the house, and wasn't able to keep it bottled up." He paused, and he went on: "Let's not forget that the images in your novels and my portfolio are selective, and they're not selecting out the merely typical; they're reaching for extremes, because it's only by going to extremes that one can get far enough away from the taken-for-granted to see it clearly and objectively. You and I aren't sick. Jane; we're just not psychically blind. Maybe it's a kind of handicap, or a kind of curse, to be psychically sighted, or partially-sighted, in a world of the psychically blind, but it's not a disease, and in itself, it's not insane, even if it might have the capacity to drive us insane if we're not careful, and even if other people sometimes think we already are."

"It might be hard to convince them otherwise, if you show them all the sketches you just showed me," Jane said, pensively. "Including the one of me crucified...which worries me a little, I must confess. Whatever story we make up to explain it...it can't reflect well on me."

"I don't know where the images I sketch in a trance state came from," Paul said, tempting reassurance, "but you know how I see you when I'm conscious, because you have the portrait I painted of you—I assume that you look at it occasionally."

She blushed slightly, and said: "It's in my boudoir, as I told you. Of course I look at it. It's more...private there."

"Well, let's not forget that while thinking about those bizarre cartoons. The portrait is you, painted accurately, consciously and with love. The others are mere doodles...and they're *my* doodles. Whatever there is about them that's puzzling, or ominous, it's my puzzle and the threat is to me. To the extent you might be involved in the explanation, or the quest to find it, I believe that our association is entirely good and healthy; I wouldn't be here otherwise."

She nodded, as if to endorse what he had said. "You're seeing both Zosima and Flammarion tomorrow," she said. You probably won't be back until late. Will you come to see me the following day, though, in the afternoon, if you're free—to tell me how it went, and what has been decided, if anything? You can stay for dinner again if you like."

"Yes, of course I'll come," he said. "And as soon as anything is decided between me and Camille, you'll be the first to know."

CHAPTER IV

The heavy sky had finally decided to release the burden of rain contained in the clouds. The downpour was not unduly heavy, but it was relentless. Paul had not brought an umbrella and became suddenly anxious about his portfolio, even though it was good quality leather. Jane offered to have her carriage harnessed, and to drive him to the hotel herself, or to give him the use of a spare bedroom, but he did not want to inconvenience her any further. It was one thing for a married woman in her position to entertain a man to dinner, but quite another for him to stay the night thereafter, or for the two of them to go off in a carriage together a dead of night. He insisted on leaving, but he accepted the large umbrella that she insisted on lending him.

"You'll need it," she said. "It's only a short walk to the boulevard, but your chances of picking up a cab immediately in this weather, even when the theaters won't be closing for some time yet, are slim. The umbrella will keep you and the portfolio dry until one comes along, or in case you have to walk to the intersection."

He thanked her profusely, and set off down the stairs. He did not attempt to open the umbrella indoors, and he ducked under the arch of the coaching entrance in order to be out of the rain while he wrestled with the mechanism, with the portfolio wedged under his right armpit.

He had his back to the road, and was taken completely by surprise when the portfolio was suddenly snatched away from its slightly precarious lodgment. Although the umbrella was not yet expanded he whipped around, tensing himself to run after the thief.

The thief, however, did not run away. He merely stood there, holding the portfolio in a sheltered position. He was a tall man, wearing a heavy overcoat and a broad-brimmed hat.

He seemed, in the uneasy gaslight filtering through the rain, to be enormous and sinister. His voice, however, was smooth and polite.

"Let me hold this for you, Monsieur," he said, "while you put the umbrella up. It would be unfortunate if you were to drop it."

Confused, Paul did not know what to say."

"It's a filthy night, Monsieur," said the tall man, exaggerating somewhat. "But if you'd care to step into the carriage parked on the pavement a dozen paces to your left, the master will be glad to give you a lift back to your hotel."

Paul succeeded in getting the umbrella erect. The big man did not hand back the portfolio.

"That's all right, thank you," said Paul. "I'll walk to the boulevard and get a cab."

"There won't be many about at present, Monsieur," said the other. "Far better to allow me to drive you."

Paul had no idea whether he was under threat, or whether the man was simply being kind. In that state of uncertainty, the hand that he reached out in order to take the portfolio was hesitant.

The tall man did not hand it over. "Please, Monsieur Furneret," he said, quietly, "walk to the carriage and climb in. No one means you any harm. Quite the reverse."

"You were waiting for me?" Paul said, drawing that inference from the fact that the big man knew his name.

"Yes, Monsieur," said the other suddenly seeming even taller, if not quite a giant.

"Why? How?"

"The master will explain, Monsieur Furneret," the burly coachman told him. "Please climb into the carriage. You'll find it much more comfortable than a fiacre."

Paul looked at the carriage that was being indicated to him. It did indeed, look a great deal more luxurious than a fiacre. He could not see the horses, because he was looking at the vehicle from behind, but if they matched the carriage, he thought, they must be fine animals. Apparently, he was being offered a lift to his hotel by an aristocrat: an aristocrat who had been waiting in the street outside Jane de La Vaudère's building for him to finish dinner. Why? And how had he known that he was there?

There was only one way to find out—all the more so as the big man showed not the slightest inclination to let go of his portfolio. Paul did as he was asked, and walked to the carriage. The coachman lowered the footstep, while carefully shielding the portfolio from the rain, opened the door, handed the portfolio to someone sitting inside, and then stood aside while Paul collapsed the umbrella and climbed in. The big man closed the door behind him.

There was a lantern suspended from the ceiling of the carriage, but the man who had accepted the portfolio from the coachman was wearing a black felt hat with a broad brim, which concealed the greater part of his face because he was looking down at the portfolio on his capacious knees, while most of the visible part was shielded by a neatly trimmed white beard.

A gloved hand waved negligently, inviting or commanding Paul to sit down facing the mysterious passenger.

Paul did so. He could not see the man's eyes, or the precise shape of the nose, but he thought: *I've seen that beard before.* He could remember or imagine, however, where he had seen it, or to whom it might belong.

The white-bearded man had opened the portfolio and pulled out the sheaf of drawings, which he set on top of the leather case, and then began to remove the sheets one by one, placing them on the cushion beside him. Paul opened his mouth to protest, but the situation seemed so bizarre, and he still had not managed to formulate his complaint when his indiscreet captor said: "This is the sketch from which you made the painting of Mademoiselle Cadelan." He tapped the image of Talia. "I am right, I assume, in thinking that the sketches were made posthumously?"

Thinking that the question took indiscretion far beyond the bounds of excess, but not unduly surprised that the unknown man knew Talia's name, given that he had evidently seen the oil painting, Paul simply said nothing.

The bearded man had turned over both sketches of Antoine. "Cros," he said, bluntly, and added, equally curtly: "Also dead." Then he turned over the pictures of Juliette. "Your so-called secretary," he observed. "The model and prostitute previously known in Montmartre as Scarab."

Paul felt a frisson at that identification, which implied that the unknown man knew far more about him than anyone should. He finally contrived to loosen his vocal chords to say: "Who are you?" His voice sounded hoarse.

The man in the hat, perhaps feeling that since Paul had failed to answer his question he was free to retaliate, only said: "Madame Scrive," evidently identifying that next sketch rather than himself.

That identification seemed far more surprising, and Paul was quick to say: "How do you know?" in a voice that was slightly less hoarse.

The question went unanswered. The carriage rocked as the massive coachman climbed up to his seat, but the vehicle remained stationary.

The man, whose white beard suggested that he might, in fact, be old enough to have known Jane's mother, was still shifting the pictures. "Don't know this one," he said, referring to the sketches of Martine Lambrunet. He repeated the comment twice more—and then came to an abrupt halt as he exposed the last sketch of a disembodied head, which he left on his knee, still covering up the picture of Jane de La Vaudère in the nude.

Finally, he raised his head so that Paul could see the whole of his face. Paul would not have recognized it, even though he knew that he had, in fact, seen it before, but he had already guessed who the man must be.

"Baron de Rochemure," he said.

The baron was staring at him, with an utterly unfathomable expression.

"Technically," he replied, "it's Baron de Rochemure de Harvanges, to distinguish my almost-extinct family from the one associated with the château in the Ardèche, but we live in an era of abbreviation. You're a very difficult man to see, Monsieur Furneret." The neutrality of his tone seemed carefully contrived.

"So difficult that you have to resort to kidnapping?" Paul countered, noting that the carriage still had not moved.

"You haven't been kidnapped, Monsieur Furneret," said the baron. "Had you collected the polite note that I left for you at your hotel, and replied to it by pneumatique, I would not have had to intercept you like this, but after the frustrations of my attempts to see you when you were last in Paris, when all my written enquiries similarly went unanswered, and when I was turned away from your studio twice by your...secretary, my patience had worn a trifle thin...understandably, I feel."

Paul had not been aware until Jane had mentioned it a short while before that Baron de Rochemure de Harvanges had attempted to visit him in his studio four years before, or that his written communications had gone unanswered, having entrusted those responsibilities to Juliette, but had he been fully apprised, he would have approved of her decisions. On the other hand, he could, in fact, understand why a man in Rochemure's position might have found the refusals offensive. The situation had now changed...but not sufficiently, given their present situation, for Paul to want to offer an apology.

"How did you know where to find me?" he demanded, curtly.

"When my valet went to your hotel to investigate why you had not replied to my letter, the receptionist told him that you had refused even to receive it and that you had gone out. You had used the fiacre that normally waits outside the hotel, and the coachman had returned to his station. Twenty sous was sufficient to obtain the address to which he had taken you—which I recognized, although it has been a long time since the days when Madame de La Vaudère and I occasionally encountered one another in passing in society and exchanged cards. I decided to cut through the formalities and wait for you. Now, if you don't mind, I'd like to talk about the important matter...the crucial matter." He tapped the sketch in which he had evidently recognized, rightly or wrongly, the face of his daughter. "She has contacted you again? You made this sketch in Toulouse?"

"I made the sketch in Toulouse," Paul confirmed. "Whether the conditions under which I made it constituted contact is...difficult to determine."

The baron's gaze flicked momentarily to the untidy pile of sketches he had made on the cushion. "I have no idea why you're to determined to play games with me, Monsieur Furneret," he said. "It seems unreasonable, not to say cruel. I do not recognize all the people whose faces you have sketched, but I know that two of them, in addition to my daughter, were dead before the séance at Juvisy to which I was not invited, and I know that three others have died since; I infer that all of these sketches were made after the people they represent had died, and that you drew them as a result of spirit visitations. Am I correct?"

"It's not as simple as that," Paul retorted. "When you say you know that two of them were dead before 1901, I assume that you mean Charles Cros and Madame Scrive. May I know how you recognized Madame Scrive?"

"Because I knew her," Rochemure retorted. "I was young at the time, and newly commissioned, but we were introduced, and...she made an impression on me. When you reach my age, you will probably be surprised, looking back, by the depth of the impressions made in your youth by beautiful women—women like Madame Scrive and her daughter, I mean, not the young woman you were living with in Toulouse or Madame Zosima's badly-damaged medium...although, to judge by these drawings, the latter do seem to have left a deep impression on your youthful mind."

Ignoring the provocation, Paul said: "Are you absolutely sure that the woman in my sketch is Madame Scrive?"

The baron's eyes narrowed, as he followed the implications of that question being asked. Instead of answering it, after a few moments' thought, he said: "You didn't believe me. You didn't believe that you'd actually drawn my daughter under Henri Lemastur's hypnosis. And you didn't believe Roimantel's identification of Madame Scrive, even though Jeanne must have..." He broke off briefly before continuing: "Must she, though? The poor child was so young that she can't possibly remember her mother as clearly as I do...which is why Flammarion was apparently running round his audience trying to get someone else to confirm Roimantel's identification instead of simply asking her. And you've been uncertain all these years...and that's why you said just now that the matter isn't as simple as I assumed. But you must know...you can't possibly be in doubt...that you really can see the spirits of the dead?"

"I don't *see* anything," Paul said, a trifle weakly. "I just draw...unconsciously. And sometimes I draw people who aren't dead, and things that aren't even people. Many of the things I draw when entranced are manifestly products of my imagination, and it's possible that they all are."

"No," said Rochemure, flatly, "it's not. That really is my daughter, and there's no way you could have seen her portrait, even if you might have seen one of Madame Scrive. But I suppose, on reflection, that it's not surprising that you were confused. I was confused myself, initially, or we'd have had this meeting four years ago, before you even went to Juvisy...but I didn't realize immediately...That explains..."

He stopped, and his head tilted forward again, so that the brim of his hat hid his eyes. Presumably, he was staring intently at the sketch of his dead daughter...the sketch, at any rate, that he had identified as that of his daughter, with complete conviction.

After a full two minutes, he looked up again. "After the séance at Madame Pommerot's house," he said, "Henri Lemastur claimed all the credit for what had happened. You were merely an instrument, he said; he was the one whose psychic magnetism had summoned the spirit and permitted you to draw her. You weren't even a good medium, he said; with the aid of a better one, he could surely obtain a much more sustained manifestation, and establish a real communication. I believed him...and continued to believe him for months, while he tried to make good on his promises. But the messages he pretended to obtain from my daughter were fabrications. I don't say that the man was a mere crook, because he did manage to produce manifestations that seemed genuine...but the messages he purported to receive from my daughter with the aid of other mediums were not.

"Initially, when I read the newspaper reports of your séance at Juvisy, I as skeptical; the pictures printed in the *Mercaba* and copied by the *Parisien* and *Le Matin* were obviously contrived. I was curious enough to want to see the originals, however, and also to question you further about what had happened at the Pommerat house, and that is why I wrote to you, twice, and tried to see you at your studio, but at the time I still considered Lemastur to be the more important figure in the equation. By the time I concluded that he was not, you had decamped to Toulouse.

"I consulted Madame Zosima about what had happened at Juvisy, and tried to ask her about a rumored second séance held at Antoine Cros's house, but she pleaded confidentiality. I engaged her to attempt to use her own magnetism to make contact with my daughter, and she tried—sincerely, I thought—but failed. Her medium was already in dire straits, and although she didn't die for some months, I suspect that her abilities were already suffering badly from the effects of her tuberculosis. When I tried to interrogate the girl about you, she became quite hostile. Even before she died, Zosima had changed the course of her ambitions and had formed the nucleus of her peculiar cult.

"I had enquiries made in Toulouse about you, but was I informed that you would no longer submit to being magnetized and had become something of a recluse, living in a remote cottage on the side of a steep hill some distance from the city. I continued trying to make contact with my daughter via other mediums, but became increasingly convinced that Lemastur had misled me, and that the key to what had happened at Madame Pommerat's house was you. When I heard that you were returning to Paris, I was very enthusiastic to make contact...and when you seemed to be refusing to do so, I...well, here we are. Now that I have explained myself, are you willing to answer my question...and to help me?"

Paul was not quite ready yet to forgive and forget, let alone to make any promises. "Who told you that I was returning to Paris?" he asked bluntly.

"This is Paris," was Rochemure's reply. "Anything that isn't a very tightly kept secret rapidly becomes common knowledge.

Paul made a quick mental review of the five people whom he had notified by letter of his imminent return. Jane and Flammarion, he felt sure, would not have broadcast the information, and it seemed unlikely that Zosima, from her present situation, would have spread it around. Victor Marvaud, on the other hand, was an enthusiastic participant in the kind of society that still qualified as "All Paris," and it was entirely possible that Auguste Chazelle, his art dealer, had mentioned his impending visit to one or two potentially interested parties. Paul remembered clearly what Antoine Cros had once told him about the void of society gossip, and how it sucked in any casual remark that might serve to ameliorate the vacuum. It was not really surprising that the news of his imminent arrival had reached the baron's interested ears.

Rochemure had obviously misinterpreted the reason for Paul's taciturnity. "I'm not a rich man by today's absurd standards," he said, "but I'm relatively well-off. I'm willing to pay for your assistance—far more, I suspect, if you're successful, than you're capable of earning at present from your painting."

"I can't choose what I sketch, and I'm not conscious of what I'm doing when I'm in a trance," Paul told him. "Apparently, I've now drawn your daughter twice, although I wasn't

75

aware of it until a few minutes ago, but I'm not in communication with her in any meaningful sense of the term. It's not a matter of payment—I'm not a professional medium and I have no intention of becoming one. I really don't think that there's any help I can give you."

"Nonsense," said the baron flatly. "The fact that this sketch exists proves that you can. It's merely a question of improving your contact with the world of the dead, bringing it to consciousness, if possible, by working with the aid of a magnetizer—Lemastur, Zosima, or anyone you care to name. I can't demand any guarantee of success, but I'm prepared to press you as hard as possible to obtain your co-operation in making whatever attempts we can to carry this quest further."

"Is that a threat?" Paul snapped churlishly.

Rochemure seemed genuinely surprised. "Of course not," he said. "Believe me, Monsieur Furneret, the last thing I would want to do is harm you, or to see you come to harm. The sum of my experiences in the world of psychic communication has convinced me—belatedly, I fear—that you might the most precious thing in the world, so far as I am presently concerned. I repeat that you have not been kidnapped, and I would not want you to think that you are under the slightest threat. I am only thinking in terms of inducements. If money is genuinely irrelevant to you, you merely have to state what you do want, and I will do everything in my power to meet your conditions. What will it take to persuade you to help me?"

"For a start," Paul suggested, "you could tell me why."

"I believe that I have explained that."

"You've explained why you think—probably incorrectly—that I can help you. You haven't explained why you're so desperate to obtain that kind of help. What is it you want to obtain from your dead daughter?"

That was evidently a more difficult question than it seemed, even though the answer, when the baron finally provided one, was utterly anodyne. "Forgiveness," he said.

"For what?" Paul asked, finally reaching the point at which he thought frank rudeness justifiable.

"I don't want to tell you that," the baron said, his voice still scrupulously even. "Lamastur is not the only charlatan, believe me, who has summoned spirit voices assuring me of forgiveness—that is a virtual cliché, as I'm sure you're aware—but none of those lying voices has been able to go into detail. If I had given Lemastur more information, or if he had been able to discover accurate information from another source, doubtless it would have come back to me from the world beyond...my secrecy is the only guarantee I have that if a medium genuinely transmits my daughter's voice, I will be able to know for certain that it really is my daughter, and not a sham. I'm sure that you can understand my caution."

Paul could, indeed, understand the baron's caution. It was not merely the quest for forgiveness that was a cliché; fifty years of American spiritualism had made the baron's challenge a virtual requirement for serious skeptics. The baron, however, was not merely playing a game—he seemed genuinely embarrassed by what he had just said, and anxious. His gloved right hand had begun to tremble, and in order to occupy it, he moved the sketch that he believed to be his daughter sideways on to the pile on the vehicle's plush cushion, exposing the sketch beneath, of the naked Jane de La Vaudère.

After a few seconds of surprised contemplation, while Paul was still trying to formulate a request that he stop, Rochemure shifted that one aside as well, and emitted a slight gasp of surprise as he exposed the crucifixion scene. Then, rapidly, he riffled through the images of the unidentifiable nude and the two sirens. Then he paused, and said: "Did you make these sketches while magnetized?"

"I suspect that the notion of psychic magnetization might be deceptive," Paul said, "but yes, I made all of those sketches unconsciously, while I was in what the popular jargon calls a trance or somnambulistic state."

"In which you're not only visited by the spirits of the dead, but phantasms of the living and creatures generally considered mythical?"

"In which I might not be visited by anything except products of my own peculiar imagination."

"Hence your doubts and confusion...which surely ought to make you more enthusiastic, not less, to accept my help in trying to prove, beyond a shadow of a doubt, that you really do have privileged access to the world of spirits, by entering into a more substantial communication with my daughter than merely sketching her face."

"I can see why you might think that," Paul admitted, evasively.

Rochemure stared at him. It only took him a few seconds to jump to a conclusion. "You're frightened," he said. "Of course—how stupid I am. Something happened, did it not, at the séance about which no one wants to talk? It sent you running to a lonely hill outside Toulouse and threw Zosima into the tangled underworld of quasi-religious cults. The Cadelan girl thought it was responsible for the worsening of her consumption. Cros has died too, and Madame de La Vaudère...well, it's difficult to judge whether she hasn't been the same since, given that she was so very eccentric before, but your refusal to submit to magnetization again presumably speaks volumes. You had a bad scare. You're frightened."

"Yes," Paul admitted, frankly. "I was. I am."

Rochemure's mind was still working hard. "But you don't know why," he hazarded. "You're not conscious while you're sketching...or, at least, you forget what you've seen and heard when you wake up. It's a kind of self-censorship, or willful blindness; it's a familiar phenomenon. I should have realized. And it all started with Yvaine."

"Yvaine?" Paul queried, startled, remembering that it was the name of a character in *Les Sataniques*—the one that Jane had referred to as her Lilith.

"Yes," said Rochemure. "My daughter's name was Yvaine. And this all started when you drew the sketch of her didn't it? I should have realized. I should have guessed when I saw those faked sketches in the *Mercaba*, and read the comment about you. I've been so stupid...I should have put two and two together long ago. But you don't know...you don't understand what happened, and why it's so imperative that you try again. But that's why you've returned to Paris, isn't it? You're going to see Flammarion again...you *want* to try again. Can't you see, Monsieur Furneret, that our interests are identical? We both want...we both *need*...to understand exactly what happened at Lemastur's séance, and exactly what my daughter might have told you that you can't remember..."

His trembling hand was now positively agitated. Again it had sought distraction while he was speaking by shifting more of the sketches; he moved the other quasi-mythological images in rapid succession, with barely a glance, and only hesitated briefly over the monstrous head with the dangling tentacles—but then he stopped again and the next image.

After a pause, during which he seemed to be trying hard to control himself, he said: "Is that what I think it is?"

"I don't know," Paul riposted, with a certain exasperation. "I don't know what you think it is."

Rochemure stared at him again, but only for a moment or two. Then he looked down again and flicked rapidly through the sketches of the beetle and the moths, and only stopped when he reached the final two images, which he held up simultaneously, one in each hand. It occurred to Paul that his attempt to find the most esthetically appropriate sequence in which to display the elected images had not misled him.

"You imbecile," the baron whispered, although it was not obvious whether he was insulting Paul or himself. "You've wasted *four years*. The *Mercaba* got it wrong—obviously. It was because you were at Juvisy, involved with all Flammarion's ridiculous fantasies. A Martian! I should have guessed—you should have guessed. It's not a Martian that you drew at Juvisy, you fool, it was a human fetus."

"Actually," said Paul, annoyed by the insult to his intelligence, "the possibility was raised at the time. Antoine Cros recognized it immediately as a fetus. It was the *Mercaba*'s so-called correspondent who jumped to the other conclusion—with a little help from Flammarion's immediate reaction.

There was no point in issuing a correction to the papers, but those of us who were involved have known all along that it wasn't a Martian..."

"And that bitch Zosima didn't tell me? She knew, but she wouldn't tell me?"

"In fairness," Paul corrected, "I think Zosima was uncertain about the identification. Talia was absolutely certain, but she didn't attempt to convince Zosima."

"Why not?"

Paul shook his head. "I can't tell you that," he said.

"Because it's a secret?" It was hardly even a question, and the baron did not wait for an answer. "Of course it was," he added. "That's why..." He broke off, presumably having reached the fringes of his own secrets.

Curiously—at least, it seemed curious to Paul, Baron de Rochemure's hand had now stopped shaking. His hands were perfectly steady as he replaced the two sketches he was holding on top of the portfolio, squared them off, and then transferred the others from the cushion, one by one, but rapidly and neatly, until he had reconstituted the entire stack. Then he replaced them carefully in the portfolio and handed the portfolio to Paul. He reached up with a long arm and rapped twice on the wall of the carriage behind the coachman's seat. Finally, the carriage moved off.

The Baron looked Paul in the face again; his stare was so intense that Paul could not help wondering whether, in spite of the relative orderliness of the baron's speech, he might be dealing with a madman.

It was, however, in a perfectly calm voice that Rochemure said: "You have given me a great deal of food for thought, Monsieur Furneret, much of it utterly unexpected. I dare say that you could say the same. I would like to invite you to come to my house in Passy tomorrow night for dinner, in order that we can discuss matters of mutual interest at length, and at our leisure."

"I can't," said Paul, apologetically. "I have an appointment to see Camille Flammarion at Juvisy, and I'm dining with him. I'll be busy all day, and I won't be back until late."

For a moment, the baron seemed annoyed, but he quickly changed his attitude. "We'll, perhaps it's not a bad thing for you to compare notes with Flammarion," he said, "especially if you intend proposing to him that you hold another séance at the Observatory. The day after, then, Wednesday. Not necessarily for dinner, if you've made other arrangements, but whenever you can make time. Name the hour, and I'll send Fabien to pick you up at your hotel."

"I'm free for dinner then," Paul told him. "I'll accept your invitation, but I'd like to bring someone with me, if I may."

"Flammarion?" the baron queried.

"Madame de La Vaudère," Paul corrected.

That suggestion did not seem quite as welcome as the guess that the baron had made, but he was quick to say: "That's perfectly acceptable. I'll arrange to have you picked up at six o'clock. Shall I send Fabien to the house we've just come from, or to your hotel?"

"I'll have to arrange that with Madame de La Vaudère. Do you have a telephone?"

"I do," said the baron. He took a card out of his fob pocket, which had presumably been placed there in anticipation of handing it to Paul. Swiftly, he went on: "I'm extremely glad to have made your acquaintance at last, Monsieur Furneret; I apologize for the unorthodox method that I adopted in order to make contact, but I'm delighted that it gave me the opportunity to see your...art-work. I believe that I might be of some assistance to you, in your career and in pursuit of your other interests, and I hope that you'll be willing to accept my help. You have my sincere, albeit belated, commiserations for the loss of your mistress—who, if the information that has reached me from Toulouse is accurate, must have been very dear to you—and I'm truly sorry if you thought my previous references to her offensive. Might I enquire as to whether you have any plans to see Madame Zosima while you're in Paris?"

Taken aback by the baron's apparent complete change of personality, Paul replied, simply: "Yes, I have."

"Excellent. In view of what you've told me, I'll probably contact her again myself, when I've thought this matter through. Again, I apologize sincerely if you found Fabien a trifle intimidating when he invited you to step into the carriage—the poor fellow can't help his size, and it's not always obvious, at first glimpse, that's he's as gentle as a lamb. And you must have thought me a trifle rude for going through your portfolio without asking your permission. Can you forgive me?"

"I suppose so," said Paul, wincing slightly at his own churlishness, feeling that it put him in the wrong, although it still seemed perfectly obvious to him that Rochemure's behavior had been appalling.

"Good," said the baron. "I'm truly grateful. As I have grown older, I have become acutely aware of the need that we all have for forgiveness—and if, possible, for redemption."

The loquacity dried up then, and Rochemure seemed to be waiting for Paul to respond.

Paul clutched his portfolio to his breast, holding it with his left arm; his right hand was still clutching the handle of the damp umbrella, which had collected enough rain during a few minutes of exposure to have dripped a tiny puddle on to the floor of the carriage.

"I'm sorry to have imported a certain dampness into your carriage, Baron de Rochemure," he said, feeling secure in the knowledge that it was not his fault and that the apology would be conspicuously unnecessary. Only a trifle reluctantly, he added: "It has been very interesting to meet you, and I hope that we can each make some contribution, however small, to our mutual enlightenment."

"We can, Monsieur Furneret," said the baron, serenely. "Have no doubt about it. In time to come, you will look back on this meeting as a turning-point in your life, and I am convinced that you will be glad of the new direction that it will enable you to take. But here we are at your hotel. Until the day after tomorrow, Monsieur Furneret *au revoir*."

Paul took the gloved hand that was offered to him for shaking, and the effort that he failed to put into the handshake was more than compensated by the enthusiasm of the other's grip. "*Au revoir*, Baron," he said, politely.

The tall coachman opened the door and lowered the footstep. The carriage had stopped directly outside the door to the hotel, and there was no need for Paul to wrestle with the umbrella again, even though it was still raining. Three strides took him inside.

Once in the reception area, he paused to collect the letters and cards that he had neglected to take when he left, but did not examine them, Instead, he went straight to the telephone booth at the back of the hallway.

The maidservant answered the telephone, but as soon as Paul identified himself Jane came on. "Paul?" she said, curiously.

"Yes," he confirmed. "I was ambushed as I left your house, and I've just had the most remarkable conversation of my life with Baron de Rochemure de Harvanges. Are you free for dinner the evening after next?"

"You know I am," she told him. "I already invited you to have dinner here."

"True. Rochemure has invited me to dinner that evening, and I asked him if I might bring you—if that's agreeable to you, obviously."

"Of course it is. It's a signal honor. So far as I know, Rochemure hasn't invited anyone to dine at his house for more than a decade. He's become a near-recluse in recent years. You say he ambushed you? You mean that he was waiting outside the house? In the rain?"

"Yes. I fear that I was taken completely by surprise, and am only now beginning to think of all the intelligent things I might have said and done but didn't. I couldn't even prevent him from looking through the portfolio that his burly coachman stole from me while I was trying to put up your umbrella, so I'm afraid that he's seen the pictures of you. More importantly, he identified the picture immediately before the ones of you as his daughter, and he also recognized the one of your mother, whom he claims to have known. Is that true, do you think?"

"I suppose so," Jane replied, after a sight pause. "He's old enough, and he probably moved in the same social circles as my parents and old Roimantel way back then, given that he was a military man and that my father was an army surgeon. But why did he ambush you?"

"Because he's still avid to make psychic contact with his daughter, and, all other supernatural means having failed, he's pinning his last hope on me—sheer desperation, and he hadn't realized how limited my supposed abilities are. But his attitude changed completely when he continued leafing through the portfolio and came across the sketch of the fetus. He'd only ever seen the mistaken drawing in the *Mercaba*, and had been misled by the newspaper coverage into thinking that what I drew at Juvisy was an extraterrestrial. When he realized that it wasn't, the revelation obviously connected in some way with the reason why he feels such an acute need to establish contact with his dead daughter, but he wouldn't tell me why—it seems to be a secret that he's been guarding jealously for a long time. Do you know anything about what happened to her?"

"No, it was before my time—my time in Paris, that is—but I know some people who might. The upper echelons of Parisian society are a small world. If anyone knows, I can find out...within forty-eight hours if not within twenty-four. You might ask Camille tomorrow—such regular social contacts as Rochemure has had in recent years have been mostly confined to the spiritist community, so far as I know, and Camille was a part of it for twenty years before I became involved. But if Rochemure saw the *Mercaba* reportage, how can we be sure that he wasn't influenced by its suggestion in identifying my mother, just as old Mère Cambourg was?"

"Because he had no reason to connect the sketch in my portfolio with the Juvisy picture...although, come to think of it, it did come directly after the picture of Charles Cros...but no, I'm sure that his identification was spontaneous, not the result of suggestion. His recognition of his daughter was certainly spontaneous, and dispels at least some of the doubts that I've always had about his identification of the picture I drew at Madame Pommerat's séance. He was immediately convinced that what happened at that séance was connected with what happened at Juvisy—a hypothesis that I'd never considered. He wants to send his coachman to pick me up at six o'clock the day after tomorrow; can I ask him to collect both of us from your house, as you've invited me to call during the afternoon?"

"Yes, by all means. You want to meet up first, I presume, in order to figure out what questions you want to ask him—and to anticipate the questions that he might have for you?"

"Indeed."

"In that case, I'll make a few enquiries, and if I discover anything, we'll have time to compare it with anything that you can glean in Juvisy. I take it from the fact that we're having this conversation that you think this is important?"

"It's definitely important to him. Is he insane, do you think?"

"If you believe salon gossip, undoubtedly—but then, if you believe salon gossip, so am I and so are you, so it might be as well to reserve judgment."

"I will. I'll see you the day after tomorrow. *Au revoir.*"

"I look forward to it. *Au revoir*, Paul."

He rang off, and sorted through the communications that had been left for him as he went upstairs to his room. One of the letters, as he already knew, was from Baron de Rochemure, asking him to meet as soon as possible and imploring an urgent reply, but that one had already become redundant. The other was from Madame Pommerat, inviting him to her next séance and mentioning *en passant* that Baron de

Rochemure de Harvanges would be sure to be present if he would kindly confirm his acceptance of the invitation.

One of the cards was Victor's with a brief note scrawled on the back cancelling the tentative arrangement they had made to meet for lunch on Wednesday because of "urgent business" and asking him to telephone to make alternative arrangements. The second was Auguste Chazelle's, again with a note scribbled on the back asking him to call urgently to discuss the possibility of arranging an exhibition. The third bore the name of Gabriel de Lautrec, which, Paul remembered, was that of a writer who had been present at Madame Pommerat's on the night of the séance. It had no message, but Paul suspected that it, too, was not unconnected with Baron de Rochemure's eagerness to make contact with him and the fact that Madame Pommerat was planning anther séance.

He decided that there was nothing there demanding such urgent attention that he needed to fill in a *petit bleu* and leave it with the hotel receptionist for immediate dispatch, so he went to bed.

Out of what was now invariable habit, he placed a drawing pad on the bedroom table, but when he woke up in the morning, it as blank. He did not know whether to be glad about that or disappointed—but that reaction too had become habitual.

CHAPTER V

Paul was punctual in arriving at the café that Zosima has designated to him as a meeting place, but she was nowhere to be seen. He ordered a pot of tea with two cups, found what seemed to him to be a suitably discreet corner, and placed his portfolio between his feet.

Almost as soon as he had sat down, one of the other customers, a slightly bleary-eyed young woman who had been sitting at a table with a man who was presumably her pimp came over to offer her services, but went away as soon as he shook his head. Having observed the interaction, two other female customers sitting together, who similarly looked as if they had been up all night looked at him speculatively for a moment or two, and then decided that he was of no interest.

He did not know whether Zosima was likely to turn up in a thick veil and a dress, a man's suit or something more appropriate to her present role as a cult-leader, but he was not at all surprised, after an interval of five minutes or so, to see an enigmatic figure wearing what looked like a friar's habit, with the voluminous cowl pulled up over the head, approaching his table. The café's limited clientele paid no attention whatsoever to the new arrival, but Paul could not tell whether that was because the strange figure was familiar to them or because they were the kind of Parisians who took a pride in never showing surprise or interest anything that happened around them, unless there was a possibility that there was money to be made.

He stood up to greet the newcomer, and bowed.

"Thank you for agreeing to see me, Madame," he said, as they both sat down. "I've ordered tea, but if you'd prefer something else...."

"Tea is fine, Monsieur Furneret," she assured him. "I was...intrigued by your letter. As you sent it to the correct address, you must be aware of the changes in my circumstances since we last met, so I'm not sure what it is you expect of me, but if I can help in any way I'll be very glad to do so. As you know, I felt that we had unfinished business when you left Paris, although time and circumstance have, I fear, reduced considerably the possibility of any satisfactory conclusion."

Having poured the tea, Paul picked up the portfolio. He took out the sketch of Talia from which he had made his oil painting—one of only a handful of items that the portfolio now contained—and handed it to the mock-friar. "I wanted to give you this," he said. "I think Talia would have wanted you to have it."

Zosima took the sketch and studied it carefully. "A slightly romanticized likeness," she commented. "Not as romanticized as the painting you made from it, or from one very like it, but that, I suppose, was the nature of the medium. Consciously made, I assume?"

"No," said Paul.

"Zosima looked at him sharply from within the cowl, as if her eyes were peering at him from a dark abyss. "I understood that you never wanted to be magnetized again," she said, flatly.

"That was true, at the time," he said. "But you'll doubtless remember that when we met at Antoine Cros's house I had slipped into a trace spontaneously during the afternoon while working on my Jeanne d'Arc, and had painted unconsciously for more than two hours."

She nodded, to confirm that she did, indeed, remember. "Does that happen often?" she asked him.

"Fairly often," Paul admitted. "Perhaps as much as once a week, but I rarely manage to produce a complete and coherent work in the interval, in spite of the fact that I can work with amazing speed on occasion."

"I remember," said Zosima. After a moment, she added: "Does she still haunt you?"

"If it is haunting," Paul countered. ""I think about her often, and I draw her, sometimes unconsciously, especially when

I try to induce an unconscious or semi-conscious state deliberately."

Zosima nodded, thoughtfully. "Successfully?" she asked.

"Very moderately," Paul confessed. "Progress has been slow...frustratingly so."

"Ah. And now, at long last, you think that it might be worth the risk of borrowing assistance—and naturally, you thought of me."

"I did...naturally, as you say."

"You know, I suppose, that I no longer use my magnetic abilities to summon the dead?"

"I know very little, actually—partly it seems, because your new institution is rather secretive. Rumor has it that you hypnotize young women in order to enable them to remember or invent anterior lives, primarily for therapeutic purpose."

"For once, rumor is not a liar. That is, in fact, an important part of what I do now."

"But the power is versatile, is it not? It can be applied to other purposes."

"Yes, it can—but has rumor not informed you that I work exclusively with women, and only rarely with women who are not psychically blind?"

"Yes. If the principle is firm, I won't ask you to make an exception for me, although I did have the thought at the back of my mind that perhaps you might want to, in view of our...unfinished business."

Zosima's head turned within the cowl to look away. When the eyes reappeared, focusing on him again, she said: "She haunts me too. Given that we share that, might I ask you an indiscreet question?"

"Yes."

"I know that Talia came to see you at least three times, on her own, before you went to Toulouse. She wouldn't tell me why, or what you and she discussed, but I presume that it had something to do with the secret she believed that she had let slip to you telepathically. Given that she is now dead, will you tell me now what that secret was?"

"No," said Paul, simply. "Given that she is still haunting you, and seems to be still haunting me, I think, if the dead were capable of speech, that she would beg me not to tell you."

The sound of a slight sigh emerged from the cowl, perhaps an admission that she thought the same. Then she said: "I suppose I ought to approve of your discretion, even though I'm troubled by certain anxieties. I presume that Talia told you that, in her opinion, I didn't love her, and regarded her purely as an instrument."

Paul thought it safe to say: "She did give that impression."

"She and I had different notions of what love entails. You might not have thought it to look at us, but hers was more carnal than mine. I will not ask you whether she attempted to seduce you, because I doubt that she would have had the opportunity, with Juliette standing guard over you like a snarling mastiff, but she was perfectly capable of it, even though her preference was for my sex rather than yours. She is disembodied now, of course, and one might have expected that to cease...but as you seem to have been trying to facilitate contact with the dead for four years, albeit in a timid and tentative fashion, do you not find, in general, that the dead seem to retain at least a shadow of carnal desire?"

That was such a surprising question that Paul had to make a long pause in order to think about it. Finally, he said: "It's not something that I've ever noticed in my drawings."

He got the impression that the lips hidden in the gloom of the hood had curled sardonically. "That's either an almost incomprehensible ingenuousness," she opined, "or an outright lie. Would you care to tell me what proportion of the people you draw while unconscious or semi-conscious are female, and beautiful?"

Paul smiled, and barely suppressed an audible laugh. "I had thought that to be an expression of my own sexual proclivities and esthetic sensibilities," he said.

"Really?" she countered, holding up the sketch that he had given her. "Talia assured me—and it is in conformity with my other observations—that people like you and her could not choose the apparitions that come to you, and are more likely to be entities that you do not consciously want to see than those that you do. If the dead come to you spontaneously, unsummoned, is it not their proclivities and...esthetic sensibilities...that are in play, rather than yours?"

"It's an interesting perspective," Paul said, "but not consonant with my experience. He reached into the portfolio again and pulled out three more sketches. One was the image of the agonized tigress, one was the fetus and the third the scarab beetle. "All those were done unconsciously," he told her.

Zosima looked at each of the three images carefully, handing them back to Paul when she had done so, but retaining the one that he had represented as a gift.

"I already knew that you don't only draw the dead," she reminded him. "I saw the drawing you did at Cros's house, albeit briefly."

"I didn't have a chance to speak to you about it then," Paul said, "but Talia told me what you had told her: that in your opinion, the field of psychic force that you had generated at Juvisy had allowed me to detect images in Antoine's mind and Jane's, and also to make remote contact with Martine."

"That seemed to me to be the likeliest interpretation," Zosima agreed, "although my impression was that Talia saw things quite differently. I didn't know, when I was first introduced to you, that you had already formed bonds with both Doctor Cros and Madame de La Vaudère in the train from Paris, probably by virtue of your unusual sensitivity, your apprehension regarding the séance, your anxiety regarding the *Palatine*'s lifeboat and their intense curiosity, but when I realized that you might have done so, it seemed to support my interpretation strongly. I underestimated the strength of all the bonds you had made, of course, which is why I made the mistake of thinking, wrongly, that a distance of a few paces might separate Talia and Madame de la Vaudère from you—although I'm still astonished that you had established such a powerful bond with your model that you were able to share a hallucination at a distance of considerably more than a kilometer. I had seen sensitive mediums before, but never one whose sensitivity was as...unusual as yours. It assists your painting, I believe...the oil painting of Talia was truly remarkable. I would have tried to buy it had my means not been so slender...but I thank you for the sketch, even though it doesn't quite have the same haunting quality. Or do I mean haunted?"

"I don't know," said Paul, "but I still suspect that it was my painting of Jeanne d'Arc that hypnotized Juliette, and acted as a catalyst in the bond that I formed with her."

"That's possible," Zosima told him. "There seems to be an aspect of contagion to what you and I do, which seems to work in mysterious ways...which we would have been able to investigate, had you been willing to try four years ago. But you might have been correct in thinking that there was a danger in that. Talia was convinced that there was, but she was fearful by nature. Did she tell you that the images that came unbidden to her mind were very often things that she did not want to see, and that they were undermining her health and sanity?"

"She did," Paul confirmed.

"And is your own experience similar? Did she manage to infect you with her fear?"

"I don't think so," said Paul, more uncertainly than he could have wished, because the second question was a hypothesis he had never considered. "Sometimes, it's true, the things I draw in a trance state are unwelcome and disturbing...as you doubtless remember. More often than not, however, they're by no means unwelcome. The two dead people that I have drawn more frequently than anyone else are Juliette and Talia. I had a close bond of affection with Juliette, and although I only met Talia briefly I felt, as she did, that we had a special bond of sympathy. I mourned her death very sincerely, and I have not been sorry about what might or might not have been her subsequent visitations."

"Perhaps you're right," Zosima conceded. "I cannot regret the fact that she haunts me...I did love her, whatever she thought." She looked again at the sketch, intently. Then, she said: "I was hurt that she would not tell me her secret, especially when I had deduced what it was. Can you understand that?"

"I can understand why you felt hurt," Paul conceded.

"I knew, of course, when I first met her, that she had suffered a traumatic experience of some kind when she was young—probably no more than twelve or thirteen. I knew that it had to be more than a mere rape, because there are few girls in her social class who aren't introduced to sexual experience at that age by rape. She, of course, was exceptionally sensitive, psychically sighted to an extraordinary degree. My first suspicion, naturally, was that the rape had been unusually violent, but subsequently, I thought it more likely that she had become pregnant as a result, had given birth in secret and had then murdered, abandoned or given away the child. That seemed the more likely conjecture—until that night at Juvisy when she had a hysterical crisis on seeing what you had drawn. You might think me stupid, but it took me some time to realize that it must be a human fetus at six or seven months of development. As soon as I had realized it, of course, I guessed that Talia must indeed have become pregnant as a result of her rape, but that she had either contrived to induce a late abortion or had spontaneously given birth to a very premature child who could not live. Either way, she must have blamed herself for its death, and was haunted by the memory...or perhaps—who can tell?—by the child. You can understand that, I think, Monsieur Furneret, if what the *Mercaba* said about the circumstances of your own birth is true?"

Paul was no longer smiling. "Yes," he said. "I could understand that, as a matter of psychological trauma. Do you really think that I might have drawn a fetus because I was being haunted by the ghost of a child who had died in the womb?"

"I do," said Zosima, "although you will note that I carefully pandered to possible skepticism by inserting the phrase 'Who can tell?' Who can, Monsieur Furneret? Can you tell where you got the image from that you drew that night, and the more graphic one that you have just shown me?"

"No," Paul admitted. "But at least we can be sure, can we not, that if such things were possible, we would not be able to credit the apparitions in question with carnal desire."

"If, by carnal desire, we simply mean sexual lust, then no, we could not...but I sometimes wonder whether that definition is a trifle narrow. There are some people, as you know, who consider that the kind of desire that some women have for one another cannot qualify as 'true' sexual desire, and it certainly requires a degree of reconceptualization. Given that carnal desire cannot be defined purely in terms of the male sexual organ, I wonder whether there might not be other forms of desire that do not involve its female analogue. But perhaps that is a peculiarity on my part, encouraged by my present situation. Do you intend to visit Flammarion while you are in Paris?"

"Yes, said Paul, slightly relieved by the innocuousness of the question and the ease of replying to it. "I'm going to Juvisy today, as soon as we're finished here—but there's no hurry."

"Is there not? And do you intend to ask him to host a séance at the Observatory?"

"The idea had crossed my mind. If I were do so, and if he were to agree, would you be interested in serving as a magnetizer?"

"Yes, I would," said Zosima, frankly, "although I might have certain reservations."

"More non-negotiable conditions?"

"No, I wouldn't feel entitled to do that, in the circumstances, but might I at least enquire whether Madame de La Vaudère would be present?"

"Very probably. She has an interest in the matter, after all."

"Yes, I know. I would have no objection, even though I suspect that she might be a disruptive presence. Yes, if you wish, you may tell Flammarion that I am willing to serve as a magnetizer, if he consents to mount the experiment."

"Perhaps I should add," Paul said, "that I have also had an invitation to attend another séance while I am in Paris, from Madame Pommerat."

"Pommerat? I know her. But she's Lemastur's mainstay—unless she's found a new young lover. I'm a little out of touch."

"She didn't mention Lemastur," Paul said, keeping his voice scrupulously level, "but she did say that Baron de Rochemure de Harvanges would be very interested to attend. He's consulted you, I believed?"

"Yes. He came to several of our séances not long after you left for Toulouse. He offered me rather a large sum of money for a private séance—it was a good opportunity, but Talia refused. She didn't like the baron at all. There was a darkness in his soul, she said. I was rather annoyed with her at the time, because it was a lot of money, but I did as she demanded and turned him down. I'd already told him at previous séances that I would do my best to make contact with is daughter but that I couldn't give him any guarantees, and he'd seemed to accept that, so I told him that I didn't feel I could accept his money because I didn't think I could meet his expectations. Surely he's not Pommerat's lover? He must be seventy-five if he's a day? It's more like that she's heard word that your mistress has died and thinks that you might be available. I presume that it's lunatic optimism, if you're still doting on La Vaudère. On the other hand, that might have been what's encouraged Pommerat, as she must be much the same age as La Vaudère and might have inferred that you have a taste for older women. Are you going to accept her invitation?"

Suppressing his astonishment regarding that flight of fancy, Paul said: "In fact, I don't think her invitation has anything to do with carnal desire."

"Yes, but you don't seem to think that anything has anything to do with carnal desire. You'll only admit to a 'close bond of affection' with your own mistress, who would probably have torn poor Talia apart if she'd thought she was a serious rival for use of your lingam. You're an innocent, as most men are...including the rapists, paradoxically, who mostly know not what they do, although, personally, I still think they ought to be clinically disemboweled. My present vocation has given me a slightly jaundiced view of the male of the species. I'm prepared to treat you as an exception, though, pending further information."

"Thank you. I remember that when you were performing you used to do preliminary background research on your clients, I wonder if you can remember why Baron de Rochemure was so enthusiastic to get in touch with his dead daughter?"

Zosima moved forward slightly in her seat in order to peer more intently at Paul. "It seemed to be a pretty standard story," she said, "odd in being such ancient history by the time he tried to involve me. I looked into it, as a matter of routine, but couldn't turn up much. Apparently, he doted on his daughter the way some men do, especially widowers. He spoiled her, naturally, and had the usual delusions about her perfect and inviolable innocence. She seems to have reacted against the shackles, and got involved with a National Guardsman while she was lending a hand to organize medical care and distributing food during the Siege of Paris. The baron was away from Paris with the army at the time and was wounded at Le Mans. He was returned to Paris after the surrender, but appears to have been thrown in prison when the Communards took over. When the regular army took control of the city they released him, and he went looking for his daughter. At that point, the story becomes very vague—the situation was chaotic, as you can imagine—but one way or another, she ended up dead. He might not even know how she died, but if he does, he keeps very quiet about it. Rumor says that she committed suicide, but there doesn't seem to be any hard evidence of that, and it was a time that gave birth to a great many horrific legends."

"Was she still pregnant when she died?"

"Who says that she was pregnant?"

"I inferred it from the way that Rochemure reacted when he saw that picture of a fetus."

"Indeed? That's interesting—but I can't tell you anything about it. If she was pregnant when she killed herself, though, and as far along as that fetus implies, that's all the more reason for Rochemure to feel bad about it—quite rightly—and to go to pieces, which he's apparently been trying unsuccessfully to pick up ever since. Perhaps he thinks that if only he could obtain a formal statement of forgiveness, he could live with himself again, or at least die in peace, the stupid old fool. Other mediums have done their best to give him that, though, and failed to convince him, seemingly because thinks he has some secret keyword by which he would be able to identify his daughter's spirit, which no one has been able to discover or guess. That was one of the reasons why I told him, honestly enough, that I didn't think I could help him."

"And why did Talia think that he had a darkness in his soul?"

"God alone knows—I'm sure she didn't. She was prone to such intuitions, sometimes justified but always vague. I don't know. Perhaps the baron murdered his daughter, or at least the boy-friend. There are other rumors about rapes and murders, including the murder of his steward, Ignatz Fell, although it seems unlikely that he would have done that. Fell used to look after his financial interests while he was away playing soldiers, and probably made a lot of enemies in the process. The baron is old aristocracy as well as army, so even if the Second Empire police knew that he'd committed crimes prior to 1870, they'd have been more likely to help cover them up than arrest him. The Communards probably took a different view, but no formal charges were ever brought against him, so far as I can tell. Maybe the darkness in his soul was simply the fact of being old aristocracy and an officer in Napoléon III's army. He must have been young at the time, but he was probably at Solferino and might even have been at Sebastopol. How could someone like him not have a soul blacker than black?

"This whole thing started because you drew a picture he mistook for his daughter under Lemastur's hypnotism, so you think La Pommerat's invitation is just whoring for the baron, hoping you can do it again. You're probably right. If you want to make some money, go for it—provided that you can remember what the picture you drew at La Pommerat's looked like...oh I know it's not your style. Innocent through and through. And that's admiration, not mockery. I never had the option, having spent my youth in Cairo and Naples. Paris likes to think of itself as a wicked city, but your average Apache wouldn't last fifteen minutes in Naples, or five in Cairo. Here, being what I am has almost become fashionable; there, it could get someone crucified—and that's not a metaphor."

"If you don't mind me saying so," Paul observed, "you seem a trifle ill-fitted to your current disguise."

"Do you think so? French literature has a tradition of bawdy friars going all the way back to the Middle Ages. But you're right. I think I'm reacting to male company, of which I don't get a lot these days. And perhaps I'm still harboring old resentments against you because you ran away when I thought that we could actually make some real progress in understanding, and I'm provoking you a little more than is necessary or laudable. And perhaps I'm just jealous—of Talia, that is. I know that her brief infatuation with you wasn't carnal and as I wasn't actually...but let's not get into that. It's ridiculous of me to be jealous because her spirit is coming to you, and I know perfectly well that your giving me this sketch is a genuine act of kindness...but there it is. It hurt me when Talia confided in you when she wouldn't confide in me, and there's a sense in which I feel that she's still doing it, and I'm irrationally jealous."

"If it makes you feel any better," Paul told her, "I feel irrationally guilty. I know that it wasn't my fault that what she thought she read in my mind that night at Antoine Cros's house caused her to have that pulmonary crisis, but even so, if I hadn't lent myself to that experiment she probably wouldn't have had it. I know she didn't die for nearly a whole year afterwards, but I had the sense then and I still do, that I killed her. And I still feel bad about it."

Zosima reached up and pushed back the hood slightly, exposing her face to the light. She looked distinctly gaunt by comparison with the last time he had seen her, but not unhandsome.

"You're serious, aren't you?" she said.

"Perfectly,"

"Well then, if it'll make you feel any better, you're virtually the only person that Talia didn't blame for what happened. She blamed me, and she blamed herself, and she blamed Antoine Cros, and even, for some reason I could never fathom, Camille Flammarion—but she didn't blame you. In her eyes you were a victim, *the* victim: the innocent—and this time, I'm not being sarcastic. She felt for you. And if her spirit is present, and heard what you'd just said, she'd be weeping...if the dead can cry. I believe they can. I'm not sure that they can talk, but I'm sure that they can weep. Believe me, Paul, if any one of us can be forgiven, you can...for that, at least. With regard to your sister, there's nothing to forgive— but you know that, and I'm only dressed as a monk; I can't actually give you absolution. Only you can do that."

"You're serious too, aren't you?" Paul said. "You really do believe that the spirits of the dead are all round us, and that even though they won't speak, they can hear us."

"I do," said Zosima. "I can't see them, or hear them, and I'm not sure that I can even feel them, but I'm sure that they can see, hear and feel me. Do you think I'm crazy?"

"No," said Paul. "you might be mistaken, but you're not crazy...unless I am too...which is not impossible."

Once again, Zosima held up the picture. "No," she said, "You're not. This is proof of it. You're not only sane, but better than sane. Talia might judge that you're too sensitive for your own good, just as she was, but if you die of it, as she did, you won't be dying for the wrong cause, and there are precious few people who can say that, believe me—especially men. But while I'm being scrupulously honest, perhaps I ought to mention that if Talia could speak, she'd probably be screaming in your ear to beg you not to allow me to magnetize you again, even in the protective presence of Camille Flammarion and Jane de La Vaudère. She'd tell you that although I mean well, I'm dangerous, that I'm far safer in my convent than out here in the world of sleazy cafés, somnolent pimps, exhausted whores and work-shy anarchists. But I'm only telling you that because I know you won't listen, that now you've made up your mind, you'll carry on. If it kills you, I'll regret it deeply, and Talia will probably hate me for it...but I want to know, you see, and I've been convinced for the last four years that you're the only innocent I've ever encountered who might have a chance of finding something out. And I even know that if things do go badly awry, you'll forgive me."

"I'm tougher now than I was four years go," Paul told her. "Things won't go awry, I hope. And with your help, I think I'd have a real chance of discovering something— perhaps not much, but something. I'll write to you again after I've seen Camille, but if, for some reason, he doesn't want to host a séance at Juvisy, could we possibly make an arrangement between the two of us...and Jane?"

The magnetizer didn't hesitate. "Yes," she said "What about Rochemure? He's sure to want to be involved."

"I'm having dinner with him in Passy tomorrow, with Jane. I'll try to figure out then how the land lies in that direction. Would you have any objection to him being present, if it seemed desirable?"

"I wouldn't have any objection personally—but I can't help imagining Talia screaming in my ear to tell you not to do it. If it were a wagering matter, I'd be prepared to wager that whenever and wherever you next submit to magnetization, whether by me or Henri Lemastur, the first thing you'll draw is Talia, perhaps doing a fair imitate of a wounded tigress."

"You think the tigress I just showed you is Talia?"

"No—I've no idea where that came from, or the beetle...although the Egyptian symbolism of the scarab lends itself to all kinds of interpretations in connection with dealings with the dead. The crucial picture, obviously, is the one of the fetus—all the more so as you've now added a third candidate to its possible identity, albeit an unlikely one. Again, if it were a wagering matter, your twin would still be top of my list."

"And mine," Paul admitted. "But it isn't necessarily a matter of either/or, is it? The Juvisy drawing obviously resonated with Talia...and although I didn't draw a fetus at Madame Pommerat's séance, perhaps it's not impossible that the reason I formed a link there with Baron de Rochemure is that it isn't only his dead daughter who was preying on his mind."

"That's an interesting thesis," said Zosima, "but it might be one more reason to be careful. Some clients need to be handled with great precaution, and even setting slanderous rumor aside, he's probably not the kind of man you want to offend."

"I have no intention of offending him—although he certainly hasn't treated me with any evident politeness. I'll make up my mind tomorrow whether I can forgive him or not, but I already have it in mind to tread exceedingly carefully...and I certainly won't ask Flammarion to invite him to the séance at the Observatory, if he's agreeable to hosting one. The baron did mention, by the way, that he was thinking of contacting you again."

"That's not a problem. I have the perfect excuse now for not wanting to perform for him...unless, of course, you decide..."

"I'll cross that bridge when I come to it, but I think he's more likely to want to repeat the experiment with Lemastur first, and Madame Pommerat seems to be eager to assist with that...for whatever reason. At any rate, I'll send you a pneumatique when I've seen Flammarion, and we can take our arrangement from there. Thank you for meeting me, and for agreeing to come to Juvisy, if Camille is willing. I'm almost certain he will be, because he's been trying all his life to find something certain, and he isn't going to let an opportunity go by. Now, I need to get to the Gare du Nord—I have a train to catch. *Au revoir*, Zosima." He stood up as he finished speaking.

She stood up too, and made the sign of the cross in mid-air, like a monk giving a blessing, evidently not knowing—how could she?—what an icy frisson it would send through Paul's soul.

CHAPTER VI

Almost the first thing that Camille Flammarion said to Paul, once the polite formalities were out of the way was: "I've just had a strange conversation by telephone with Baron de Rochemure. He's invited me to dinner in Passy tomorrow night. He says that you'll be there."

"That's right," said Paul, frowning. "I saw him last night and he invited me. He didn't say anything about other guests, but I asked him if I could bring Jane, so perhaps he felt that he might as well invite others. Did you accept?"

"It's very short notice, but I didn't have any other commitment, and the weather forecast is poor, so I agreed—but perhaps I ought to have asked your permission first?"

"Not at all. In fact, I'll be glad of your presence. I found the baron...a trifle intimidating."

"He was quite charming in the telephone, although we have had our differences in the past. He said that he wanted to meet me urgently in order to discuss matters of mutual interest, and that he felt that his discussion with you might benefit enormously from my expert judgment. He didn't go into detail, but I got the impression that you had devastated ideas that he had taken for granted for a long time."

"Did I? But I hardly said anything—he did most all the talking. Although...well, he did leaf through all the sketches that I'd just shown to Jane and have now brought to saw you. He didn't say a great deal, but more than one of them gave him considerable pause for thought, and it may be that once he'd begun thinking, he began to see more significance in the whole array. He'd been thinking about what I did at Madame Pommerat's séance four years ago as the essence, and perhaps the limit, of my...ability. He might have a very different perspective now. May I show you the full set?"

"Of course. I've had some forewarning, of course, by virtue of our correspondence, but I'll be very interested to see them."

At the Observatory, there was room to spread out all the sketches on the large table where star charts, maps of the Moon and compilations of mathematical data were normally distributed. Their usual contents had been tidied away into huge chests of drawers containing drawings that Flammarion and others had made of the disks of the planets of the solar system, including originals made with the aid of the Juvisy telescope and the Paris Observatoire, and copies of drawings made by other observers in the south of France and other countries.

"It's all virtually redundant now, of course," said Flammarion, referring to his stock of drawings. "Astronomy has changed drastically in the course of my lifetime, as the human eye and hand have gradually been replaced by photographic apparatus. As the twentieth century advances, observatories like this one will become quaint, replaced by much larger devices, placed at higher altitudes, in locations where the sky is much clearer for much longer periods, and the observation will be carried out almost entirely by photographic apparatus rather than the human eye.

"The problems will never disappear, of course; the objectivity of photography has inherent flaws of its own, in terms of the chemistry of the development process and the quality of the substance on which images are recorded. There is always scope for distortions, and the three great enemies still remain: cloud, the atmosphere itself, and reflected light. The third is getting worse with every decade that passes as electric light spreads. It's ironic, is it not, that the three things most vital to life—air, water and light—should be the curse of the observational sciences?"

Paul agreed, while he set out his sketches carefully and neatly.

"The science will make more rapid progress, of course," Flammarion mused, "vast progress, I'm certain, and many of the errors introduced by the limitations of observation with which I and my colleagues have had to cope will soon be overcome. How I've envied the astronomers privileged to work at Pike's Peak in the Rocky Mountains, at such an elevation!—but even there, bad weather reduces the windows of observation to frustratingly narrow intervals, and such is the perversity of nature that when the weather is at its best, in summer, the nights are at their shortest.

"Soon, I hope, the American observatories, by virtue of their advantageous placement, will be able to correct many of the errors of the eye and mind that have cursed astronomy during my lifetime, but I'm beginning to fear that there, as in the other fields of my observation that have attracted derision, I might find myself on the wrong side of the controversy. When Schiaparelli first published his account of *canali* on Mars I was skeptical; I couldn't see them. Then I began to see them, and began to make every effort to map them more carefully and more accurately. When the American Lowell began to publish more detailed accounts, and to offer more elaborate accounts of their probable nature, and the *canali* became canals, I was convinced. Already, though, Lowell is becoming isolated in the American community, and the astronomers of the old world are withdrawing support for me. I very much fear that the canals of Mars might be a delusion, belief in their existence being impelled by the power of the myth rather than the virtue of the telescope and the reliability of human brain."

While he was speaking, the astronomer was studying the sketches in a careful and orderly manner, sometimes leaning forward to study them individually, sometimes stepping back to consider the entire array.

Paul waited patiently for his eventual judgment, but when it came, it was not quite what he had expected.

"You showed these images to Baron de Rochemure yesterday evening?" he said.

"He saw them," Paul corrected him, uneasily. "The matter was taken out of my hands—literally. Can you see why he was startled?"

"Yes, I think so." Flammarion reached out with his right hand, the index finger extended. "Did Rochemure identify that portrait as his daughter?"

"Yes. Do you agree then, that it really is an image of his daughter?"

The astronomer sighed. "It's not as simple as that, alas. To identify the picture as one that Rochemure would identify as his daughter is not quite the same thing as saying that it is, in fact, an image of his daughter. It's now 1905, thirty-four years since Yvaine de Rochemure died. I was in my late twenties at the time, Rochemure might have been forty, certainly not much older. Yvaine was not yet twenty. How reliable do you think that my memory can be, or his? It's common knowledge on the séance circuit that he's long been convinced that he can remember her precisely—as if it were only yesterday, as the saying has it. But how reliable are our memories of yesterday? And how many times in a month, or even a week, while we are walking in crowds like those at a railway station or the Parisian boulevard, do we see someone that we think we recognize, and continue to think that we recognize as we look more closely, only to realize, on scrupulous inspection, that we have made a mistake? Sometimes, it might come to the point where we salute the person concerned, or even speak to them before the mistake becomes apparent. Rochemure has already identified one sketch you have made as his daughter, and he must have been avid to see another."

"But when I drew that one, I couldn't remember the one that I'd drawn at Madame Pommerat's. Until Rochemure paused at it and looked at it so intently, I had no idea who it was. I only brought it from Toulouse to see whether Jane recognized her, but she didn't. Antoine Cros, of course, would say that even though I didn't remember the earlier sketch consciously, it would have been stored quasi-photographically in my unconscious, and that it's not surprising that it would pop up again, in a period of four years."

"It's a pity that Antoine has passed on—he'd be a much more able that I am to judge how closely the picture resembles its supposed model."

"Antoine knew Yvaine de Rochemure?"

"Undoubtedly. Even if Antoine wasn't consulted with reference to Rochemure's wound, he and Yvaine were both part of the emergency relief system during and after the siege, and they both continued working when the Commune assumed control. You do realize, I suppose, that the baron will want to be a part of any séance that you and I might organize here?"

"So it seems, if he's asked you to join us at dinner," Paul said. "Jane has already asked me if she could be part of such an...experiment, and I saw Madame Zosima immediately before taking the train to Juvisy. In spite of the fact that she now has a very different career, she immediately volunteered to serve as a magnetizer if we do attempt to repeat the experiment of four years ago. Obviously, I said that I would have to discuss it with you first."

"I've been taking it for granted that you wouldn't have come all the way to Paris, and to Juvisy, if you didn't have that possibility in mind. Nor am I surprised that Madame Zosima wants to be part of it, and that Madame de La Vaudère wants to be present. Personally, I have no objection to Rochemure also being in attendance, although it's a complicating factor that might well affect the outcome. Do you know by any chance, whether the baron has also invited Henri Lemastur to dinner in Passy tomorrow night?"

"No—I didn't know he'd invited you until a few minutes ago. But I have had a letter from Madame Pommerat inviting me to attend a séance at her house, which included a note to the effect that Rochemure would be sure to be present. Gabriel de Lautrec, who was present at her first séance also left a card at my hotel."

"I see. There's a possibility, evidently, that the baron might try to arrange a séance of his own tomorrow. What would you think about that?"

"I'd think that the notice was rather short, and that I'd far rather collaborate in the planning of an experiment here. Will he take no for an answer, though?"

"He will if Madame de La Vaudère and I back you up. Even if Lemastur and Madame Pommerat are there, and Madame Pommerat is prepared to surrender her own proprietary interests to Rochemure, it still leaves the sides even...not that we should be thinking in terms of sides. The real issue is your safety. From my point of view, obviously, I'd far rather that the experiment were conducted here, and I'm certain that Madame de La Vaudère will agree. I do not think the situation in Passy will be conducive either to a careful experiment or to your comfort."

"You're probably right," Paul agreed. "I hadn't been thinking about visiting Rochemure as an experiment at all, and the circumstances of our meeting made it very difficult for me not to think in terms of battle lines—which is why I immediately thought that Jane's moral support might be invaluable. Initially, of course, I had intended to ask you whether we might conduct a very private experiment here, with no one present but you me and Zosima, but when I mentioned it to Jane yesterday, she immediately decided that she wanted to be present, and...well, I couldn't refuse her."

"To tell you the truth, Flammarion said, "I'm a little surprised that Zosima was so quick to volunteer her services. She seems to be employing her psychic force as the leader of one of the cults that have sprung up in such profusion in Paris in the last thirty years. There were already thirty-four when Papus organized his first Spiritist Congress in 1888, which was supposed to unite the community, but actually set the spiritists and the Rosicrucians at one another's throats and helped to generate so many schisms and splinters that there must now be nearer three hundred groups than thirty. Hers, I believe, makes much of the notion of serial reincarnation, but not in an interplanetary context...although I only have rumor to go on, which might not be reliable."

"She feels that she and I have unfinished business, left over from the catastrophe at Antoine Cros's house," Paul supplied.

Flammarion nodded his head. "I can understand that. I saw your painting of poor Talia when it was put on display. Is that the sketch from which it was made?" His index finger extended again.

"No, I gave that one to Zosima. This one's very similar, though." He added: "There are others."

"How many others?" Flammarion asked.

"Perhaps a dozen...some of them are unclear."

"And how many of the girl that featured in the picture to which Cros laid claim...the one who jumped off the Pont Neuf?" The index finger moved to indicate the three sketches of Juliette.

"More than a dozen, drawn over a shorter period of time. You know that we were living together in Toulouse, and that she died?"

"You mentioned it in passing in letters. And Antoine?"

"Perhaps half a dozen sketches. All the examples you see here are the clearest, most unambiguous examples. Sometimes, I don't know who, or what, it is that I've tried to draw. This set gives a false impression of the precision of my...second sight....if that's not too loaded at term."

"You know very well that it is, but we have no terminology that isn't loaded, alas, and any new terms we invent in order to discuss the phenomena more objectively immediately become loaded. I'm not sure exactly what you expect of me, Paul. You already know my opinion regarding the products of automatic writing and drawing. Rochemure probably thinks, or hopes, that you can confound me, but you learned very rapidly four years ago, from Antoine Cros, how the intellectual game is played."

"For me, Monsieur Flammarion," Paul said, quietly, "it's not a game. I know that you believe, as Antoine did, that the one and only source of the visual images that I produce, like the literary imagery that Jane produces, is the unconscious mind. Zosima, on the other hand, has no doubt that some of them really are inspired by the spirits of the dead, undoubtedly manifest via the unconscious mind, but emerging nevertheless from some kind of supernatural realm beyond it. It's not a game for her, either, because for her the question of whether she really is haunted by the spirits with which she makes direct or indirect contact, or whether they're delusional, affects every aspect of her life and work."

"You're right, of course," Flammarion said. "I've known other artists who have taken part—or who have refused to take part—in my experiments, who have taken a different view, saying that it doesn't matter where their inspiration comes from, but only what they produce. I can understand the refusal even to investigate the question, their preference for mystery, even though it's not my own mental inclination. Obviously, I sympathize far more with your determination to investigate and discover the truth, because it's what I hope I would do in your situation, but I understand that your motivation is far more intense than mine. I think I can understand how disturbing it must be for you that for long periods—hours at a time, at intervals of only a few days—your consciousness becomes lost, utterly helpless, while your hand continues to be active, sometimes active with a marvelous rapidity and acuity, producing genuine works of art, possessed of considerable talent.

"My own visions are far less imperious, and consciousness is always only a slight mental effort away...but I believe that I have enough in common with you to appreciate how deeply upsetting it must have been on that night at Antoine's when you were mentally absent for some four hours, unable to return even in response to the signal implanted in your mind by Zosima's suggestion. Antoine was unworried once he had decided that you were merely asleep, and he never had an atom of doubt that you would eventually wake up—but Jane was certainly frightened by the possibility that you might not, or that if you did, you might not be able to take up your existence exactly as you had left it, and so was I. We both understood, I think, the fear you had when you did wake up, fortunately unimpaired, and realized the danger you had been in."

"If you'll give me or saying so, Monsieur Flammarion," Paul riposted, "I'm not sure that you do understand. Yes, the fact that my hand sometimes operates without the guidance of my consciousness is disturbing in itself, creating the fear that I might lose control permanently, as my will, my self or my soul slips into oblivion, or madness...but there's another factor, even more important. If it had only been me, that night at Antoine's, who was temporarily lost, that might have been a near disaster, perhaps a narrow escape for me—but it wasn't just me. It was also Talia, and Juliette, who were caught up in the same...psychic vortex. Both of them suffered real physical injuries, and both of them came distressingly near to death.

"You can tell me, as I tell myself, that it wasn't my fault, that their troubles originated in themselves, in their physical debility and the labyrinthine darkness of their own unconscious minds, in their own neuroses. That's true. Perhaps I was only a catalyst—but even so, there's a sense in which it really was my doing, my fault...not entirely, but partly. And having seen Zosima this morning, I now know for sure what I had already suspected—that she feels responsible too, that she believes that it was her doing and her fault...and that awareness, or feeling, changed her life overnight, just as it changed mine...which is why she agreed without hesitation to emerge from her refuge this morning to met me in a sleazy café, and why she agreed with similar immediacy to come to Juvisy in order to magnetize me again, even though she warned me, very dutifully, while pretending with all her might that it was just flippant eccentricity on her part, that it might be dangerous for both of us...and not just for us."

"For Jane, you mean?" Flammarion asked, a trifle disingenuously.

"You had a vision too that night at Antoine's," Paul reminded him. "A familiar, harmless vision, of the kind you've long since accommodated into your life and your career, but a revelation of vulnerability nevertheless. I know that, unlike

111

Rochemure, you've recanted your earlier belief in the reality of the spirits of the dead supposedly manifested by mediums, but you haven't abandoned your belief in psychic force, although you're wary of the magnetic analogy. In fact, following the spirit of Occam's razor, you think that thesis is the only hypothesis required to explain all the other phenomena of hauntings. You don't believe that Zosima's psychic magnetism can summon the spirits of the dead, but you do believe that she can exert a psychic force of some kind, and that her suggestion has an uncommon potency. Is that a fair summary?"

"Broadly, yes," the astronomer confirmed, "and thank you for your concern regarding my own safety if and when I host a further experiment matching your unusual psychic sensitivity with Zosima's exceptional psychic force. But once again, I'm not sure what you expect from me in reaction to showing me these images. You already know that drawing images of dead people who were known to you, even peripherally, let alone those who were dear to you and for whose loss you grieve, is easily explicable by the presence of such images in your memory, albeit sometimes cryptomnesially, to use Flournoy's term. You know, too, that images whose presence seems difficult to explain, notably Madame Scrive and Mademoiselle de Rochemure, are subject to inevitable doubts regarding the accuracy of the identification. The presence in the set of sirens and other chimerical figures obviously proves beyond a shadow of a doubt that the creative imagination plays a significant role in producing the images that you draw while in a trance state. What more can I add?"

Pal used his own index finger to select out the image of the bloated head with the tentacles dangling therefrom. "Have you ever seen an image similar to that one in your own visions of extraterrestrial life?" he asked, bluntly.

"You must know that I have," Flammarion replied. "You doubtless remember that when I first saw the sketch you made here—the sketch that I still have—that was the first thought that spring to my mind. Does it really qualify as a vision, though? Is it not more likely that it's akin to the siren and the manticore, produced by a process of imaginative hybridization? When we try to imagine what things might exist in other worlds than ours, what recourse to we have but recombining the features of known life-forms by means of eccentric juxtapositions? When I was young, I was fascinated by the products of my own imagination, and I'm familiar with the seductive temptation to regard such products as visions. When I first read Jean Reynaud's *Terre et ciel*, not knowing at the time that his idea of extraterrestrial reincarnation had been around for a century and more, it struck me with the force of a revelation, and I didn't doubt that he was a true visionary. Now...I'm doubtful. Certainly, if reincarnation is real, there is no reason why it should be confined to one species or one planet, in a world where there are countless species and a universe where there seems to be an infinite number of stars, but I wonder now whether the concept of reincarnation even makes any sense, if analyzed philosophically?"

"Zosima uses her psychic force to enable her sisters to remember anterior lives," Paul suggested, mildly.

"To remember or to create," Flammarion countered. "That she delves into the unconscious minds of her sisters I have no doubt, but as to the nature and origins of what she finds there, or persuades them to synthesize...that is another matter."

"True," said Paul. "But to return to that particular image, and the one that I drew here four years ago, do we need to assume that my duplicating something that you were able recognize, albeit tentatively and uncertainly, as something you had previously imagined, was a mere coincidence—given the time, the place and the context in which my drawing was made?"

"It's a hypothesis that can't be proven," Flammarion sad, "but you know very well that my acceptance of the notion of psychic force has among its corollaries the notion that some kind of communication between minds is possibly—what the modern jargon calls telepathy. Talia Cadelan, if I remember correctly, was convinced that you and she were telepathically linked, and that both of the hysterical crises she experienced, here and at Antoine's house, were caused by that telepathic linkage. Did she convince you?"

"She did," said Paul. "And she also convinced me that a telepathic linkage was established on that second occasion between me and Juliette. I'm convinced, too, that neither link, once formed, was ever entirely broken. In fact, I also suspect, very strongly, that links were formed between myself and the other people present, which have also never even broken."

"Including me?"

"Including you...not as strongly, evidently, as the other links, which varied considerably in intensity, but sensible nevertheless."

Flammarion pointed at the images of Jane de La Vaudère. "And these, in your opinion, are the consequences of a psychic bond?"

"I believe so—but one that is only of secondary interest, for the moment. You'll notice that I've juxtaposed the image of the hypothetical extraterrestrial with an image, very similar in many ways, of a human fetus?"

"Yes. Antoine told me, after a brief lapse of time, that he had immediately identified your original drawing as a fetus, and that he had told you what it was on the train on the way back to Paris. He also told me what he had inferred from the identification...he loved playing his little games of psychoanalysis. He said that you accepted his explanation fully...he was crowing a little, I think, at my mistake, although he no longer found it so amusing when the *Mercaba*'s repetition spread to the daily newspapers, and created an item of modern legend. Can I assume, given your production of the alternative images and your decision to juxtapose them, that you still have some doubt regarding the identification?"

"Not consciously," Paul told him. "Consciously, I have no doubt that Antoine was right, not only that what I drew was a fetus, but that it was probably a vague image of my sister's fetus, which had been preying on my mind all my life because of feelings of guilt I had regarding the fact that I succeeded in being born while she did not, and that her failure caused my mother's death. I say *probably* because I was very rapidly presented with an alternative explanation of the fetus and the feelings of guilt associated with it...and after all, one fetus looks so similar to another that the issue of specific identification hardly even arises."

"That's true," Flammarion observed, presumably marking time while he wondered where the argument was leading.

"So true, in fact," Paul said "that when Baron de Rochemure, after having stared at the picture that he identified as his daughter for some considerable time, was leafing through the remainder of the sketches absent-mindedly, he stopped dead when he came to that one, and underwent a complete and instantaneous change of attitude and manner. He too recognized the fetus, not as a generalized fetus, such as might be seen in a medical textbook, as Antoine Cros did, but as a very specific fetus. Exactly what he inferred from that recognition, I have no idea, but the recognition itself was indubitable. Whatever happened to Yvaine de Rochemure was before Jane's time, and Zosima was only able to tell me what rumor had handed down—a very banal story, as she put it. But you actually knew her, and presumably have a much clearer notion of what happened than old rumor. Can you offer any conjecture, then, as to why Rochemure, after seeing that picture, immediately invited me to dinner...an invitation that he seems now to have extended to you, and perhaps also to Henri Lemastur?"

Flammarion was frowning deeply, as if searching his memory assiduously. While doing so, he said: "Forgive the indelicacy, but in view of what you've just said, I need to ask: when you say that you were given an alternative explanation of the image of the fetus, do you mean an explanation provided by Mademoiselle Cadelan, or by Mademoiselle Scarran?"

"Does it matter?" Paul parried.

"Yes...but not, I suppose, with regard to the psychoanalytical interpretation, as either one of them might have endured...an incomplete pregnancy giving rise to feelings of guilt, rational or irrational. Except that...but if it's a sensitive subject. I'll pass on. I have no accurate knowledge of what you're asking with regard to Yvaine de Rochemure. I too have nothing to go on but rumor, suspicion and inference—I certainly never obtained any sort of confidence from Rochemure, and I would be astonished if anyone else ever has.

"For what it is worth, though, there was some speculation at the time that Yvaine de Rochemure might have been pregnant at the time of her death, and even some speculation that she might actually have given birth. Nowadays, of course, there would have been a autopsy, the findings of which would inevitably have leaked out, but in 1871...believe me, Paul, when I assure you that you have no conception of what conditions were like in Paris after months of siege, days of heavy bombardment, the German invasion of the city and the subsequent attempt by the Communards to reorganize life there while the treaty was being negotiated.

"History has demonized the Communards, as the voices of the Third Republic felt obliged to do, in order to justify the appalling cruelty of the way they treated them when the regular army took back control of the city and slaughtered the national guardsmen that had only been recruited, often forcibly, as a measure of desperation under German fire. History records it as a mere formality, but it was a massacre, although it is unsafe to say so even today. Antoine and Charles Cros were not the only men scarred by the experience for life, and it is probably safe to say that no one as closely involved with the events as they were escaped unscathed. What Antoine and Charles did was to render aid to the wounded—all the wounded, without discrimination—trying to save lives as best they could, and they came within an inch of being condemned, perhaps executed or transported, for their common humanity. Others I could name, whom I knew, were not as fortunate. I was not proud, afterwards of the slightness of my involvement, but rather ashamed.

"Antoine survived not because of his innocence of any wrongdoing but because of the quality of his connections. He was the physician of important and influential people, and was therefore shielded from the fury—which was, I can assure you, pure and simply fury, a violent madness. I do not know whether Baron de Rochemure was among his clients then—I don't believe that he was afterwards—but it was people of Rochemure's ilk who had the authority to intervene, who somehow retained the authority to exercise a literal power of life and death over those accused, accurately or fatuously, of having taken part in what was retrospectively described and condemned as an uprising, an insurgency, although the vast majority of the Communards were only interested in the survival of the people of Paris, of supplying people who might otherwise have starved to death with food, and people who would otherwise have died of injury and disease with elementary medical care.

"I don't know whether it's true that the Communards actually put Rochemure in prison when they took over, but he would in any case have been one of the enemies of the Commune during the violent and vengeful aftermath of its attempted rule. Yvaine, on the other hand, had become actively involved with relief work during the siege, like thousands of young women who volunteered to do whatever might be necessary to keep the city functioning in direly difficult circumstances, when every able-bodied man from the lower orders was pressed into the National Guard, many of them sent out of the city, without adequate weaponry or equipment, to serve as cannon-fodder for the German guns. In the beginning, her father probably wouldn't have opposed that, had he been in Paris, and might perhaps even encouraged it. Over time, however, it would not have been surprising if his attitude had changed drastically.

"All I can tell you for certain is that Yvaine did not survive 1871. So far as I know, there is no official record of how she died, when or where, but if there were, I would not trust it. If she was pregnant at the time, I saw no evidence of it, but the last time I saw her cannot have been later than November 1870. As to who the father of the hypothetical child might have been, I have no idea. As to whether their blood is mingled with the other blood that Rochemure probably has on his hands, I do not know. Probably no one does any longer, except Rochemure...but the interval between the catastrophes of January and the Bloody Week of May 1871, was a time when a great many men who were not intrinsically evil committed violent, murderous and evil actions. Some of them never fully recovered from the trauma.

"I know no more than that—but given your description of Rochemure's reaction to seeing a fetus drawn by you, in the same batch of sketches as one that he had identified as his daughter, I agree than there can be little doubt as to what fetus it was that he believed he had identified."

"But he was wrong," Paul observed. "About that we can surely be certain. Even if some doubt remains with regard to the precise identity of the fetus I drew four years ago, if it were not just a generalized image, it could not have been one with which Yvaine de Rochemure was pregnant."

"Agreed," said Flammarion, "but if the occasion arises when you have to convince Rochemure of that, you might not find it easy. Even though he has seen this entire array of images, and could easily deduce that you are haunted by at least a dozen real and imaginary ghosts, so far as his tunnel vision is concerned, you only exist as a conduit for contact with one. From his standpoint, there is only one ghost, and therefore only one ghostly fetus, if his daughter was, in fact, pregnant before her untimely death; your entire *raison d'être*, in his thinking, is to enable him to make contact with his daughter, with whom his conscience has unfinished business...if it is possible that you can, in fact make some such contact."

"It's not," Paul said. "Even if that sketch really is a sketch of his daughter, made by virtue of a telepathic link induced between his mind and mine by Henri Lemastur's psychic catalysis, I can't possibly meet whatever evidential standard that Rochemure has invented as proof of that contact, and I can't hear his daughter speak. The dead, insofar as they manifest themselves to me, are silent."

"I believe you," Flammarion said. "But it's not what Henri Lemastur will have told him. I know Lemastur, and he's not a bad fellow. He's certainly a skilled hypnotist and an artful manipulator of mediums, but you heard Zosima's account of the logic of mediumistic performance. He cheats. Authentic as his ability is, he neither understands it, nor has any significant degree of control over it. So he cheats. And Madame Pommerat colludes with his cheating, for psychological reasons that are a mystery to me, but no less powerful for that. I'm out of touch with salon culture, but I know how it operates, and I can imagine the gibes that their relationship attracts, although I have no sympathy with that kind of malice. Be warned, though, that if Lesmastur is present at the dinner at Rochemure's house tomorrow, he won't be on your side even to the limited extent that Zosima was at Antoine Cros's house. He will have his own agenda, in which Rochemure's money probably figures large, all the more so if he's been frozen out for some while, after the last time he failed to come through in promises that he made. If you consent to his hypnotizing you, given the extent of your apparent sensitivity, you might become a pawn in his scheme rather than master of your own."

"Mastery of my own," Paul muttered, "is something I've been trying to achieve for four years, with no conspicuous success."

"I've seen others strive for the same result, with a similar lack of success—but that doesn't mean that success is impossible."

"It might, if I'm simply insane."

"There's nothing simple about insanity, or about sanity. I'm routinely accused of insanity, and so are countless other people whose only abnormality is that they attempt to think about things, while supposedly normal people would rather not. How is that normal? Commonplace, I'll admit, but normal? For a mind capable of thought, for which thought is the most precious faculty and the greatest glory, to refuse to do it?

That, to me, is the ultimate in perversity, an extreme abnormality."

"I couldn't reasonably refuse to accept Rochemure's invitation," Paul said, pensively. "It might not be easy to refuse to allow Lesmastur to hypnotize me, without being rude."

"But you can make a reasonable counter-offer—one that he can't reasonably refuse. It's not ideal, I know, but if you are backed into a corner, you could invite both Rochemure and Lemastur to come here instead, to witness, and perhaps participate in Zosima's magnetization. On the other hand, the greater confusion of presences might make things worse. I can only point it out as a possibility; I can't honestly recommend it, and rudeness might be the best option. From my own viewpoint, I'd rather see an experiment conducted with a minimum of potentially-confusing factors. I'm sorry if that's not much help."

"But you will be at Passy tomorrow, and you will take my side there, won't you?"

"Yes, certainly. It's an observation I wouldn't want to miss, whatever the outcome."

"Good. I'll feel a lot better with you there, as well as Jane...covered on two flanks, as it were."

Flammarion frowned. "I'm not sure that I'm comfortable being cast as your protector," he said. "I'm glad to be considered your friend, but a protective role would be too much responsibility, and beyond my competence. I'd prefer you to think of my presence as that of a sympathetic but essentially objective observer."

"I apologize," Paul said. "But if I may, I'd like to ask you a question about the last time you played that role."

"Of course."

"Jane told me that you had experienced a vision under the force of Zosima's suggestion, but that you had dismissed it as something familiar and insignificant: a cosmic vision of some kind. Did you have a similar vision, however brief, during the séance here, and if so, did it involve any imagery of extraterrestrial life?"

"Ah!" said Flammarion. "You haven't entirely abandoned the hypothesis that the fourth image you drew might only have resembled a fetus, then, and might actually have been something else entirely? The answer isn't simple, I'm afraid, but it might be better to approach it from the opposite direction. Manifestly, there is a visionary element in such works as *Lumen, Uranie* and *La Fin du Monde*, but, as I'm sure you must have discussed with Jane, writing, as a process, cannot be entirely automatic in the way than your drawings apparently can. Save for short bursts, usually no more than a page long, with little in the way of punctuation or syntax, automatic writing cannot capture visionary experience; that requires logic, organization and focused consciousness. My images of hypothetical extraterrestrial life are, I believe, almost entirely the result of conscious processes. I can make no comment on the exotic moths in your sketch, which certainly resemble images that I have produced of alien beings, but I suspect that my imagery is more likely to be the *agent provocateur* of yours than something that emerged from a common source.

"The vision that I experienced at Antoine's house while you were formulating your drawings was not so much something seen as a shift in attitude. I imagined for a few moments, that I was looking at the sky, as I very frequently do, and understandably so, being a professional astronomer who lives in an observatory and makes a living popularizing the discoveries of the science. But you must remember that 'seeing the sky' is not a simple process. What a photographic apparatus produces as an image of the sky is a pattern of white dots on a two-dimensional black backcloth. Some people, I am assured, see the actual sky in the same way, but I cannot believe that there are many, and I suspect that what most people experience when they look up at a starry sky is quite different.

"It is impossible, I suppose, to obtain any definite estimate of depth in gazing at the sky, in the way that one can conceive the placement of objects on the earth's surface, but I would suggest that it is equally impossible to gaze at the sky without an awareness of depth, and of immensity. Even in the days when the earth was imagined by intelligent people to be the center of a relatively small universe, with the empyrean forming the outermost of a series of crystal spheres, anyone with an ounce of imagination must have obtained a sense of immensity in gazing at the stars, and since we have discovered the true configuration and dimensions of the universe, there is an implicit challenge posed to the imagination to comprehend and to contend with that immensity. That challenge, and the effort to meet it imaginatively, is the heart and soul of my personal visions of the macrocosm.

"What that implies about the nature and contents of my unconscious mind, I don't know, but what I sense is very numinous, a kind of attempted identification with creation: almost an effort to recreate the universe, the existence of which science assures me, within the limited frame of my mentality. conscious and unconscious. That is what my mind was striving to do, automatically, when it drifted during the séance— perhaps in a dereliction of duty, as I was supposed to be there as a scrupulous observer. I am not aware of having suffered any such loss of concentration during the séance at Juvisy, over which I was presiding conscientiously, but if I did, momentarily, I certainly did not visualize any form of extraterrestrial life. When I made the suggestion after seeing your drawings, my thinking was that you might have come to Juvisy with preconceived notions of what you might be expected to see in my company. I do not believe that there could have been any telepathy involved...not with me, at any rate."

"Thank you," said Paul. "Might I also raise a point that you mentioned in one of your letters, when you suggested that if the dead leave ghosts behind, then, given the world's current population and its rate of replacement, the number of shades surrounding us must be enormous...unless, you suggested, those disembodied souls were, in fact, reincarnated, here or elsewhere, thus preserving the earth's surface from excessive overcrowding. But the figures you suggested would have to be increased very considerably if deaths during or prior to birth were included, and the question of their possible reincarnation might become more complex. The question seems significant to me, as you'll understand, if I am to entertain the notion seriously that I might be being haunted by the phantom of a sister who died before birth. As I said, I know that, you don't believe any longer that the entities that spiritist mediums apparently make contact really are the spirits of the dead—but you do still believe, nevertheless, in the existence of spirits of the dead. Is it conceivable, do you think, that individuals who die before birth do leave behind spirits—silent spirits, obviously, but spirits that might, under certain conditions, become sensible, at the least to the psychically sensitive?

"The simple answer," Flammarion told him, "is that I have no idea; it is a realm of pure conjecture. But if there are such things as souls, which survive the death of the individual, I can see no reason why individuals that die before birth should be excluded *a priori* from possessing one. The Church might disagree with me, but that is hardly relevant. Whether fetal ghosts might haunt the living is another question, but if any spirits of the dead can be credited with a motivation to haunt the living, or even some kind of attraction to the living, then again, I can see no logical reason to exclude from consideration the phantoms of little children, or children that did not quite contrive to be born. Are you seriously anxious that the ghost of your twin sister might be literally haunting you, intent on punishing you for surviving her?"

"Actually, no," said Paul. "I've managed to convince myself, consciously at least, that if the spirit of my dead sister were still lurking in my vicinity, or in my unconscious mind, it wouldn't be for reasons of vengeance, or even mere psychic gravity, but simply because I'm the only living person of whose proximity she ever had the opportunity to experience. For the moment, however, I was thinking about the fetus that might be haunting Baron de Rochemure, or which he might imagine to be haunting him...which, at the very least, seemed to give him such a profound shock when he saw my drawing."

"Ah! Yes, I see. I should have thought of that. Well, I repeat, it's purely a matter for conjecture...but if Baron de Rochemure really is being haunted by a fetus, whatever that allegation might imply, then the precise circumstances of Yvaine's death, and the exact extent of her probable pregnancy, might be very significant factors in determining the precise configuration of his feelings of guilt. But if it were not, in fact, his daughter's forgiveness of which he had been in search all these years, one would have to wonder whether a fetus, or the spirit of a fetus, is actually capable of forgiveness? I don't suppose you've had a chance to discuss that question with Zosima...or Juliette or Talia? After all, if such hauntings can and do exist, they are surely far more likely to afflict women than men, are they not—your case being highly exceptional?"

"It's not a topic I've so far raised with any woman," Paul said, blandly, "and it's not a topic that I feel that I could— certainly not with Madame de La Vaudère, for instance."

"Or Madame Pommerat," mused Flammarion, "unless you wanted to be extraordinarily provocative."

"Is that a suggestion?"

"Merely an observation. I agree that it's not a topic that could safely be raised with very many women...and perhaps not with certain men, if you have some such plan."

"It *was* a very intriguing reaction," was Paul's only comment—and he began gathering his sketches together, into a neat pile, ready to be replaced in the portfolio, before the discussion continued in the dining room.

CHAPTER VII

When Paul returned to the hotel there was only one note waiting for him at the reception desk; it was from Victor Marvaud, inviting him to telephone after ten. It was quarter past, so Paul went directly to the booth at the back of the hallway and dialed Victor's number.

The telephone was answered by a woman, who was clearly not a maidservant. Although Victor was not married, Paul was not particularly surprised. He was almost tempted to ask whose wife it was, but thought that it might be stretching the bonds of camaraderie a little too far.

"I just got in from Juvisy and picked up your note," he said.

"Is old Flammarion well?"

"Very well," Paul told him. "We had a long talk and an excellent dinner. His wife and children are perfectly charming. There, I thought, is a fortunate and enviable man. Would that we could be so lucky,"

"Indeed. Look, I'm sorry about having so little time. Parisian life, you see—hectic and relentless. But we'll get together soon for a long chat. Do you have news of Gaston?"

"Not recent, I fear. He travels a great deal, and hardly spends three months a year in Toulouse. He's well, though. The loss of his mother and Martine hit him hard, as you know, but he's moving on with his life. The family business keeps him fully employed."

"No sign of a marriage there either, then?"

"He's only the same age as us; he has plenty of time."

"Of course. How's your girl-friend—the painter of flowers and the holy grail, I mean, not the lady who writes the smutty books?"

"Clémence isn't my girl-friend, merely an acquaintance. And Jane's books aren't smutty."

"Have you read *L'Androgyne?* Of course you have. And *Le Harem de Syta?* I still remember the way she looked at me in your studio that day when you were painting your Jeanne d'Arc—poisonous. But no matter. What does your dealer say about organizing an exhibition?"

"I'm seeing him tomorrow morning to talk about the possibility," Paul told him.

"Good—get down to business; no point coming otherwise. You really ought to move back here, you know. I know you were too embarrassed to show your face while you were shacked up with Scarab, but there was really no need, and it's two years since she died. No one remembers her anymore."

"I do," said Paul, mildly.

"Well, of course you do, but that's not what I mean. Your old studio is occupied, of course, but I have contacts; I could find you a better one in no time. It's not as if you're a landscapist always prattling about the light of the Midi; your forte is portraits, and that's what you should be doing: portraits of wealthy Parisians for hanging in the villas that are springing up like mushrooms in Sèvres, Meudon, Auteuil and Passy. There's a fortune to be made from the *nouveau riche*, and you have the talent to do the spade-work, if only you can stimulate a little talk, of the right sort. I can help with that. You weren't ready four years ago, but now, the city's your oyster, if you'll only stir yourself."

"I'm dining in Passy tomorrow," Paul commented.

"Really? That's good—a step in the right direction. Anyone I know?"

"Camille Flammarion will be there. I've been invited by Baron de Rochemure. Do you know him?"

There was a momentary pause before Victor said: "Not personally; only by sight and by reputation. He doesn't come into society much, except for popping into town to participate in the occasional spiritist séance or to trawl the bouquinistes. You met him at La Pommerat's four years ago, didn't you? That's what got you the invitation to Juvisy, with a little assistance from me. He thought you drew his daughter while you were playing the somnambulist, although you were dubious."

"That's right."

"He probably wants to have you put under again, to see whether you can repeat the trick, and go a little further."

""Probably," Paul agreed, "but I'll approach the possibility slowly and cautiously, if I can."

"You do know, I suppose, that rumor credits him with having driven his daughter to suicide by having her lover castrated?"

"No, I hadn't heard that particular detail. Do you know who her lover was, then?"

"Some poet who got tangled up with the Commune, I believe."

"Does rumor say what happened to him?"

"Not that I've heard. Probably transported, banished, or shot...or maybe killed himself, like her. Take your pick."

"But do you think that Rochemure had him castrated?"

"I've only heard it whispered. It was long before my time, obviously. Didn't you ask Flammarion about it?"

"I did but either he didn't know the detail you just cited or he left it out for squeamish reasons."

"You aren't going to bring it up at the dinner table, I hope. Rochemure might haul you out into the garden with a pair of pistols. He's an old army man, remember. I think he resigned his commission immediately after the war, but he can probably still shoot straight, and he probably wouldn't hesitate. He's old school aristocracy, and probably thinks the rest of us are just serfs. Have you seen his coachman? He comes into town more frequently than his master, running errands of various kinds."

"We've met," Paul confirmed.

"Probably need more than one bullet to stop him. But seriously, though, tread carefully. I don't say there isn't money to be made there, but it probably isn't easy to lay hands on. Others have tried and failed, I believe."

"So I'm told."

"Can you remember what the drawing you made looked like well enough to draw another, assuming that that's what he wants you to do?"

"There's no need. I already have. Rochemure saw it last night when he kidnapped me."

"Kidnapped you? Baron de Rochemure?"

"Well, technically it was his coachman, and not for long. But it's probably your fault."

"My fault? How could it be my fault?"

"Because I only told five people when I'd be arriving in Paris, and you're the one with the loose tongue."

"Oh. Well, yes, I did mention it to a few people...and, come to think of it, when I told the art critic Dujardin you were coming, we were in the Moulin Rouge, and there were other people around."

"You didn't, perchance, mention it to someone named Gabriel de Lautrec?"

"The hashish-eater? Not directly, but he was in the Moulin Rouge that night, and might have overheard. Does he know the baron?"

"He was at the séance where I drew the picture, and he left his card for me at the hotel reception desk yesterday."

"Oh. It probably was me, then—but you didn't ask me to keep it a secret. And your five must include your dealer. Chazelle's lips aren't exactly glued, and Rochemure's a known collector."

"Known collector of what?"

"Of you. Well, maybe not a collector, but he bought that painting of a girl that you did...the one that Zosima used to use in her double act before she went into the cult business."

"Baron de Rochemure bought my picture of Talia?"

"Yes. I took an interest, naturally, when that one came on to the market, and caused a bit of a stir. Didn't you know?"

"No. The dealer just forwarded the money, less commission."

"That's odd. Normally, he'd have bragged. I suppose Rochemure must have asked him not to mention it, although there are no secrets here for people in the know."

"The baron had the opportunity to mention it when we were talking about Talia," Paul said, pensively, "but that was before he invited me to dinner, and he hadn't yet become chatty."

"Well, he is reputed to be an eccentric, with esoteric interests. Probably going senile too. Are you going to do it, then?"

"Do what?" Paul riposted, disingenuously.

"Do a new drawing for him. If he likes it, he might commission you to turn it into a portrait. I don't suppose he has one. The kid can't have been very old when she killed herself, and it was way back in 1871—not exactly prime time for portrait painters. You might be able to bargain him up to a fat fee."

"Too difficult to arrange a sitting. I only produce sketches while in a trance. Oil painting has to be done consciously."

"It didn't that day I found you painting the flames of Jeanne d'Arc's pyre. You were well away. I know I always used to joke about you going mad, but that afternoon I was seriously worried about you—even more so when La Vaudère came along and just whipped you away, as if she owned you...as I suppose she thought she did."

"What's that supposed to mean?"

"Only that she'd commissioned you to paint her portrait...although I did wonder..."

"You would. No, nothing improper has ever happened between Madame de La Vaudère and me, nor will it."

"She does have reputation, you know. Not for that specifically, but...well, just a reputation. Can't write books like that and not have a reputation. I quite like them, mind. Racy. Not your type, though, suppose, since you ran off to Toulouse with Scarab. That caused some talk, I can tell you. In fact, I did, as I recall. And when that picture of Jeanne d'Arc in armor waving that sword went on display...do you know who bought that one?"

"No. Do you?"

"Can't help you there, I'm afraid. Ask Chazelle. You really must tell me how it goes tomorrow though...that could be juicy. Don't worry—I'll tell it so that you come out smelling of roses...which is why you have to give me the story first. As it's Passy, I dare say you'll be late back, especially if you're going to play the ghost game, but don't worry—I'll still be awake."

"I don't like to disturb you when you're clearly busy."

"Oh, subtle...don't worry about that; she's a good girl. Ring me anyway, the next day at the latest, and we'll find a slot for lunch. And do be careful. Joking aside, Rochemure isn't the kind of man you want to upset. He isn't someone you want to be on the wrong side of. This is Paris; money and status still talk, even if the lips are sealed. Humor the old goat, if you can."

"That might not be easy, but I'll do my best. *Au revoir*."

He replaced the receiver, and opened the door of the booth. There was a man standing outside, obviously waiting.

"I'm sorry to have been so long," said Paul, reflexively, as he moved to steer around the other and make for the stairs, without even glancing at his face.

"That's perfectly all right, Monsieur Furneret," the other said, in a smooth, cultured voice, "But might I have a word with you, if it's not too late."

Paul looked the man directly in the face. He was not very old, perhaps thirty-five, and his hair and beard were still black, as were his neatly-trimmed eyebrows. His eyes too were dark, but his complexion was rather pale, and very smooth. He was dressed very neatly, but did not give the appearance of being a conscientious dandy, in spite of his swagger-stick.

"We have met," the man said, "but you might not remember me."

In fact, Paul did remember the face quite distinctly, and even if he had not, the voice would have triggered a memory.

130

"You're Henri Lemastur," he said.

The magnetizer smiled. "That's impressive," he said, unctuously, "given that we only met very briefly four years ago. I did try to renew the acquaintance then, but you were very busy...understandably so, after your sensational performance at the Juvisy Observatory. Quite a masterstroke, as it turned out...but you can't have very fond memories of it, in view of the *Palatine* lifeboat disaster, which wrecked the denouement. If only it had come safely to land...but fate has a nasty habit of failing out fondest hopes, alas. Might we go up to your room, perhaps? I won't keep you long, but I really think it might be wise for us to have a short discussion."

Paul was not entirely certain about the wisdom of the move, but he could understand why Henri Lemastur might think that it was a good idea.

They went up to Paul's room, and Paul offered his guest the armchair, while he perched on the bed.

"Rochemure hasn't wasted any time, obviously," Lemastur said. "Personally, I'd have preferred to go slowly, and to arrange a séance at Madame Pommerat's place, although she isn't at all put out at having been invited to dine at Passy tomorrow, even at such short notice—it's quite a privilege, in its way, in the circles in which she moves. Her priorities aren't exactly the same as mine, as you can imagine. Well, I won't beat round the bush; doubtless you've heard some bad things about me, and I won't bother to deny them, but you know from personal experience that I'm not a charlatan, and I'm certain that you're not a charlatan either. What we did four years ago was real, and it was honest. I'm not saying that we really summoned the spirit of Yvaine de Rochemure, but we did something out of the ordinary, and we weren't running any kind of fraud. I don't know what happened between you and Zosima, but I know that she's not a charlatan either, and I'd almost be prepared to bet my skin that you didn't make any prior arrangement, and played it absolutely straight at the Observatory. In fact, I'd be willing to wager that you were more astonished by what happened there than anyone else. Am I right?"

"Yes," said Paul, curtly, still trying to digest the information that Baron de Rochemure appeared to be turning what had originally been represented as an intimate dinner into a circus.

"Good. Except that it doesn't make things any easier for us in trying to prepare for tomorrow. We both have good reasons for not wanting to disappoint the baron, but there's no point even thinking about trying to put together some kind of trickery. That's been tried and done to death—it doesn't wash. Nobody even knows exactly what he wants, or if they do, they're keeping very quiet about it. Do you have any idea?"

"I fear not. I've arrived on the scene very late, and the few people I've been able to talk to today don't seem to have any inkling as to what happened in 1871. You must have made much more extensive enquiries than I have—surely you can't have drawn a complete blank?"

"Not exactly, but it's all hearsay, and somewhat contradictory; not surprising, as there appear to be two or three stories tangled together. The Baron was said to be a bad landlord, although that might have been partly the fault of the steward who ran his estate for him, a man named Ignatz Fell. Rochemure was involved in the catastrophe at Le Mans, but most of his men had already deserted before the serious shooting began and he got a couple of bullet wounds, one of which nearly cost him his leg. He came back to Paris after the surrender on a stretcher, but was no sooner able to stand up again than the Communards took over and threw him in prison, although they never got around to drawing up a formal charge-sheet, let alone organizing a trial. There were rumors of rape and murder, but nothing specific, and rumors of that sort were common currency back then for a man in his position."

"But his daughter worked with the Communards?"

"Apparently. She probably didn't have any sympathy with them, but who can tell? Young and romantic...well, at any rate, she seems to have simply carried on doing what she'd been doing during the siege, helping to get food and medical attention to people in dire straits...of whom there was no shortage, as you can imagine. The story is that she got tangled up with some fellow who'd been pressed into the National Guard during the siege and had joined the rebellion. Some versions make a great romance out of it, but they would, wouldn't they? Unfortunately, no one seems to know for sure what happened when Rochemure was released from prison by his old army friends. Some say that he had already sent Ignatz Fell after the boy, telling him to take care of him—which, if rumor can be trusted, he did in a gruesome manner. The baron seems to have gone looking for his daughter himself, but whether he found her or not, before she turned up dead, or what happened between them if he did, nobody knows—nobody, at any rate, who's talking. Fell was murdered shortly thereafter—no one knows by whom, although there was probably no shortage of suspects. Nobody knows, either, whether Yvaine gave birth to the child she was carrying, or what happened to it if she did. As you can imagine, more than one person has speculated that the reason Rochemure is so keen to get his dead daughter to talk is to find out what happened to her child, but it's pure conjecture. I'm sorry I can't be more definite."

"It probably wouldn't help if you could. When you said 'prepare for tomorrow,' what exactly did you mean?"

"It's fairly obvious that he's going to ask me to hypnotize you again, if not tomorrow, then soon—no later than Madame Pommersat's next séance. As I said, my inclination is to stall for the time being, but your friend Marvaud has been telling people for years that you would never allow yourself to be magnetized again because of something that went awry at Antoine Cros's house. Is that true?"

"I've certainly been very reluctant," Paul told Lesmastur, warily, "but I've been trying for years to make sense by myself of what I produce while I'm in a spontaneous trance state, and have become rather frustrated with my lack of progress. I've come back to Paris because I thought the time might be ripe for a further experiment, under controlled conditions, preferably at Juvisy. The baron's involvement is a complicating factor, but it's already obvious that he isn't going to be put off, and might want to proceed a lot more rapidly than I do— but at least I'll have your support, it seems in trying to slow him down."

"Mine, certainly," Lemastur said. "Madame Pommerat might have a different agenda. But Flammarion will be there, I understand, and he'll obviously be keen to set something up at Juvisy, even if he feels obliged to let the baron in on it."

Paul decided that there was no reason to keep secrets from Lemastur, if his own hypothesis were to be explored seriously. "I don't know exactly why the baron has invited us both to dinner," he told him, "but he reacted very oddly last night to a picture that I'd drawn, of a human fetus at approximately seven months' development. If that meant something to him in connection with his daughter..."

Lemastur was obviously no fool, and he was familiar with the parameters of the puzzle. "You think she never got to give birth?" he queried. "You think she was seven months pregnant when she died? But that should be ascertainable—it would be, if the official records for that period weren't in a complete mess. But somebody still alive must know...if only we could have done this four years ago we could have asked Antoine Cros. Even if he wasn't directly involved, he'd probably know who was. Damn. Let's see: Louise Michel probably had contact with Yvaine during the Commune, but she died at the beginning of the year. Jules Lermina's alive but he wasn't in Paris—he was sent to face the German guns when he was let out of prison to be drafted into the Guard—but he did knew all the Communards. and he's still at the heart of the movement, albeit discreetly. He might know Rochemure, too, through Henri Chacornac, who married his daughter. On the other hand, he's probably been asked before, and nothing has fed back into the rumor mill. And then again, even if it's true, it doesn't get us any closer to guessing what Rochemure wants...and even if we did, would you actually want to use the information to...cook something up?" Lemastur looked at Paul speculatively.

"No, I wouldn't," said Paul, "and I couldn't—I have absolutely no control of what I draw when I'm entranced."

"You might think that," Lemastur countered "but that might only mean that you haven't learned to take control. I can't promise anything, but I might be able to help you with that...the problem is that it would take time. You really should have come back to me four years ago...or stuck with Zosima. She's an odd one, for sure, but she's a powerful magnetizer, perhaps the most powerful in France. On the other hand, that might be a double-edged sword. You're an artist, and the last thing you'd want, presumably, is to take risks with your brain, in case it affected your hand-eye coordination."

"Precisely," Paul agreed. "You can appreciate my dilemma, then?"

"I've been in the game for quite a while, and I've seen some of the casualties. I don't think I've done any serious damage myself, but perhaps that only reflects the limitations of my hypnotic abilities. Obviously, I have an ax to grind, but quite honestly, if I were you I'd see what you and I can achieve before you go to Zosima Remember what happened to her last medium."

"That wasn't her fault," Paul said curtly.

"She didn't give her tuberculosis, but she didn't do much to help either. Too ambitious. And bear in mind that it was me who put you in touch with Rochemure before, at Madame Pommerat's house. It might be worth re-creating the circumstances, as closely as we can."

Paul could see the logic of the argument, but had no intention of making any decisions yet. "Would that involve inviting Gabriel de Lautrec?" he asked.

"He was there, wasn't he, with Magre? I don't know—he was marginally crazy even then, and I'm not sure that his subsequent dealings with the baron went well. Nor did ours, obviously, but if Lautrec recommended that he try to enhance his own psychic sensitivity with Indian hemp...well, I'm wary of all stimulants and soporifics myself. Have you tried it?"

"No," Paul said. "I'm trying to obtain more control over my wayward unconscious, not trying to let it off the leash. Surely the baron wouldn't..." He left it there, realizing that he had no reliable grounds for any such judgment.

"That's not obvious" said Lemastur. "He was out of the army before the last big Tonkin campaign and he wasn't in the Opium War, but he's bound to have known men who went, and a lot of them came back having sampled opium copiously. Then again, the leg wound he sustained at Le Mans was apparently nasty—he almost certainly had morphine for that, and it can be a difficult habit to kick. The fact that he ever gave Lautrec the time of day is suggestive...but I don't know whether they're still in communication. Why do you ask?"

"He left a card at the desk, as you did. No message, but he must have had a reason."

"Possibly—but if he contacts you again, tread carefully. A charming fellow, and he means well...but when you add the hashish and the Martinism to the fact that he's a poet, whose originality sails a little too close to incomprehensibility for my taste...and we're straying from the point, aren't we? How are we going to handle the baron tomorrow night? It's difficult, I know, as we don't know exactly what he has in mind, but...am I right in thinking, now, that you don't want to refuse point blank to play ball, but that you want to steer him in Flammarion's direction rather than Madame Pommerat's?"

"At present," Paul told him, "I'm not sure what the best course of action is. Twenty-four hours ago, I had no idea that I'd produced a second drawing that the baron would recognize, and I haven't the slightest idea what it signifies that I have. Originally, I thought that the baron's identification of the first image I drew as his daughter was just wishful thinking on his part—and the fact that he's done it twice, somewhat to his own surprise, might only be a reflection of the intensity of his wishfulness. Do you really believe that you summoned the spirit of his dead daughter four years ago?"

Lemastur laughed, briefly. "Twenty-four hours ago," he said, "I thought exactly as you did. But now I know that you've done it twice, especially unknowingly...that's a complication. Flammarion, I assume, thinks it's entirely explicable in terms of your unconscious mind...and Zosima's equally certain that you really are visited by the spirits of the dead on a routine basis?"

"That's an accurate summary," Paul agreed.

"And your inclination is to believe Flammarion...but it still leaves puzzles unsolved?"

"Indeed. You side with Zosima, I assume?"

"In theoretical terms, yes...but in this particular case, I don't have enough information to make a judgment. If I could hypnotize you again...oh, don't look like that, I don't mean here, and certainly not now...and not in Passy tomorrow, if we can help it. But if you and I could get together, in private, perhaps the day after tomorrow...I really think that we might at least be able to get a clearer idea of what's happening."

Paul sighed. *If only...*, he thought. "But you do believe that the spirits of the dead do communicate with mediums during your séances?" he said.

"Certainly—but how much of what they appear to say is due to the effect of my suggestion and how much is due to their efforts is difficult to say."

"And you believe that the spirits of the dead are all around us, although they only become manifest to certain individuals, on certain occasions?"

"I do. It's rare, obviously, for them to make any effort to communicate, or to respond to attempts to communicate with them, but they can and do. There are evident difficulties on both sides, but it happens. You know that as well as I do."

Do I? Paul thought. Or *do I simply fall for the same tempting illusions?* "And do you believe that the spirits of the dead can be reincarnated?" he persisted.

"Yes, I do," Lemastur said, unhesitatingly. "The cost of that reincarnation, evidently, is almost-complete forgetfulness of previous incarnations, but the hidden memories sometimes resurface spontaneously, and can sometimes be recovered by hypnotism. Whether spirits can be reincarnated on other worlds, I don't know, but I agree with Flammarion that it's an intriguing possibility. Whether they can be reincarnated as animals, I'm also not sure, but I certainly wouldn't rule it out. Why the interrogation? You can't have expected me to say anything different."

"I suppose not—but they're all issues about which I'm profoundly uncertain. Given that Monsieur Flammarion has been trying to ascertain the answers for forty years and more, without reaching certainty, perhaps it's a hopeless quest, especially as my experience is...idiosyncratic—but I feel obliged to try."

"I can understand that, even though most people don't, and most of those who do are prepared to settle for the first plausible story that they're told. Flammarion's not the only person who's been searching assiduously for forty years. Henri Chacornac's bookshop on the Quai Saint-Michel does a roaring trade in every species of occultism. When Rochemure gave up soldiering he became an assiduous reader, an esoteric scholar of sorts, but all his reading doesn't seem to have slaked his thirst for understanding, any more than hundreds of spiritist séances have brought him a single message from his daughter that he's prepared to believe. Let's not discount the possibility though, that some of them were genuine and accurate, but they simply didn't tell him what he wants to hear."

"Or perhaps it's because they told him exactly what he wants to hear that he can't believe them," Paul mused, remembering Zosima's lecture four years ago, when she had mentioned perverse individuals who did not believe that the forgiveness of which they were ostensibly in search was possible."

"You think he's unconsciously seeking to punish himself? It's become a fashionable notion in the last decade or so that most or all hauntings are imaginary: the torments of guilt feelings that can't be exorcised. Do you think that applies to your own case?"

Paul though that a good sportsman might simply say *touché*, but he was too weary. "If what happens to me is a matter of my tormenting myself because of what happened in the womb, or the way I came to interpret what had happened in the womb," he said, "then I'm a seriously disturbed individual." *But there isn't any doubt about that*, he added, silently. *The question is, where does the disturbance originate, and can anything be done to ameliorate it?*

Diplomatically, Henri Lesmastur made no reply. Instead, he stood up and said: "It's late. I think we've clarified the station as far as we can. We'll pick things up tomorrow evening, and meet again to decide how to proceed when we know what the baron's intentions are...and when we've had a chance to gauge the extent and nature of his serious disturbance. But however that comes out, my offer stands. I can help you, with or without Flammarion's assistance." He extended his hand, and Paul shook it, considerably more firmly than he had shaken the baron's the previous evening.

Then they bid one another good night, Lesmastur left, and Paul went to bed. Again, when he woke up in the morning, the drawing-pad on the bedside table was blank.

CHAPTER VIII

Paul's conference with Auguste Chazelle did not go as well as he had hoped. Paul delivered four new paintings that he had brought from Toulouse, none of them developed from sketches made while entranced. "Too *trouvère*" was Chazelle's verdict—by which he meant that they were showing too much influence of Provence and the floral games, even though they certainly did not qualify, in Paul's estimation, as "troubadour art." Like Victor, Chazelle thought it would be wise for Paul to return to Paris and devote more effort to portraiture—the "bread and butter" of the profession.

"The posthumous portrait you did of Talia Cadelan is your finest piece to date," the dealer told him, "and proves what you're capable of accomplishing when you put your mind to it. If you can capture the same magic with living models—and Paris is where all the beautiful women in France accumulate—you'll make a comfortable living, and leave yourself time to follow your...personal inclinations. Even if you're determined to stay in the Midi, though, we ought to plan a serious exhibition for next year. The time is ripe. We should be able to include some of your existing paintings, on loan from their purchasers, including the Jeanne d'Arc diptych."

"And the portrait of Talia?" Paul queried.

"Perhaps. I'll enquire."

"I can do that," Paul told him. "I'm having dinner with the baron this evening."

Chazelle looked at him in frank surprise, tinged with annoyance. "He's contacted you directly? That's odd. Not his style—but then, portraits aren't his style either. He used to buy a lot of his paintings from the old Salon de la Rose+Croix, but that's long dead. I gather that he'd met the model, though, at a séance. He asked me not to reveal the purchaser's name, but that's not unusual with aristocratic collectors. Is he going to commission you to do a painting for him?"

"I don't think so. He's a collector of Symbolist art, then?"

"Occult art, certainly. He's become quite a scholar, I believe. He was invalided out of the army—caught a bullet in the Le Mans fiasco, I understand, and nearly died; had to find a new hobby. Had quite a traumatic experience, being carried all the way from Le Mans to Paris in the dead of winter with an infected wound. The surgeons got him through it, but as soon as he was on his feet the Communards threw him in prison. Then his daughter died—suicide, some said. He's never got over it—but he's not mad, whatever people say, and he's not senile either. He doesn't get around much because he still walks with a limp, and I suspect the leg still gives him a lot of pain, but he knows his art, unlike the *nouveau-riche* bandwagon-jumpers. He hasn't bought a lot from me over the years, but anyone will tell you that he's a good client—not exactly a trend-setter, but if you can get a commission from him, or even sell him a couple more canvases, it'll be a significant boost. Send him along to see me, and I'll do my level best to persuade him to take one of these...and we might well be able to interest him in some of your more esoteric material, if we pitch it cleverly. Let me know how it goes tonight—and sound him out about lending the Cadelan portrait for exhibition. It could be the nail, as they say in the theater."

"I will," Paul promised.

Chazelle had a great deal more to say, about anything and everything, and Paul had essential purchases to make, so the afternoon was well advanced by the time he returned to Jane de La Vaudère's house. She assured him that she had been in her study, engrossed in writing, and had not even been aware of his absence, but he didn't believe her, if only because she was already dressed for dinner when he arrived, in a magnificently elegant pale blue evening dress, and had obviously taken great care in the arrangement of her hair and the application of her make-up.

His hostess offered him tea, and Paul accepted gratefully, having built up a thirst while running around, and not having paused when he returned to the hotel to deposit his purchases and change. They sat down in the drawing room in the same chairs they had employed two days before, but the situation seemed to Paul to be very different.

"It was quite a surprise when you telephoned last night," she said. "I remembered, obviously, that you had caught the baron's attention at La Pommerat's séance, and I heard while you were painting my portrait that he was making enquiries about you, but I didn't think it was anything serious—certainly nothing that would lead to him waiting for you outside the house. Why didn't he just call on you at the hotel?"

"He'd tried. When the receptionist told him that I hadn't even picked up his letter he became impatient."

"Yes, he does that, so I'm told. He doesn't have many social contacts now, but my maidservant knows someone who knows his coachman, Fabien. Apparently, he's not a bad employer, by the standards of his generation, but he still suffers sometimes from an old war wound, and it makes him cantankerous, especially when he can't walk and has to rely on Fabien for support."

"Did you manage to talk to anyone who was in Paris at the time of the siege and its aftermath?"

"I made a couple of visits this morning to members of the geriatric brigade—old acquaintances who were surprised to see me, as you can imagine. They both remembered Yvaine, who doesn't seem to have borne the slightest resemblance to my wicked Yvaine, and they depicted her as an angel, but neither of them knew what had become of her after the siege ended. They had heard rumors of a romance with a National Guardsman, but had no direct knowledge of it. They remembered that the baron had been searching for her desperately when the army released him from the clutches of the Commune, but he could hardly walk and was apparently in a bad way."

There was a brief pause while Valérie brought in the tea—just one pot, this time, with less ceremony than the first time, and poured it into the Sèvres cups, and Jane resumed even before the maidservant had closed the door.

"They both said that he took her death very badly, but they couldn't say whether there was any truth in the rumors about her having committed suicide and the guardsman being murdered. The fellow would very probably have been killed doing the Bloody Week, though, either in the fighting or thereafter, when so many of the insurgent guardsmen were put before firing squads. If Yvaine did kill herself, that's probably why—she wouldn't have been the only one, by any means. The whole city was hysterical, one of the old ladies said. Nobody talks about it, the other said, because everybody has things they'd rather forget."

"Not everybody can, apparently," Paul observed, scalding his tongue slightly as he took a sip of tea while it was still too hot. "I wasn't even born in 1871, and haven't spent much of my life in Paris, but I've been able to observe that some people here are still haunted by it, even after thirty-four years—probably more than are prepared to admit the fact."

"I was still in the convent," Jane said, "and hardly saw Paris for ten years thereafter, but the wounds were still very raw when I moved here. They weren't the kind that scars over easily, even for people who didn't have actual bullet wounds to remind them, or the deaths of close relatives to mourn. Some people, of course, can even get over those things...whereas other can be haunted by things that seem far more trivial."

The tea was now cool enough to drink without danger to his tongue or palate, and Paul was able to slake his thirst a little before making what seemed to him to be an anodyne remark: "It's a familiar syndrome, alas. Obsessions are sometimes triggered by trivial things."

"Is that gibe aimed at me?" Jane retorted.

"No," said Paul, startled. "It wasn't a gibe at all, and certainly wasn't aimed at you. Insofar as it was more, or less, than a general observation, the person I had in mind was me."

Jane set down her teacup, still almost full, and took a moment to gather her thoughts. "Of course it was," she said. "I'm sorry. As you can imagine, this isn't a normal conversation for me at a five o'clock tea, here or elsewhere, but the situation isn't quite normal...and I don't mean because I'm already dressed or dinner, no matter how shocking that might seem to some of the people with whom I associate. I don't mean it unkindly—anything but, in fact—but your presence...your return...has stirred up more than memories. I'm sorry."

Paul set his own teacup down, almost empty. "I understand," he said, not entirely sure that he did, but feeling that it was the right thing to say. He added, pensively: "I assume that the reason why you felt a bond of sympathy for me, during that journey to and from Juvisy, is that you thought you understood how I must feel, and I dare say that you were right. Would we be here now if we weren't both haunted, and unable to shake our hauntings? Hauntings that have become entangled because of that sensation of mutual understanding?"

She picked up the teapot and filled his cup, putting the forefinger of her left hand on the knob of the lid to steady the pot.

"No," she said, baldly, in answer to the question.

"In which case," Paul suggested, thinking that it would return the conversation to safer ground, "perhaps we ought to feel some sympathy for the baron, who appears to have suffered a compound trauma infinitely worse than yours or mine. The accounts I've obtained from Zosima, Flammarion, Auguste Chazelle and Henri Lesmastur don't add anything substantial to yours regarding Yvaine de Rochemure, but having pieced them all together, I think I'm beginning to get a clearer picture of the baron."

Jane followed his direction. "Henri Lemastur, you say? You've seen Lemastur?"

"Yes. He ambushed me too, last night, as I came out of the telephone booth in the hotel, where he'd come to seek me out. The baron has invited him and Madame Pommerat to dinner tonight as well."

"You mean that he's planning to hold another séance?"

"Possibly—but Lesmastur and I have agreed to stall him, if we can. Camille will be there too, and he'll support us in trying to organize something at Juvisy. It won't be what we originally envisaged, but on the basis of what I've heard in the last twenty-four hours, I'm not unsympathetic to the idea of the baron being in attendance. We'll probably be able to come to a satisfactory arrangement at tonight's dinner, although it will be a little more crowded than I would have liked."

"Indeed—La Pommerat's a crowd all on her own, and the baron might be thinking about a séance at her house rather than Juvisy. Is anyone else going to be there tonight?"

"I don't know. The baron did mention the possibility of contacting Zosima, but whether he did, and whether he would consider her an appropriate dinner guest, I don't know. Mention has also been made of Gabriel de Lautrec—do you know him?"

"As a writer, certainly, and in person, a little better than slightly. Like me, he has the reputation of being one of the most Decadent of Decadent writers, and he's always affable when we meet, but we generally move in different social circles. He probably met the baron through his Martinist connections; the baron used to attend the Salon de la Rose+Croix assiduously a few years back, leaning on his walking-stick, and Lautrec was a regular there too."

"Lautrec left a card at my hotel, and Victor thinks that it might have been him who told the baron where to find me; Chazelle didn't give me any indication that he had informed the baron of my return, although he might have been drawing a discreet veil over the information. Apparently, he sold my painting of Talia to the baron.

"Really? Well, Rochemure is apparently a serious collector, more so than me. But why would Gabriel de Lautrec have told him where to find you?"

"Perhaps simply because he knew that the baron would be interested. The baron might have consulted him at one time regarding the effects of hashish, probably with a view to employing it as a pain-killer rather than a hallucinant, if the leg wound he sustained at Le Mans gives him occasional trouble..."

"Or both, if the wound is intimately connected in his memory with the loss of his daughter. Trauma can be cumulative, I understand, and the combinations can sometimes be peculiar. I've read the visionary prose-poems that Lautrec wrote under the influence of hashish. If the baron read them too—and he's reputed to collect esoteric books as well as esoteric paintings—he might well have concluded that you and Lautrec are two of a kind, both seers, either of whom might be able to aid him in his quest to deal with his haunting. And if he bought your portrait of Talia, perhaps it's because he recognized her as a seer too, if he attended some of Zosima's séances four years ago?"

"He did—and he wanted to arrange private sessions with Zosima, but Talia refused. She said the baron had a darkness in his soul. Zosima took that to mean that he was nursing direly guilty secrets there, but I'm not sure that's the right interpretation, given what I now know, and comparing my situation with his, as he clearly did last night. It's possible that he's simply hurting, in more ways than one. Rumor says different...but rumor always does, doesn't it?"

"It's never short of malice, that's for sure. But if you're right, it's not necessarily good news from your point of view. The links between your mind, Talia's and Juliette's were entirely sympathetic, but that's exactly why they were nearly catastrophic. If, as you say, the baron's anguish is deeper than theirs, it might not be a good idea for you to be hypnotized again in his presence."

"I have considered that, and I've wondered whether the link that was forged the first time might have affected me more profoundly than I thought, and might have had something to do with what happened at Juvisy and at Antoine's house. But I also reminded myself that the sympathetic link forged between you and me has done me nothing but good. If the effects of the links I forged with Talia and Juliette are considered as a whole, and not just as a matter of a temporary shock with which none of us was ready to cope, then it would be difficult to evaluate them as catastrophic. What Zosima told me yesterday about Talia's attitude to me, and what I know about Juliette's attitude suggest that both of them were grateful that the bonds had been formed."

"I didn't mean catastrophic for them," Jane said. "I meant catastrophic for you."

"They're the ones who are dead. I'm fit and well, and, according to you, better looking and not insane. What happened was disturbing, and it certainly alarmed me, but from the viewpoint of today, it doesn't seem to have done me any lasting harm."

"Are you sure about that? Oh, don't look at me like that—it's not a gibe, or an accusation. Just call it sympathy, if you want to be kind. But it's two years since Juliette died, after months that must have been harrowing, in spite of your stubborn insistence that you didn't love her, and you've only now gathered the courage to come back. We've only spent a few hours together but, and please forgive me for saying so, you don't give me the impression of someone who hasn't suffered any lasting damage."

Paul put down his teacup again, emptied for a second time, and the excused himself. He took slightly longer than was strictly necessary, feeling that he needed a moment to compose himself, although he was not entirely sure why.

When he returned, the teapot and the cups had been cleared away.

"I don't feel damaged," he told his hostess. "Not, at any rate, by the brief relationships I had with Talia and Juliette as a result of the seemingly-telepathic bonds we formed. Juliette's death was harrowing, as you say, but on the whole, I think my relationship with her enriched my life rather than damaging it. Even though it didn't qualify as love in the way that people usually use the term, it wasn't without value."

"No wonder you took so long if you had to compose and rehearse that ridiculous circumlocution" Jane observed, not bothering, this time, to ask for forgiveness for saying so. "In fact, I took the inference from your little homily the other day that what you had with Juliette was superior to any mere carnal desire, or anything that we mere humans experience. And, as you undoubtedly knew, having read my books, I took that suggestion very seriously."

"Ah," said Paul. "No, I didn't know it, in the sense of having consciously thought it...but since you mention it, the relationship that seems to exist between the two of us..."

"Don't be naïve, Paul. We may have succeeded in setting aside mere lust, for various good reasons, but that doesn't make our relationship asexual. And the fact that you and Juliette fooled yourselves into thinking of the sexual component of your relationship was a mere physical convenience, while Talia thought she was only capable of being sexually attracted to women, doesn't affect the fact that those relationships were inherently sexual too. You can't imagine for an instant that any bond formed between you and Camille, or between you and Antoine, was remotely similar...or that any bond you might form with Baron de Rochemure de Harvanges could be similar."

"Zosima said much the same thing to me," Paul confessed, frowning in confusion and wondering how the conversation had reached such a strange juncture, "making exactly the same charges of naivety and self-deception. But you'll forgive me for thinking that it isn't as simple as that. After all, the relationships you've quoted aren't the only ones I have."

""Of course not. There's the mysterious Clémence...mysterious to me, at any rate, although I suspect that's more a matter of teasing my jealousy than polite discretion."

"Actually," Paul told her, feeling that the juncture as becoming even stranger, "I was thinking about Martine."

"Marine? I thought your relationship with her was entirely imaginary?"

"It was. It is."

"Is? You mean she's still haunting you?"

"Yes. Perhaps not as much as Talia and Juliette, or even the mysterious fetus, but yes, in her case, I do sense her presence in a different, more intimate way."

"And me? Am I haunting you more intimately too, naked and crucified?"

"That's different. You're not dead. When my somnifabricatory hand draws you, I don't think you're even a phantasm of the living, as people like Gurney and Myers understand the term."

"You mean that I'm more like the wistful siren, the sphinge and the tortured tigress?"

"No...except perhaps in the sense that the image of the crucifixion is presumably symbolic, like many of the others. Although, obviously, they might all be symbolic. Just because a face is a face, it doesn't mean that it isn't symbolic of something else.

"Don't get carried away," she told him, although it seemed to Paul a case of the pot calling the kettle black. After a slight pause, she went on: "So, even though you don't remember making any of the drawings, you feel differently about some of them when you see them? But there's nothing surprising about that—and nothing surprising about your adding Martine to your list of phantom not-quite-lovers, given that you thought you loved Martine, after a fashion, just as you had special relationships with Juliette and Talia?"

"I suppose not," Paul admitted, having no idea what agenda his interlocutrice might be following in her own mind

"And if Antoine were here, he'd tell you that, as they're not really the spirits of the dead, but only illusions entirely

149

generated by your unconscious mind, it would be very odd indeed if you didn't feel differently about those you once loved...or had feelings akin to loving ones."

"Doubtless he'd tell me exactly that—and doubtless I'd counter with the same argument Flammarion once used: that just because the images I draw come from the depths of my unconscious mind, it doesn't demonstrate *ipso facto* that they aren't the spirits of the dead."

"That's just wordplay."

"Is it?" he countered. Then, feeling that he was entitled to counter her probing of feelings that were not being stirred without a certain discomfort, he added: "What about the images of your mother? Are they or are they not manifestations of her spirit?"

She looked at him with her blue eyes in a fashion that immediately made him wish that he had resisted the impulse. "I thought we'd agreed not to talk about that," she said.

"No, we hadn't," he told her, and went on, defensively: "and how can we avoid it, give that it's a crucial test case, a significant aspect of our collective haunting. We'd decided, I think, to accept that my ability to draw your mother was dependent on the fact that a psychic link had been established between my unconscious mind and yours—but that still leaves unanswered the question of the existential status of the image in your unconscious mind. Is it, in fact, a manifestation of the spirit of your mother, or an illusion of your own mind?"

"I don't know," Jane retorted. "How can I possibly tell?"

"And that," said Paul, with a sigh, "is the nub of the matter. How can we possibly tell? How can I possibly tell whether the image of the fetus that haunts me incessantly is or isn't the spirit of my sister? How can we tell whether the image that I presumably plucked out of Baron de Rochemure's unconscious mind in Madame La Pommerat's drawing room, and stored away for later recovery, is or isn't the spirit of his daughter? What evidence could ever be adequate to settle the question? And in either case, is there anything than can be done about it, if anything needs to be done about it? In either case, is the entity in question something capable of granting any of us forgiveness and facilitating our redemption?"

Jane smoothed the pleats of her gown over her knees. The sight and feel of the fabric seemed to remind her that they were about to go to dinner, to embark upon a familiar social enterprise, to which all the rules of etiquette applied. She put the slender fingers of her hand to her forehead then, as if to press a button in her brain. Then she reached for her gray gloves, which were on the table from which the tea-tray had been removed, and began to pull them on. When she finally spoke again, it was in a markedly different tone, although she picked up the continuity of the conversation exactly where it had been left.

"I can't believe, my dear Paul," she said, mildly, "that you're in need of redemption."

Paul took note of the fact that she had said nothing about her own need, or possible lack of it, but he tried to match her changed, bantering tone.

"I fear that I am," he said, lightly. "And although a generous judge like you might grant me clemency, that doesn't mean that I'm not guilty."

The doorbell rang at that point, just as Jane completed the adjustment of her gloves. A brief conversation, perhaps longer than was strictly necessary, was engaged at the door between the visitor and the maidservant; Paul tried to hear what was being said, but couldn't. Eventually, the maidservant came in and said: "Monsieur le Baron's coachman apologizes for being a little early, but says that he has other guests to collect, and that the journey will take a little longer than the baron originally anticipated."

"That's all right, Valérie," said Jane. "Please ask him to wait for a few minutes, Paul; I'll come to join you in a few minutes." She disappeared into another room, while the maidservant escorted Paul to the door where Fabien was waiting.

The tall coachman did not seem quite as intimidating by day as he had by night, because he was not wearing his bulky overcoat, the weather being cloudy but free of rain; even so, he was a good six inches taller than Paul, who was not usually required to think of himself as a short person. It occurred to Paul, however, that if the baron's coachman routinely had to lend him assistance because of his lameness, a certain burliness was a requirement of the position.

The two of them waited by the portière of the carriage for Jane to finish her final preparations.

"Is it Madame Pommerat and Monsieur Lesmastur that you have to pick up?" Paul asked, for the sake of something to say.

The tall man seemed surprised. "No, Monsieur," he said. "Madame Pommerat has her own carriage, and she has kindly agreed to meet Monsieur Flammarion at the railway station. I shall be picking up Madame Zosima and Monsieur de Lautrec."

"Indeed? We shall be eight for dinner, then?"

"Yes, Monsieur."

"That must be unusual. I'm told that the baron rarely entertains nowadays."

"That's true, Monsieur, but have no fear; the service will be adequate. Madame Louvot, the housekeeper, has been with him for a long time, and is very adept. I shall do my best to match her dexterity."

"Have you been with the baron for a long time?"

"All my life, in a manner of speaking, Monsieur. I lost both my parents when I was very young, and the baron was kind enough to allow my aunt, Madame Louvot, to take care of me in the house long before I was old enough to be of any use."

Paul studied the big man a little more carefully, trying to estimate his age. He was certainly no older than thirty, perhaps less. "You must be a great asset to him now," Paul observed, "given the limitations imposed on him by his lameness."

"I'm glad of the opportunity to be of use to him, Monsieur," said the coachman, meekly. "I owe him my life."

"He must be very old now," Paul observed, "He was at Solferino, I believe, with the Emperor."

"So I believe, Monsieur, but it's not something he talks about frequently."

Jane came out then, and Fabien offered her his gloved hand in order to help her up into the carriage. Paul took his place beside her.

"Lautrec is invited," Paul told her, as Fabien climbed back on to the seat. "So is Madame Zosima. Perhaps the baron is hoping to hold a séance, with either Lemastur or Zosima, or both, supplying the magnetic fluid, psychic force, suggestion, or whatever."

"Probably not both of them at once," was Jane's opinion. "Magnetizers rarely operate in pairs. I've heard them opine that influences are more likely to cancel one another out than supplement one another. In any case, Zosima is unlikely to oppose you if you want to wait. There might be a certain tension in the party, though, between Madame Pommerat and Zosima, or even between Madame Pommerat and me. She feels entitled to disapprove of me, I fear, although there's almost as much hostile gossip about her as there is about me. Mercifully, there should be a sufficient gap between us at table to reduce any possible friction, and Gabriel is said to be a delightful table companion; he's a professional humorist nowadays, who can probably be relied upon to dissipate any tensions with his wit, especially in combination with Camille's wisdom. Given that the food and wine are sure to be excellent, there's no reason why we shouldn't all enjoy ourselves, and make any future arrangements that need to be made very amicably."

Paul hoped that she was right.

The next person to join the group was the poet and humorist, whom Jane introduced to Paul. Lautrec was tall and slim, exceptionally well groomed, with a dandy's monocle, a silk hat and an ebony swagger-stick, but his manners were so graceful that Paul forgave him the later affectation, although he could not help feeling that he was being made to look distinctly dowdy by comparison with his fellow guests.

"I'm delighted to meet you, Monsieur Furneret," said the alleged hashish-eater. "Your painting is a fine addition to the baron's dining-room, fully deserving of its pride of place above the mantelpiece, where those haunting eyes can survey the guests with an admirably plaintive cynicism. And Madame de La Vaudère, it's a great privilege to meet you again. Your recent work is wonderful, although I do think that your caricature of my old friend Jean Lorrain in *Les Androgynes* was very harsh. Still, he has done worse to others, and I could forgive you anything for *L'Amazone du roi de Siam* and *Le Harem de Syta*. This, I thought, as I read them, is a woman who certainly knows her poisons—which, coming from a reprobate of my stripe, is high praise. Would you believe that I've given up the struggle to make sense of life, and have settled for finding it absurd and laughing at it? But what can you expect? I'm married and happy, which is fatal to the seriousness of a once-determined pessimist like me."

"I'm married myself," Jane replied, ironically, "but my pessimism is probably more than a match for yours, and as a woman, I can only weep at the cruel absurdity of life."

Lautrec's gaze flickered back and forth between Jane and Paul as if he were trying to weigh up the nature of their relationship, but he made no moment, even in jest. Instead he said: "You deserve every congratulation, Monsieur Furneret, for having finally woken the baron from his social torpor. It will do the dear fellow the world of good to have convivial company for an evening. I believe that Madame Pommerat and Henri will be joining us, and Camille Flammarion too. An expert mixture! And we shall be seven for dinner—a magical number."

"We shall be eight, I fear, Monsieur de Lautrec" said Jane. "Madame Zosima will be joining us."

Lautrec shrugged his shoulder expressively. "All numbers are magical, each one in its own way," he said, "and I renew my congratulations. To stir the baron qualifies as a marvel, to persuade him to invite the legendary Madame Zosima, and for her to accept, is surely little short of a miracle.

I fear that I shall be something of a psychic lightweight, though, in such august company. Perhaps I am to be cast as court jester—but it's an honorable employment, which I shall do my best to fill adequately."

"Have you known the baron long, Monsieur de Lautrec?" Paul asked, curiously.

"A little more than seven years. Henri Chacornac introduced us, not long after he had moved from his bouquiniste's pitch into an actual shop, much to the comfort and delight of his regular customers. The baron and I have literary interests in common, and we have lent one another books on occasion. As Madame de La Vaudère knows, there is no great intimacy than that of book-lovers able to trust one another to the extent of lending precious volumes. The words chalk and cheese might spring to your mind, Monsieur Furneret, but the baron and I are friends nowadays, and we count one another valuable in a world where amities wither so easily."

It seemed for a second or two that the poet was about to add something more, but he hesitated, and Paul judged that he would probably have remand silent even if the portière had not opened then in order to admit Madame Zosima, who had abandoned her monk's habit for a man's suit of the kind that she had worn routinely four years previously. Jane introduced the magnetizer to the poet, and vice versa.

"I had not expected to see you again quite so soon," Paul said to Zosima.

"It comes as a surprise to me, too," said Zosima. "I hardly recognized myself when I looked at myself in a mirror; but there are certain invitations that simply cannot be refused—and Baron de Rochemure baited the hook by telling me that he would be careful to seat me opposite your painting of Talia, which, he says, is truly magical. From anyone else, I would take that for polite hyperbole, but the baron's reputation does not encourage that suspicion."

"Oh, please don't judge the baron by his reputation," Lautrec put in. "I shiver at the thought that I might be judged by mine, and even Madame de La Vaudère might wince at certain aspects of hers. Society is neither an honest nor a generous judge. We all have our crosses to bear, with various degrees of fortitude, but the baron has a heavier one than most, and if he is sometimes bad-tempered, that is the effect of his wounds, not his soul. On the other hand, he is not prone to hyperbole, and I can vouch for the fact that when he says that Monsieur Furneret's painting is magical, that is exactly what he means—and it is surely true. Do you not agree, Madame de La Vaudère?"

"I only saw the painting of Talia very briefly," Jane replied, "but I am the privileged possessor of three of his paintings now, and I have been fortunate enough to see his recent sketches, so I am in a perfect position to testify that his work is, indeed, extraordinary, and I am very proud to have played a small but significant part in aiding his career. If the baron wishes to commission a painting from him, I shall be almost as delighted as Paul."

Again the poet's gaze flicked back and forth between Paul and Jane, still trying to calculate the precise nature of their relationship.

"Extraordinary is certainly an accurate description," Zosima supplied, perhaps a trifle ironically. "Like you, Madame, I have been privileged to see Monsieur Furneret at work, and even to lend him a certain modest assistance. I hesitate to declare that he is one of a kind, the world being so large, but there are certainly not many like him, and I still feel that ours was a fateful meeting."

"Doubtless Henri Lemastur feels the same," Jane put in, mischievously. "I certainly do, having been depicted by Paul's magical hand no less than three times. No one else alive can claim that distinction, I believe." She stressed the word "alive" mildly but conspicuously, and then added: "Unless his new muse has been more prolific in her inspiration than he has yet been prepared to admit."

"Have you a new muse, Monsieur Furneret?" Zosima asked.

Before Paul could answer, Jane continued: "Her name is Clémence, after Clémence Isaure. She paints fanciful flowers and images of the holy grail, and is in mourning for her late husband, who drowned in the Garonne. All very *trouvère*, to borrow a phrase from Monsieur Chazelle.

"I approve entirely," said Gabriel de Lautrec. "What better muse could a Toulousan painter have than a reincarnation of Clémence Isaure? Shall we see a portrait of her soon?"

"Possibly," said Paul, defensively. "I shall not be making any definite plans until I return to Toulouse, but Chazelle is urging me to paint more portraits of the living, in order to rebalance my reputation as a painter of the dead, and I have not found many suitable models on the mountainside where I live or the village below. Clémence considers it to be a magical place, but the ruins of the ancient fortress and the long-uninhabited convent seem bleak to me, and the local village is positively banal. It's both peaceful and rugged, though, a combination very conducive to meditation and the exercise of the imagination."

"But there would be a certain symmetry, it seems to me," Zosima suggested, "in following your portrait of Talia with one of Juliette? You mentioned—did you not?—that you have several sketches of her, in addition to those that Antoine Cros claimed as the fee for the séance held at his home, although, strictly speaking, I believe that I was the one who was owed a fee. Or would it be too painful for you, even after a interval of two years, to paint a portrait of your late lover?"

Before Paul could improvise an answer to the deliberate provocation, Jane intervened again. She said, addressing Gabriel de Lautrec: "Juliette was the model for the Jeanne d'Arc diptych that Paul sent to Paris before the portrait of Talia. Although they were not really lovers, in Paul's account of their relationship, they were very close, and he maintained a long vigil by her death-bed. Perhaps it is too sensitive a subject for discussion in a circumstance like this."

"I apologize," said Zosima, not sounding in the least repentant. "Perhaps the almost-exclusive company of women

157

during the last three years has left my social graces a trifle rusty. But for art's sake, I really do think that Monsieur Furneret ought to make more use of his sketches, if only those where there is no emotional involvement at stake. Perhaps, Madame de La Vaudère, as you are the most prolific collector of his work, you might commission him to turn one of his sketches of your mother into an oil painting?"

This time, it was Paul who was quick to interrupt. "It's very kind of you to take such an interest, Madame Zosima. Given that you did, indeed, play a significant role in my development as an artist, and might well have had a moral entitlement to the sketch I made at the doctor's house under the effect of your hypnotism, you're making me feel a trifle mean for only having made you a present of a single sketch, after a four year interval. Madame de La Vaudère has my siren and my sphinx, but perhaps you'd like a tigress?"

Zosima laughed. "Oh, very good," she said. "I accept the rebuke. We really ought to focus our attention on Baron de Rochemure, though, who has been kind enough to bring us all together, with Camille Flammarion and Henri Lemastur too. We must try be worthy of the honor. I fear that I might seem a trifle vulgar in such elegant company, as the daughter of a Marseillaise matelot and an Egyptian lady of the night, but I shall do my best not to offend anyone again."

"I'm sure Madame Pommerat will be grateful for that," Jane could not resist remarking.

"A delightful lady, Madame Pommerat," Gabriel de Lautrec put in, smoothly. "It was at one of her séances that I first saw Monsieur Furneret—I cannot say that I met him, alas, because we were not introduced—and it's always a privilege to see Monsieur Lemastur at work. My friend Maurice Magre was with me that night. Do you know him? An excellent fellow, and a fine writer. You know him, Madame de La Vaudère, I believe?"

"Vaguely," said Jane, with a negligent flick of her right hand, as if it were holding a fan that was only present in phantom form. "A handsome young man, and a fine poet. But you've known so many fine poets, Monsieur de Lautrec. You knew Verlaine, I believe, and Oscar Wilde?"

"I did—very briefly, I fear. Both dead now, alas, along with Mallarmé. Those of us who remain will be in their shadow for a long time, will we not, Madame?"

"Undoubtedly," said Jane—but she was looking at her empty hand, and it seemed to Paul that she suddenly remembered that she was his guest, and that they were embarked on a serious mission. She frowned slightly, perhaps chiding herself for having allowed a habit of artifice to take over in her interchange with Zosima that was not only inappropriate to the situation but reflected a hypocrisy of which she would rather not be guilty, She glanced at Paul, apologetically, but Paul had no idea how to manifest forgiveness in a swift smile.

"But here we are in Passy, almost on the baron's doorstep," Gabriel de Lautrec supplied, coming to the rescue, "and if I'm not mistaken, the carriage ahead of us is Madame Pommerat's. Fate and Fabien's fine horsemanship have brought us together. It's a sign, I believe, that the evening will be fruitful. I shall offer my own private prayer of thanks to the Sacred Fire silently, for fear of offending anyone else's beliefs. The setting sun is hiding behind the clouds, as if behind the veils of Isis, but it is infusing them with the color of blood and life, in order that we might rejoice. Monsieur Flammarion will not regret his telescope tonight, I think."

"Only the one at Pike's Peak," Paul murmured, as Fabien turned into the coaching entrance of the baron's villa, immediately behind the slightly smaller carriage carrying the other three guests.

CHAPTER IX

"Please forgive me for not getting up," said Baron de Rochemure de Harvanges, when the company entered the drawing room, were he was sitting in a carefully-placed arm-chair. "After years of relative quietude, the wounds in my hip and thigh that I sustained thirty-four years ago, have begun to misbehave again, atrociously."

The baron was elegantly clad in a frock-coat that was very old-fashioned, but seemed all the more appropriate for that. The room was only illuminated by candlelight, with made his hair and beard seem so white and his complexion so pale that he might almost have been a ghost displaced in time by half a century or more. Paul and Jane were the last to present themselves to him formally, the occupants of Madame Pommerat's carriage having preceded them into the villa. Gabriel de Lautrec had offered his arm to Zosima as if it were the most natural thing in the world and had led the way, as it was appropriate for an habitué of the house to do, so had introduced the magnetizer to their host before Jane.

"I'm delighted to receive you in my home, Madame de La Vaudère," the baron said, after brushing Jane's gloved hand with his lips. "I should have invited you here many years ago, given that I owe my life, albeit indirectly, to your father."

"To my father?" Jane queried.

"Colonel Scrive was the surgeon-general of the army when I was a mere lieutenant. I never had the privilege of being treated by him personally, of course, but I was in the Crimea with him, and I saw at first hand the effects of the reforms he introduced into the military medical services. They saved a great many lives—including mine, albeit many years later, at Le Mans. Twenty years earlier, the after-effects of the two bullets that struck me in 1870 would certainly have killed me, after a long agony, but the surgeon who treated me was able to remove both bullets under chloroform and sow up the wounds hygienically. I would have escaped infection altogether had it not been for the terrible conditions I which in was obliged to return to Paris. Did Monsieur Furneret tell you that I recognized the sketch he had made of your mother?"

"Yes, he did," Jane said.

"A truly beautiful woman. I hardly knew her, of course, although we were formally introduced at a regimental banquet, and I danced with her once, in my turn—but as I explained to Monsieur Furneret, when one gets old, and one is trying to make a summary assessment of an entire life, a momentary contact with a beautiful woman sticks in the memory with an astonishing obstinacy. I met Empress Eugénie too, on several occasions, but she did not make the same impression. I am not sure that I would recognize her if I saw her again, but your mother...yes, I recognized her instantly in the sketch. Please forgive my fit of nostalgia."

"There's nothing to forgive, Baron," Jane assured him, in a slightly colorless voice.

The Baron turned his attention to Paul. "I owe you an apology too, Monsieur Furneret," he said. "I should have realized as soon as I saw the drawing of Madame Scrive what a truly remarkable seer you are, but it was not until I found the second sketch of Yvaine that I took the full measure of your importance...and it was not until I had had several hours to ponder the matter that I realized that it was necessary for me to rethink my entire attitude to my situation. It is too easy, alas, for ideas to fall into an obsessive rut and for convictions to become set in stone. I hope you can forgive me for engaging you in a slightly larger gathering tonight than you were expecting."

"There's nothing to forgive, Monseigneur," said Paul, semi-automatically.

"Yes, there is," the baron assured him. "My impatience, last night and in the hasty arrangement of this conference, must seem to you to be frightfully rude, but I hope it isn't inexcusable, in the circumstances. When a man discovers that he only has a matter of a few weeks to live, it gives one a re-markable sense of urgency."

"A few weeks?" Paul queried, taken aback by the asser-tion.

"Months, perhaps, but less than a year. There's no doubt, I fear. The cream of the Faculty of the Sorbonne and the Pas-teur Institute are in complete agreement. It is, apparently, not very uncommon. A wound that appears to have healed, even one that leaves a literal hole in the flesh because of the effects of a secondary infection, can lie dormant for years while re-maining a fertile site for the eventual development of what is nowadays called a cancer, which can spread from its initial site, slowly but inexorably, to other organs of the body.

"In my young days, of course, we had no knowledge of such things. Infection and contagion were credited to mysteri-ous miasmas, and it was not until men like Scrive, Raspail and Pasteur realized the importance of strict hygiene in medical treatment that the modern notion of organisms invisible to all but the most powerful microscopes was able to clarify the matter. Cancers are still mysterious in many ways, but histolo-gists and anatomists, with the support of improved micro-scopes and X-rays, are delving into the body nowadays as never before. So much new understanding is becoming possi-ble, almost by the day...you seem very surprised, Monsieur Furneret. You formed a bad impression of me on Monday night, I dare say...and you have doubtless spent the last forty hours collecting rumors. Then again, you have looked around at the paintings on the walls of this room...the Delville and the Knopff, in particular...but you are a belated Symbolist your-self, I believe, and you can surely appreciate them, even if they seem a little out of place in the home of an old soldier?"

"I love the paintings," Paul said, parading a circular glance around the capacious drawing room, where his fellow guests were still separated into two groups, Gabriel de Lautrec still loyally keeping Zosima company, while Madame Pommerat seemed to have monopolized Camille Flammarion, "and they do, in fact, strike something of a chord in my unconscious, but..." He stopped, uncertain as to whether it was polite or wise to add any kind of *but* to his judgment.

"But you have difficulty reconciling an innocent interest in Symbolist painting and my friendship with a humorist and dandy like Gabriel Lautrec with the rumor that I drove my daughter to suicide by commissioning Ignatz Fell to castrate her lover?" said the baron, with a sudden brutality that was not concealed by the deliberate lightness of his tone.

Paul winced and blushed. "I know what a terrible liar rumor is...," he began—but Rochemure cut him off.

"You're attacking the problem from the wrong angle, Monsieur Furneret. He question is not whether the rumor might be false, but whether the notions are really at odds." He made the mildness of his voice even more conspicuous. "But I am being impatient again, and such matters are best addressed in a disciplined manner." As he spoke he made a signal with his right hand, and a maidservant who had been standing beside the door of the room like a sentinel, immediately hastened to his side.

"This is Madame Louvot, my housekeeper, and lately my nurse," the baron said to Paul. "Could you possibly excuse us for a moment?"

"Of course," Paul bowed, and allowed Jane to draw him away. "I fear that we have misread the situation," she whispered in his ear.

"I fear so," was all he had time to say before a middle-aged woman wearing a dark blue evening dress appeared before him, on the arm of a younger man, forming a couple that Paul could not help imagining as a caricature of himself and Jane, with an appropriately larger mass, painted in a suitably darker shade.

"It's a great pleasure to see you again, Monsieur Furneret," said Madame Pommerat, extending her gloved hand to be kissed or shaken. Paul contented himself with brushing the fingers with his own. "And a great pleasure, as always to see you, my dear Jane," the lady added.

Paul estimated that Madame Pommerat must, as Zosima had remarked, have been the same age as Jane, a year or two short of fifty, but whereas Jane had aged very gracefully, assisted in that by her slim figure and delicate features, Madame Pommerat, being several inches taller, had thickened out proportionately, and although she did not have Zosima's quasi-masculine solidity, she nevertheless had an intimating bulk. She had obviously once been pretty, but her looks were fading far more rapidly than Jane's, and there was little that make-up could achieve in compensation for the damage, in spite of an obvious effort.

"Thank you for your letter, Madame Pommerat," Paul said, pulling himself together. "I'm sorry, as I said in my note, that I wasn't able to accept your invitation immediately, but some years have passed since I was last in Paris, and it has been very difficult for me to organize a timetable for the brief time that I'll be here."

"Then we must all make what effort we can to persuade you to extend your stay, or to return as soon as possible, must we not, Jane?" said Madame Pommerat, in a falsely honeyed tone.

"It's very kind of you to add your pleas to mine, Henriette," Jane replied, "and I hope they will be able to tip the balance that mine has not been able to incline in that direction."

"You remember Henri, of course," Madame Pommerat said, addressing Paul again—by which Paul inferred that Lemastur had not told her about their conversation of the previous evening.

"Of course," said Paul, shaking Lemastur's hand.

He did not have to say anything further, because Madame Pommerat continued: "Has Jane explained to you what an honor it is for us all to have been invited here tonight? I suppose that she must have done, as you seem to have made room for it so promptly in your timetable."

"It seems the least I can do," Paul muttered, "to grant the wish of a dying man."

He realized immediately that he had been thoughtlessly indiscreet. Madame Pommerat contrived to go pale even under the layers of her make-up. Henri Lemastur started as if he had received a galvanic shock.

"Dying?" repeated Madame Pommerat. "The baron is dying?"

"So it seems," said Jane, keeping her voice deliberately low, to emphasize the confidentiality of what she was saying. "Hence the urgency with which his invitation was issued."

"That is why he asked me to arrange another séance, and to be sure to invite you as soon as your train arrived from Toulouse? And why he became so annoyed when he heard that you had not even picked up my invitation?" Madame Pommerat seemed to have received the news with all the shock of a revelation.

"The poor fellow must be nearly seventy-five years old," Lemastur observed, "and he never recovered fully from the wounds he sustained at Le Mans. It's a miracle that he's lasted as long as he has." He looked at Paul, significantly. "You think, then, that he does intend to ask us to hold a séance tonight...and that it might not be easy to refuse him?"

"Perhaps," said Paul, warily, unable to help wondering whether he had just fallen into a trap set by the wily baron.

Madame Pommerat was looking at Zosima, who was standing half a dozen paces away, now in conversation with Flammarion, while Gabriel Lautrec's gaze was wandering over the slightly garish painting by Fernand Knopff, presumably acquired from the Salon de la Rose+Croix ten or a twelve years before, which was hanging over the mantelpiece and which might well have originated as a illustration for one of Sâr Péladan's occult novels.

"If so," the lady opined, "there would be a measure of unwisdom in inviting two magnetizers. Everyone knows that the effects are more likely to cancel one another out than to combine. I had assumed, when I saw the four of you descending from the second carriage, that the baron merely wanted to decide which of the two he wanted to consult first."

"If you'll pardon me saying so, my dear Henriette," Lemastur put in, with scrupulous politeness, "what 'everyone knows' is not always the truth. The baron has always prided himself on being an independent thinker."

Madame Pommerat had returned her attention to Jane. "You were present, of course, at the mysterious séance at Antoine Cros's house in 1901, were you not, my dear—of which all the survivors are here present?"

"That's true," Jane conceded.

"And it was on that occasion that you commissioned Monsieur Furneret to paint your portrait—the mysterious portrait that no one has ever seen?"

"In fact," said Jane, "I had already asked Monsieur Furneret to paint my portrait before that evening. I had visited him at his studio, had had bought an excellent picture of a siren, as well as seeing his first Jeanne d'Arc while it was in progress. It's true, though, that only a select few people have seen his portrait of me, because I hung it in my boudoir. It is miserly, I know, to hoard a work of genius in that manner, but I might lend it to Chazelle for display in next year's exhibition; perhaps you'll be able to see it then if you wish. Or perhaps you'd rather commission him to paint your own portrait?"

"And Monsieur Flammarion organized the séance at Juvisy, whereas Gabriel was present at my séance, when Monsieur Furneret kindly volunteered to make a drawing under the influence of Henri's hypnotism," said Madame Pommerat, stubbornly sticking to her own point and ignoring the final suggestion. "At which Monsieur Marvaud, as I remember, was not present, although he had suggested the experiment."

"Victor has a very hectic life," Paul observed. "He wasn't present at Juvisy, either, although he still claims the credit for suggesting that experiment to Monsieur Flammarion, and he was certainly responsible for my meeting Doctor Cros and Madame de La Vaudère. One could almost see him as the hand of fate, although he seems rather ill-fitted to the role."

"He does work in a bank," observed Jane, her mischievous impulse intervening again.

"The hand of fate is invisible," said Madame Pommerat, still obstinately following her own train of thought. "Nevertheless, its presence is palpable here, is it not?"

She looked around at the various works of art as if they were emblems of the supernatural, although all of them were modern, and could not content in exoticism, in Paul's opinion, with Jane's Buddhas and other Orientalia. The old-fashioned candlelight, however, did lend a slight supernatural implication to eyes accustomed to gaslight.

"If Madame Zosima is correct about the spirits of the dead being all around us," Paul observed, "and the eight of us who are dining tonight have all brought our hauntings with us, there will be no shortage of invisible hands at table." He turned as he spoke to look back at the chair where Baron de Rochemure had been sitting only a few moments before, but it was empty. Madame Louvot had disappeared as well. Even in the quasi-magicality of the candlelight, however, Paul assumed that the baron had simply been discreetly assisted to make his way to the dining room, in order to be ready to receive his guests there when the meal was ready to be served.

Gabriel de Lautrec, evidently having become surplus to requirements in the earnest discussion at Flammarion had engaged with Zosima—or vice versa—had drifted to Paul's elbow. As Henri Lemastur replied in anodyne fashion to Madame Pommerat's comment about the palpability of the presence of the hand of fate, Paul leaned over toward the poet's ear and said: "You didn't think it worth mentioning in the carriage that the baron is dying?"

Lautrec did not seem embarrassed. "Not my place, Monsieur Furneret," he murmured. "It did occur to me, however, when I received the telegram inviting me, that the baron might be planning some kind of...announcement. He has a slightly theatrical temperament. I'm surprised that he told you so quickly; I would have expected him to save it for dessert."

Observing that Madame Pommerat and Jane were still listening to Lemastur, Paul drew Lautrec a little further aside, and said, in a low whisper: "That was not the only confession he made."

The humorist clearly did not take any immediate inference from that, but after a moment's hesitation he ventured a mistaken conclusion: "He told you about the pills? Surely you're not holding that against us? It's purely medicinal. The Faculty wanted to dose him with morphine, but he had a bad experience with that back in the seventies. Rightly or wrongly, I'm reputed to have a certain expertise in the careful use of poisons, and the hashish has certainly helped with his pain, even if it has had...side-effects."

"I don't blame you in the least," Paul assured him. "I'm just trying to figure out what I'm dealing with."

"So is he, Monsieur Furneret," Lautrec assured him. "I've tried to help, but it's beyond my wisdom. If the people gathered here can't give him something that will put his mind at rest, I far that it might not be possible—but to be honest, I see more potential here for argument than agreement."

"You might be right," Paul conceded, not entirely certain that etiquette would be capable of repressing all the hostilities that seemed to be haunting the room for the duration of an entire soirée.

"What are you two whispering about?" Jane de La Vaudère demanded. "It's a little early in the evening to be formulating conspiracies isn't it? All the more so as you hardly know one another?"

"My dear Madame de La Vaudère," said Lautrec, radiating an admirably-simulated sincerity, "you must forgive us for not wanting take the slightest risk of offending your ears. You're a woman of the world, and you understand that young men—especially reprobate artists like us—often whisper things to one another that they would hesitate to say loudly in the presence of ladies."

Jane did not believe for an instant that they had been exchanging bawdy remarks. She looked at Paul with a wounded expression, and drew him aside herself, while Lautrec oblig-ingly stepped between them and Madame Pommerat.

"Lautrec has been feeding the baron with hashish," he whispered. "Purely medicinal, he says, and I believe him...but the drug might have intensified the baron's haunting. God only knows what conclusions he's drawn from seeing the sketches in my portfolio...especially if what he just implied about rumor can be taken seriously."

"But the baron really is dying, according to Lautrec?" she queried. Apparently she too had wondered whether the admission might have been a ploy.

"It seems so. But if he wants me to submit to hypnosis tonight, it might be as well to hope that two magnetic influ-ences operating simultaneously will tend to reduce one anoth-er's effect rather than multiplying it, perhaps by more than their arithmetical sum."

Zosima and Flammarion approached them then. "Either our instincts are deceiving us," Zosima said, "or there is a se-cret being passed around that has not yet reached us."

"The baron has cancer," said Paul, bluntly. "He thinks that he only has a few weeks to live."

"Ah! I suspected as much. "Hence the urgency of his summons. Does he see this old-fashioned gathering, then, as a last-ditch attempt to evoke his daughter's spirit, in whatever form we can contrive? Have we been summoned in lieu of a priest, to administer some kind of extreme unction?"

"Perhaps more accurately than you suppose," Paul said. "The baron seems to be in a confessional frame of mind."

"I already told you that I can't grant absolution, even when in quasi-religious garb," Zosima observed. "Do you see anyone here who can? I don't—although I have to admit that I wouldn't, even if the Archbishop of Paris were here with a crucifix the size of a halberd."

"That isn't the point, Madame" said Flammarion. "The apparatus is irrelevant—what matters is whether sincere re-pentance can be achieved, and hence authentic redemption. Let us not be too harsh in our judgments. I see more than one person here who might be able to assist the baron to achieve that, since he seems to be prepared to put his trust in us."

"*But I can't control what I draw*," Paul hissed.

"No one is saying that you can, my dear, or that you ought to try," Zosima said. "And don't simply look around and count to seven. The dead are present too. Silent as they may be, they are not impotent."

"I wish I were able to believe that," said Flammarion.

"I don't," Jane put in, "but I suppose it's not an occasion to be selfish. Quite the reverse, in fact. If there are manifestations, of whatever sort, we shall need to support one another."

"And your not being selfish will doubtless, as usual, take the form of clinging to Paul like a leech," Zosima snapped. "At least you'll have the advantage over your competitors of being alive—but we're not at Juvisy or in Antoine Cros's house now, and the dead have proprietorial rights as well as the living. There's an atmosphere here that doesn't bode well...and in spite of a lifetime's effort, I have only a little more control over the application of my psychic force that Paul has over his. As for that male whore Lemastur..."

"That's not a polite way of expressing it, Madame," observed Henri Lesmastur, who had moved inquisitively to stand behind her without her noticing, "accurate as it might be. Whatever happened to professional courtesy, I wonder? But let's not fight over the moral high ground, which I, for one, am perfectly willing to yield to Monsieur Flammarion, probably the only one of us entitled to throw stones, albeit the person least likely to do it. Am I to understand from what I just overheard, Madame Zosima, that you intend to deploy your magnetic power here tonight?"

"Do I understand," Zosima retorted, "that you think we'll have a choice?"

"Certainly I do," said Lesmastur "What about you, Monsieur Furneret? Do you think we no longer have the choice of setting our own terms and conditions?"

"I think that this argument is entirely redundant," Paul opined, "until we've heard what the baron has to say. Whatever proprietorial rights the dead might have, those of the living are his, and we're his guests. He hasn't brought us here to quarrel, with him or among ourselves, and I believe that he's entitled to our courtesy, if nothing else. If Antoine Cros were here, I'd probably look to him for advice, because his advice has helped me in the past. 'Be kind,' he would say. 'Whether it helps anyone else or not, it will do you good.' For want of anything better, that's what I shall try to do."

"Be careful, Monsieur Furneret," Lemastur said. "In my experience, it's best not to fight over the moral high ground."

"Your experience," Zosima said, waspishly, "might not be a reliable guide. Have you ever tried?"

Lemastur shook his head—not as a sign of negation but as a pantomime of sorrow. Paul was surprised that Zosima was manifesting such hostility, when she had been so consummately polite last time he had seen her clad in a frock-coat, plastron and cravat, four years ago. He did not know whether she had simply lost the habit since she had changed her mode of performance, or whether she really did sense disturbing invisible presences around her.

"The baron evidently feels that he needs our help," Camille Flammarion said, "and Monsieur Furneret is right to remind us that he is entitled to do so. There is no reason why there should be any differences between us, but even if there were, we should surely be prepared to set them aside, just as we should set aside any prejudices we might have acquired by listening to idle rumor."

"Agreed," said Lesmastur, swiftly.

Again, Paul attempted to whisper to Lautrec, although the group of seven had now contracted in such a way as to make that difficult. "How long as the baron lived in this house?" he asked.

"I don't know exactly," said the poet. "Far longer than I've known him—but not since 1871, if that's what you mean. The house can't be more than twenty years old. If it's haunted, the ghosts must have come from elsewhere; they're not the residues of any tragedies that unfolded here."

"The dead are not anchored," Zosima put in, obviously having kept track of Paul's attention. "An entire cortege seems to have followed you to Toulouse, including Yvaine de Rochemure. They are with you still. Which is not to say that the baron does not have an elaborate cortege of his own...and whether Henri and I are capable of harmonizing our forces or not, you know full well, Paul, the effects that proximity and sympathy tend to have on your manifestations. I'd advise you not to feel sorry for the baron if I thought you were capable of resisting the temptation, but try to remember what he was, and what he might have done."

The glass in which Paul had been served an aperitif was empty, so he could not mark time by taking a sip. He looked again at a large painting by Jean Delville, carefully hung so that it would not by exposed to direct sunlight from the window. It depicted, in a rather numinous fashion, a figure that might have been an angel, contending with two creatures that looked more like insects that conventional demons, in what might have been a remote corner of the ethereal battlefield on which the war in Heaven had been fought. Paul knew that Delville had founded his own Salon d'Art Idéaliste when Péladan had abandoned his annual showcase of the "décadent esthétique," and the "esthétique du Temple du Graal," but it had not lasted long enough for him to submit anything to it, and the artist was now teaching in Scotland, which seemed to Paul's imagination a more apt location for symbolist hauntings that Belgium, although he had never visited either country.

"It's a fine work," said Gabriel de Lautrec, following the direction of his gaze. "The demons seem to be winning, and it's left to the mind of the beholder to remember that, in fact—or, to be strictly accurate, in fiction—the battle was lost and the angels with fiery swords were victorious. Unless, of course, the reportage is unreliable..."

Fabien appeared in the doorway then, effortlessly dominating the entire population of the room, and his voice seemed to have a majestic ring as he said: "Would Mesdames et Messieurs be good enough to make their way to the dining room, where dinner is about to be served?"

Madame Pommerat took possession of Lemastur's arm, while Flammarion offered his to Zosima. Gabriel de Lautrec stood aside theatrically in order to leave Jane's to Paul, and dropped back to bring up the rear of the procession, while Fabien led the way.

Jane leaned over to whisper in Paul's ear: "I am *not* clinging to you like a leech."

"I know that," he replied, in a similar whisper. "She doesn't understand. She can't. Perhaps we don't either, but it doesn't matter. It is what it is, and it's good for both of us."

They arrived in the dining room then, and Paul saw his portrait of Talia again.

She looked different.

CHAPTER X

Talia was not different in the sense that the colors of her portrait had deteriorated or the contours blurred; the paint was still exactly where Paul had placed it. The baron had reframed the picture, though, and he had set a lamp with a tall glass beneath and in front of it, so that it was illuminated from below; the effect, because the picture was slightly inclined, was slightly eerie. The expression of the phantom's eyes, which had seemed hypnotic even before, now seemed doubly so, and the line of the mouth, which had never been suggestive of a smile, now seemed even sterner. Paul was seized by a momentary anxiety that the invisible smoke of the lamp might eventually stain the paint, but noted that the glass was not precisely vertical, so that the updraft was angled away from the painting.

The baron was placed at the head of the rectangular table, directly below the portrait, but it did not seem to be looking down at him so much as staring over his head at the far end of the able—where, as the baron had promised, Zosima was seated. In spite of the disproportion of the sexes, a symmetry of sorts had be contrived by seating the other two women in the center of the long sides, Jane to the baron's left and Madame Pommerat to his right. Jane was flanked by Gabriel de Lautrec, seated immediately to the barons left, and Lemastur, seated to Zosima's right. Madame Pommerat was flanked by Paul, to the baron's right, and Camille Flammarion.

The service, as Fabien had promised, was carried out with a remarkable smoothness and dexterity by Madame Louvot and himself. Paul watched Madame Louvot at work, and tried to estimate her age, Fabien had told him that she had been his adoptive mother, so she was likely to be in forties, at least, but she might have been even older, probably over fifty but not as old as sixty. She was thin and a trifle gaunt, so her face was not conspicuously wrinkled, but her skin seemed hardened, like parchment. She might once have been beautiful, and still had a certain presence. She moved around the table very smoothly and efficiently, but paid particular care to her employer, with what seemed to Paul to be a genuine affection rather than duty.

The antique oak table was not too long and broad to dissuade individual conversations, but it was not so small as to make them awkward. Paul, not entirely to his surprise, was engaged in conversation amidst immediately by the baron while Gabriel de Lautrec turned to Jane, emanating a somewhat theatrical charm.

"Do you approve of the manner in which your portrait is hung, Monsieur Furneret?" the baron asked.

"It's not quite the effect I had planned," said Paul, "assuming that it would be lit more brightly by gaslight, but it's certainly not ineffective. It gives her a slightly ghostly quality, not inappropriate to a portrait made posthumously. In the long term, though, in spite of the slight angle of the lamp-glass, the smoke from the candles will darken it, if you don't substitute gas or electric lighting,"

"Excessive light can also cause oil paint to deteriorate," the baron said. "There is no permanence in art, even in sculpture. But even in bright light, your portrait's eyes were hypnotic, were they not?"

"Hopefully," Paul said. "That was the effect at which I was aiming—but not everyone is equally vulnerable to their effect."

"Of course not. Some of us are more sensitive to such influences than others—and perhaps some of us too sensitive for our own good, as I believe was the case with Mademoiselle Cadelan. But when you say that it was the effect you were aiming for, you mean that it was the effect that you were trying to reproduce...that her eyes, as you experienced their gaze, really were hypnotic?"

"She was a magnetizer's instrument rather than a magnetizer herself," Paul said, "but yes, once the link between us had been formed, there was a special quality in her gaze, which I felt quite intensely, and which I tried to reproduce in colors, although I'm not certain that it's something capturable by technique."

"She still haunts you, does she not—Talia, I mean."

"It certainly appears so," Paul said, cautiously, "but not in a conventional fashion. When I draw her, I'm not conscious of doing it, and I don't actually see her. When I think about her while I'm not in a somnambulistic state, I'm not sure that it can qualify as being haunted. I seem to sense her presence occasionally, but that must surely be an illusion."

"Must it? You don't feel the touch of her hand occasionally?"

"Not Talia's hand, no. I imagine that I feel Juliette's, occasionally. Juliette and I had...a more tactile relationship. But I sometimes have the sensation of being observed by someone unseen, and I recall Talia's gaze."

"And the others? Do you ever sense their presence, and feel their touch?"

"If you mean the other people whose faces I draw, I don't know. The only apparent phantom whose touch I believe that I can identify reliably is Juliette's. But how can I tell, when I can't see?"

The baron, who was sipping his soup with a regular, mechanical action, nodded his head vigorously during one of the intervals permitted by the movement of the spoon.

"That I understand," he said. "My daughter's touch I can identify. The others...as you say, how can I possibly tell? I do not think, however, that Talia Cadelan is among them. I have, I fear, prostituted her portrait. I only met Talia briefly, and she did not like me. I didn't buy the portrait because it represented her, but because she reminded me, a little, of my daughter. My daughter was taller, and more robust, but there was something about her eyes, and lips. Perhaps it's an illusion, but at any rate, when I look at the portrait, it isn't Talia Cadelan that I see. Can you forgive me for using your work in that unintended fashion?"

176

"You bought the picture," Paul replied, guardedly. "It is yours to use as you wish." For himself, he could not see any particular resemblance between the image of Talia and the sketches that the Baron had recognized as images of his daughter—which were, indeed, of a seemingly robust and healthy young woman"

As if he has read his thought, the baron said, softly: "But you see Yvaine as she was *before*. You don't see her as she was at the end. I try to see remember her, always, as she really was, as a child and as a young woman but...it isn't easy. Has Zosima told you that Talia did not like me because she saw a darkness in my soul?"

"Yes," Paul admitted.

"She was correct. And she was correct to be frightened by it. If Zosima had agreed to the private séances that I wanted her to hold here, Talia would probably have suffered distress in consequence. I feel obliged to warn you, Monsieur Furneret, that if you are kind enough I help me, as I hope you will, it might not be without distress, or even danger. I cannot tell—no one can—exactly how you will make contact with my daughter, if you can. I have reason to be hopeful, because of the images that you have so far produced, but I cannot offer you any guarantees that you will not find the contact hurtful. I am prepared to break the habit of a lifetime for you, Monsieur Furneret, because I have nothing left to lose in so doing, and I will tell you the truth about how the child in my daughter's womb perished, but I want to give that explanation in an orderly manner, to the whole table. I cannot in all conscience ask you to do likewise, but I would like to tell me now, quietly, if you will, whether you really are haunted by the idea that you might have killed your twin sister in the womb, and thus caused the death of your mother?"

Paul had to take a very careful spoonful of soup himself while he considered that question. "May I use a formula of your own," he ventured, in the end, "and say that you might be coming at the question from the wrong angle? You've seen the drawings—some of them, at any rate. You know full well, therefore, that I'm haunted by the image that is almost certainly a fetus, at approximately seven months of development. I have always assumed, and now think it almost certain, that the fetus in question is that of my sister rather than the either of those that other people might have recognized therein; but I have never taken seriously, at least not consciously, the notion that I was responsible for my sister's prenatal death.

"Perhaps, as Antoine Cros once suggested, that is because I have repressed the guilt I felt, which only surfaced in the form of a stupid joke. If what I have heard recently about the theories of the Viennese psychoanalyst Dr. Freud can be trusted, he would find that thesis entirely plausible. But I have given a good deal of thought over the last four years to the question of what ghosts might be, and why they haunt people. I do not find the thesis that they are essentially vengeful spirits seeking reparation for wrongs done to them in life plausible, in the light of reportage by others, or consonant with my own experiences.

"Specifically, I cannot believe that my sister, prior to her death, could have had any kind of consciousness in the womb, but if she had, or if she acquired some kind of consciousness after death, I do not believe that she could have or would have held me responsible for her death. If she exists in some fashion independently of my strange perception of her, then I am inclined to think that she haunts me for exactly the same reason that Juliette—and, for that matter, Talia—haunts me: because we had a psychic bond of some kind."

"Can you tell me anything more about the nature of bonds of that kind?" the baron asked, very quietly.

"I wish I could. I would like to think of it as a kind of love, but that word implies both too much and too little."

"It always does," observed the baron. "Go on."

"I'm not sure that I can. When I suggested to Zosima yesterday that such bonds are unconnected with carnal desire, she laughed at the assertion, and accused me of naivety and self-deception. She would not be alone in that assumption, but I can't accept the criticism. Perhaps it is absurd to say that my sister and I could have loved one another, in a fraternal fashion, in the womb we shared, but I do believe that any bond that I might have now with my dead twin is essentially affectionate, not hateful and destructive. I make no claims for ghosts in general, and I suspect that there might be different kinds of haunting, but I do not believe that any of my own haunters are vengeful."

"Thank you, Monsieur Furneret," said the baron. "That is exactly what I wanted to know, and I am very glad to find that we think along broadly similar lines, in that regard. For what it might be worth, I think you are absolutely correct about your own hauntings. Have you considered the possibility that the reason that Talia Cadelan formed such an immediate bond with you is because she once lost an unborn child of her own after approximately seven months of pregnancy?"

"The idea had occurred to me," Paul admitted, guardedly.

"But you'd rather draw a veil over the matter? I know the feeling. I have been drawing veils for my entire life. It's the way that I was educated—a familiar item of education for boys of my class. In England, I believe, they call it a stiff upper lip—a matter of turning oneself to stone, of denying feelings, if humanly possibly, or, at a minimum, of never allowing them to show: a matter of discipline. I was brought up to have the utmost respect for discipline—always destined for the army, of course, even as a child; it was an old family tradition, which had somehow survived the Revolution, the Empire and the Restoration, while the army went through enormous changes. Such changes made no difference to the Rochemures de Harvanges, who did not go back to the crusades, but certainly would have done if they could. I can see now that I was not cut out for it, but what chance did I have of seeing it then? None at all. I loved the idea of the army, before I joined it. I wanted to be a hero, until I discovered what heroism actually entailed. But I did my duty. For twenty years, I was a professional murderer...and after that length of time, it can become a hard habit to break, like morphine and drawing veils. But at least I broke the habit of murder in the end, and I became...a scholar, of sorts. A madman, some say.

"I also became a lover of art...again, a madman, some might say. Belgian symbolists! Who on earth—or in Paris, anyway—collects Belgian symbolists? But you understand them, do you not? Even when you're in a somnambulistic state, and unconscious of being bothered by the dead...in fact, especially when you're in a somnambulistic state and unconscious of being bothered by the dead, you produce symbolist art: sirens, wounded tigresses and martyred women. And the moths—I liked the moths, by the way. They're souls, are they not? Counterparts to the dung beetle, which symbolizes flesh and mortality, the moths symbolize the immaterial and immortality, just as the hybrid creatures symbolize the essential duality of conscious existence, of animal urges compounded with the aspiration to something higher, something that can't be described but only implied, something essentially mysterious, even absurd, but nevertheless important."

"I honestly don't know," Paul told him.

"Nor should you," the baron told him. "As a painter, your part is to do, not to know, to produce rather than to understand...even as a seer, as the unconsciousness of your actions clearly testifies, your part, at least initially, is to act without understanding, without the hindrance of the veil of rational censorship. Later, of course, you have no alternative but to make the effort of understanding—when you attempt to elaborate a spontaneous sketch into a detailed oil painting, for example. Then it becomes a matter of a curious mental compromise. I discussed the matter with Jean Delville about it once, at some length. Have you met him?"

"No," Paul said, regretfully.

"Well you must know from your own experience that those who can understand inevitably find the understanding getting in the way of the doing, once they bring it to bear, and have to attain a kind of hybridity...unless they have some way of transcending the understanding temporarily, like Gabriel.

Have you read his detailed account of the effects of hashish in *L'Initiation?*"

"No," Paul admitted, again.

"You should read the third episode, at least. It's a brave confession, although credited to a fictional character: a determined attempt to talk about the unmentionable, to penetrate one of the veils. The pills help with the pain, although I'm not sure how or why. Hashish doesn't blot it out, as ether and cocaine do, until you become accustomed to them, but it transforms the pain into something strange...strange but bearable. I sincerely hope that you never need it, though. How do you like the wild boar? And the Beaune?"

"Excellent," said Paul, slightly surprised to und that they had moved on to the main course without him being fully aware of it, so smoothly had Fabien or Madame Louvot removed the soup bowl and substituted the platter. "You maintain the table of the old aristocracy, I see."

"Traditions," said the baron. "Hard to break."

Paul refrained from asking him whether he had hunted the beast himself, given that it was all too obvious that the baron could hardly stand up nowadays, let alone ride a horse. He understood, now, why the baron had waited for him outside Jane's house, sitting in his carriage, and had asked Fabien to fetch him, rather than waiting for him in the hotel, as Lemastur had.

Madame Pommerat, perhaps tiring of Flammarion's conversation, claimed his attention while his pensiveness had distracted him momentarily from the baron.

"Whatever might happen tonight, my dear Monsieur Furneret," she said, "I do hope you'll come to my next séance."

"I'll certainly try, if I'm still in Paris," Paul assured her, but added, for safety's sake: "May I bring Madame de La Vaudère, if I do?"

"Of course," said the lady, with a slight moue "If she'll come, that is. She disapproves of me, I fear."

"I'm sure that's not true," said Paul, insincerely.

"Society becomes a thorny path, alas, when one reaches a certain age, especially for widows. That status carries all kinds of unfortunate associations. I did not turn to spiritism until I was widowed—an all-too-common story, alas, which gives rise to cruel gibes whispered behind one's back. If any of my children had lived, my life would be different, but all three died in infancy. Misfortune, or a curse? I wish I knew. Madame de La Vaudère is still married, of course, and her only son is a fine young man now, I hear. Have you met him."

"No, I haven't," Paul replied.

"Her husband is a charming man, but he very rarely comes to Paris. You haven't met him either?"

"No," Paul admitted, gritting his teeth slightly, "I haven't."

"But you have read her books, of course?"

"Yes, I have," Paul declared, preparing to spring to their defense in case of an attack, but the lady contented herself with a casual dismissal.

"They're very popular, I believe. I hear that Auguste Chazelle is planning an exhibition of your work in the new year, so you'll be returning to Paris for that, I imagine?"

"I imagine so," Paul confirmed.

"You must come to visit me when you do. I see your friend Victor occasionally, of course—he seems to be everywhere, but always on his way to somewhere else. I met his other friend from Toulouse once, while he was staying with Victor for a while; Gaston is his name, I believe. Gaston Lambrunet?"

"That's right," said Paul.

"You must see a good deal of him in Toulouse, I assume."

"At irregular intervals, yes. He's still a close friend, but like Victor, he's a businessman, always making money, traveling hither and you. I was the odd one out in our little trio, but they were always very good to me, and still are. I couldn't wish for finer friends."

"I'm sure they'd say the same of you. Madame Lambrunet and her daughter were lost in the *Palatine* lifeboat disaster, I remember, a week after the séance at which Henri hypnotized you?"

"That's correct," Paul confirmed, knowing perfectly well that the affected vagueness of her memory was a sham.

"A terrible thing. And then—was it one or two days later?—the young woman who was modeling for your Jeanne d'Arc pictures threw herself in the Seine. A terrible time for you. But the latter affair worked out fortunately, I believe?"

"Fortunately for my diptych, at any rate. Juliette died two years ago, alas. Turberculosis, the curse of the Parisian poor."

"But you draw sometimes draw her? As you sometimes draw the young woman on the wall up there?"

"Yes."

"And the baron's daughter? Moe recently than the drawing you did at my séance?"

"Apparently," Paul agreed. "Obviously, I never knew her."

"The baron took possession of that first sketch, although technically, one could argue that it was my property."

"I'll be happy to let you have another," Paul said, wondering if this was what the conversation had been leading up to.

"Oh, it wouldn't be the same of it weren't drawn at one of my séances. You really must try to come to my next one. It seems that I might have assumed too much in promising that the baron would be there, but that wasn't my fault—the suggestion came from him. I had no idea that he was so ill. He's been walking with a stick for years, of course, but his condition has obviously worsened dramatically since the last time I saw him. It's a tragedy—he must be one of the last surviving heroes of Solferino. How long ago that must seem! Before I was born, obviously. I've seen Gabriel recently, though—he really should have told me about the baron's condition. The baron would have told him not to say a word, but commands like that aren't made to be obeyed. I really would like you to do another drawing at one of my séances, though. Perhaps you could regard it as a commission. I'd be glad to pay you for the sketch...unless you'd like to paint my portrait?"

"That would take too long, alas," Paul told her, with carefully feigned regret, unable to help imagining what Jane's reaction would be if he told her that he had decided to extend his stay in Paris because he had accepted a commission to paint Madame Pommerat's portrait. "I really do have to return to Toulouse soon. The baron's intervention has already disrupted my timetable considerably. I'm very sorry."

Madame Pommerat sighed, ostentatiously, but evidently without astonishment. "It can't be helped, I suppose. Madame de La Vaudère, I understand, has hung the portrait you did of her in her boudoir?"

"I wouldn't know," Paul said, taken by surprise by the blatant indiscretion of the question. "I've never been in Madame de La Vaudère's boudoir,"

He could not tell whether Madame Pommerat's smile was smug or incredulous. "You seem to be getting along very well with the baron," she observed. "Should I assume that if he asks you to consent to being hypnotized after dinner, you'll consent?"

"I haven't made up my mind," Paul told her, "but I'm not sure that I'd be able to refuse decently, after eating his roasted wild boar and quaffing his Beaune."

"It's a very good year," she commented, "but he's obviously not thinking about conserving his cellar stock for future years. And if he were to give you the choice of being hypnotized by Henri or Zosima, which would you choose?"

"I haven't made up my mind about that, either," Paul lied. "Do you have a preference?"

He meant the question ironically, but he was taken by surprise again when she answered: "Yes. I'd rather you chose Zosima."

"Really? Why?"

"Because I suspect that this is one of those duels in which it's better not to fire the first shot."

"I'm afraid I'm not very familiar with the etiquette of dueling," Paul said, "So I don't know what kind of duel that is...and in any case, I haven't actually thought of this civilized candlelit dinner as a duel."

"I believe you. I'm not so sure about the baron...but Zosima certainly seems to think of it that way. She doesn't like Henri...or me."

"To tell you the truth," Paul said. "I don't think that Zosima likes very many people, and none of them are men."

"She seems to like you well enough."

"She's always courteous to me, it's true, albeit without affection, and sometimes without sarcasm, which might make me something of an exception; she seems to find me interesting as a specimen—but she I can't believe that she likes me. As a matter of interest, what kind of duel is it in which it's better not to fire the first shot?"

"The kind in which the pistol is likely to blow up in your hand."

"You think that the person who undertakes to hypnotize me, if the baron requests it, might be in danger?"

"I do. Not as much danger as you, perhaps, but more than sufficient to make one wary. You know, I suppose, that the baron is rumored to be a multiple murderer?"

"He has mentioned that to me, in a spirit of fair play, but it seems that neither of us believes in vengeful spirits."

"They might not care whether you believe in them or not. I can understand why the baron might now be prepared to take the risk, after a lifetime of caution, but you and Henri don't have his reasons. So, if you do have a choice, I'd rather you chose Zosima. I'm very fond of Henri."

"But not of me?"

"How could I be fond of you, Monsieur Furneret, when I haven't had a chance to get to know you, and don't seem likely to be given one?"

"A fair point," Paul conceded. "You can be sure that I'll bear your preference in mind, if I do, in fact, have to make a decision.

Madame Pommerat, apparently having made her point, turned back to Flammarion, even though the astronomer seemed to be in discussion with Zosima again. Paul turned back to the baron, who appeared to have been waiting patiently for him to do that.

"Gabriel is right, as usual," the baron remarked, "I should have done this years ago. As one gets older, one becomes stuck in one's routines. I have not been solitary, of course, in my reclusiveness. Madame Louvot has been inestimably valuable, and Fabien too. I could almost wish, sometimes, that the rumors about him were true."

"I haven't heard any," Paul said.

"No?" said he baron. "Well, sometimes rumor simply die. You can't judge precisely, at present, because I'm sitting down, but I'm considerably taller than average. Inevitably, when a small boy that I'd taken into my household grew to be abnormally tall, people began to speculate that he might be my illegitimate son. You'll understand the kind of whispers that inevitably circulate about a widower and his housekeeper, and rumor was very ready to make Madame Louvot his mother, which she is not, and me his father, which I am not. Kindness is often misunderstood, don't you find? Gossip will always look for a base motive, and rarely has any difficulty improvising one. But as I say, I sometimes wish that I could have had a son like Fabien. I sometimes wonder...but that only leads to tears.

"I won't deny that I have recently been tempted to make a testament in Madame Louvot and Fabien's favor, and to damn the cousins who happen to share my name...but it wouldn't be right. The name is the property of the family, and so is the wealth that goes with it. So, I shall make a fair provision for Madame Louvot and Fabien, which will make sure that they're never in need, but the core of the estate will go to its rightful heirs. Am I right in assuming that the financial incentives I offered you two nights ago really are irrelevant to you? I can still make good in the promise, if you wish. Unless I'm much mistaken, Madame Pommerat was just impressing

upon you that what I intend asking you to do might be dangerous, and I can't promise you that it won't be."

"I'm here because I want to understand," Paul told him.
"I won't say that I don't care about money, because that would
be ludicrous in today's world, but I don't want to ask for money for this. I feel that not only wouldn't it be decent, but that
taking money might actually prejudice the likelihood of success. I'm glad to have taken your money for Talia's picture, all
the more so if it has been useful to you, and I'll be glad to sell
you more of my art-work if you'd like to buy more, but it
seems to me that if I'm to try to facilitate your communication
with the spirit of your daughter, I ought to do it as a matter of
generosity rather than mercenary interest."

"Well, perhaps you're a fool," said the baron, "but at
least you're a noble fool. I'll buy the sketch of the moths, and
the picture of my daughter, and, if Madame de La Vaudère is
amenable, the picture of her mother. I'm assuming that the
pictures of her aren't for sale, and that I shouldn't even have
seen them."

"That's correct," Paul said. "Would you like me to ask
her about the sketch of her mother?"

"If you would. I think the request might stand a better
chance of being granted than it would if it came from me. And
thank you."

"It's no trouble," Paul assured him.

"Not for that—for the kindness you've so far shown me,
in spite of the vague confessions I've made you. It gives me
confidence that when you hear the whole story, your horror
will be directed at the appropriate targets, and that only my
fair share will be reflected on me."

"It is a horror story, then, that you've assembled us to
hear?"

"Oh yes. It's most certainly a horror story: one that has
been haunting me for the last thirty-four years. There are
things that can never be forgotten, and never be overcome."

"But you still hope for forgiveness?"

"Only in the measure that it's possible, and only from the one source. To be honest, I doubt that you can find it for me, and somehow make it manifest, but if you can't, it won't be your fault. The fact that you're willing to try is something. Shall I ask Lemastur and Zosima to attempt to exert their influence simultaneously, or would you prefer them to take turns?"

"I don't know whether it's true that two magnetizers necessarily impede one another's action, but in the present circumstances, given their naked hostility, I think it highly likely that they would. I'd rather keep things simple for the time being, and I'd rather you invited Zosima to try first."

"Because of what Madame Pommerat said to you?" Rochemure asked. Obviously, his hearing was still sharp.

"No. I have reasons of my own—but since she asked, there's no reason to deny her the satisfaction of thinking that she might have been successful."

The baron smiled. "You're not as naïve as you pretend to be, are you, Monsieur Furneret?"

"I don't pretend," Paul told him. "I'm simply misunderstood, by those who have motives for misunderstanding. Unlike beauty, naivety is often in the eye and mind of the beholder."

"Everything," said the baron, "is in the eye and mind of the beholder. That is the whole point of what we are about to attempt. And I hope with all my heart that you can find beauty in yours, where I have the difficulty, much of the time, in finding anything but appalling ugliness. Do you believe, Monsieur Furneret, that ugliness and horror can kill?"

"No," said Paul. "And I think, too, that much of what is sometimes seen as ugliness in painting—or in prose—is misunderstood. Art is art, and the notions of beauty and ugliness, and horror too, that we commonly apply objects seen in the world need to be transformed when applied to matters of art, which partake of the ideal in a fashion that the natural world cannot. As a connoisseur of Delville you obviously know that. You obviously understand that imagery that some people find simply distasteful can, if properly appreciated, enhance life rather than detracting from it. So no, I don't believe that I will be in any danger, even if Zosima's powers of suggestion enable me, for the first time, to catch a glimpse of the images that my unconscious mind is evoking while I'm in a somnambulistic state. In fact, I'll go further, and say that that I would be privileged, even if the experience is initially distressing. Nor is that simply foolish egotism. I only have a second-hand account of how Talia felt when she had recovered from the shocks that she suffered at the two séances that bound her to me four years ago, but I was with Juliette for almost every hour of every day during the last months of her life, and even though the hypnotism of my painting had almost caused her to drown in the Seine, she assured me repeatedly that it had been the necessary prelude to the most fulfilling period of her life. I believed what she said, and I still do, in spite of the cynical attitudes adopted by more than one of the people at this table."

"You're a remarkable man, Monsieur Furneret," said the baron. "Perhaps foolishly optimistic, but no less remarkable for that. I truly hope that if a psychic bond can be forged between the two of us, it will not do you any harm...but I repeat that I can make no promises, and in looking back at my own experience of life, I cannot be optimistic. If, when you have heard my confession, you would rather refuse my request, I will not hold it against you. In your place, I suspect that most people would."

"And Zosima would tell me that if I could hear Talia's spirit," Paul said, "she would be screaming in my ear bidding me to run away. But Zosima would also say that I would not listen, and she would not mean it simply as a disdainful challenge. By your own admission, there is a darkness in your soul, but I am not afraid to look into it, and even, to the extent that it might be possible, to share it...not because I'm a hero, but because I'm an artist, a devotee of art for art's sake."

"It's a pity that the hand of fate kept us apart so assiduously four years ago," the baron said. "I won't say that perhaps it had its reasons, because it has no reasons, no matter what religious men want to believe. Your secretary had no reasons either, but perhaps she had an instinct. And she loved you—be honest now—did she not?"

"She always denied it," Paul told him, "and she was honest in so doing. But yes; it was certainly a transfiguration of what is ordinarily called love, although not as grotesque as many of the representations that novelists have made of the ideal in question, but it *was* love. I wish that I had been able to reciprocate it, but all I could offer her was kindness."

"I believe you," said his host, "although I am certainly prejudiced. And here, at last, comes the dessert. I hope I can tell my story clearly, given that it's the first and last time that I shall ever tell it. It would be terrible would it not, if rumor were to transmit a garbled account, once you've all dispersed?"

"That's surely unlikely," Paul said, meaning the exact opposite.

The baron smiled again, although his face was sufficiently drawn to suggest that he was still suffering a certain amount of untransformed pain, no matter how much hashish he had eaten.

CHAPTER XI

"My marriage was arranged by relatives," the baron said, addressing the entire table. His voice was not unduly loud, but it carried well enough, and the attention was rapt, not only among the guests seated at the table but also, it seemed to Paul, on the part of Fabien and Madame Louvot, who were still present, standing to attention against the wall to either side of the door. "All marriages were in those days, in the social class to which I belonged. Marriages made for love were the stuff of popular fiction. My parents thought that marriage would be a steadying influence, something of a shield against the riotous proclivities of young officers in a time of distant war. Many would have regarded my wife as fortunate, in being traded to a handsome young officer rather than an old man, and perhaps she reckoned herself fortunate as well, but she did not love me. How could she, in that circumstance? I was not her choice, but an imposition. She was dutiful, but she did not love me.

"On the other hand, I loved her, because it was easy to do. She was beautiful. Love comes easily to a young man in such circumstances. I loved my daughter too, because it was equally easy. I was supposed to be disappointed, because my wife had not given me a son and heir to the title, especially when she had the misfortune or the discourtesy to die after having done it, but I was only disappointed by her death, which seemed to me to be a terrible and unwarranted tragedy. I loved my daughter very dearly, although I did not see her frequently, precisely because of the distant war. It was a filthy war, in every possible sense of the term. I hated it. I did my duty, but I hated it. I did what I was required to do, consciencelessly, and other things, which it was merely convenient to do, equally consciencelessly, but I hated it. And I was sustained through my distress, even in the Crimea, by the

191

knowledge that although I did not have a wife waiting for me at home any longer, I had a precious child, who loved me.

"By the time of Solferino, that awareness had become enormously important to me. As some of you in this room probably know, and some of the others might yet have the opportunity to discover, there is a kind of spontaneous affection of which only certain very young children are capable: a kind of automatic, unthinking love, expressed in action and reaction. By the time they are eight or nine years old all children have become socially conditioned to the extent that their affection has become conscious and guarded, confused by various awarenesses and agendas, but there is a brief period when it is utterly wholehearted, and when a father who has been away for some time returns, their faces light up with an ecstasy that is unique, the vision of which unforgettable. It is certainly etched in my mind forever, and it is the most precious of all my memories.

"So, although Yvaine and I were separated for long periods throughout her childhood and youth, there was a special bond between us, enhanced on either side by the fact that she no longer had a mother and I no longer had a wife, which made each of us additionally precious to the other. I won't bother to describe the horrors of Solferino—of which I actually saw very little, only a very tiny fraction of a vast action being visible to me—but once again, I did my duty, as a soldier had to do, and the men under my command did theirs, without overmuch excess. Perhaps you know that, however emperors, generals and officers might regard war as a matter of politics and career advancement, from the point of view of common soldiers, war is essentially and almost entirely an opportunity for licensed looting and rape, and the necessity of facing occasional gunfire is seen as a high price to be paid for subsequent rewards that are very often meager. Military discipline, while it holds, keeps such behavior within bounds, but accepts it as an unavoidable necessity.

"I make that point because you might not be able to understand what happened in Pars after the siege unless you understand that way of seeing. History does not mention it, but that is the way history operates: it is a form of selective perception, which lies by massive omission even more than by deliberate deception. History records what happened in the region of Le Mans in December 1870 and January 1871 as a tactical retreat followed by a battle, but it was not a battle, in the almost-meaningful sense that Solferino was a battle, with two rival armies clashing after a period of preparatory maneuvering with some semblance of strategy. What happened in the west while Moltke was carefully besieging Paris was a disorderly flight followed by a massacre.

"It was the dead of winter and the roads were in an appalling condition. That hampered the German advance as much as it impeded Chazny's retreat, obviously, but the hindrance did not have the same effect. The Prussians were on enemy soil, surrounded by implicit hostility. Their discipline held firm; they remained an organized fighting force, with a determined objective, toward which they moved methodically in spite of the awful conditions. Our discipline did not hold, and although Chazny and his general staff were continually making plans and calculations, they could not put their intentions into practice

"During the retreat, tens of thousands of men deserted, seeking ready refuge and hiding-places among a population assumed to be sympathetic. When we reached Le Mans we were in no condition to put up a fight. The Germans knew that, and decided to destroy us—which they did, with reasonable efficiency, in spite of the difficult conditions. The Prussian forces were superior in their armaments, but the most important advantage they had was simply the capability to operate as a co-ordinated force, organizing the movements of their units and their individual operations in a rational manner. Chazny did everything he could, and the men who came under fire in Le Mans did what they could, bravely and dutifully, but our strength, such as it had been, was already gone.

"As at Solferino, I only saw a tiny fraction of the action that took place around my position, but we were better placed

193

than many, and even so, it was a massacre. There were many more desertions. I have heard the total reported as fifty thousand, twice as many as were killed, and I have no reason to doubt that, but many of them probably did not represent what they were doing, even to themselves, as desertion. Many of them undoubtedly considered it a sage tactical retreat, and whereas many of them hid out, temporarily, among the civilian population in and round Le Mans, many eventually headed for Paris, where they joined up with the forces accumulating outside the German lines, without being asked any serious questions as to how they had made their way there.

"All things considered, I was fortunate. I was hit by two bullets, in the hip and the thigh, but we still had some semblance of a position and there were surgeons on hand. The bullets were removed quickly and safely, under anesthetic, in hygienic conditions. When I woke up, I was dosed with laudanum to suppress the pain. Rank has its privileges. I was assured that the bullets had missed both the bones and the arteries. Had I been able to remain in a field hospital, I might have made a full recovery—but that, of course, was out of the question. I had to be moved, swiftly, and once I was on the move the movement became continual.

I do not know whether the men who carried and protected me while I was transported on a stretcher would be classed as deserters or not, but I think not. They really were part of a tactical retreat, perhaps not organized by Chazny's direct commands, but which at least had his blessing. However, it was the depths of winter, the roads were in an appalling condition, and the entire country was in chaos. Perhaps mercifully, I only have the vaguest memory of the journey, because I was opiated and delirious much of the time, my wounds having become infected. I survived the fever, though, with the aid of a previously-robust constitution.

"By the time we reached the vicinity of Paris and were integrated into the encamped French forces, the siege was over; Bismarck's bombardment had put an end to the resistance in a matter of a few days. The surrender had already been negotiated, but the terms had not yet been fully implemented. They included the disarmament of the French troops, but that was a very slow and incomplete process. Because I was wounded, and not yet able to walk, I was taken back into the city before the Germans had completed their withdrawal. I was able to see my daughter again, who found me not long after I had reached the city center and had been transferred to a hospital there. It was extremely crowded, but my rank, again, obtained privileges.

"My daughter's face was no longer capable of lighting up the way it one had, but she was delighted to see me, wounded as I was, and I was delighted to see her, apparently thriving in spite of the deprivations of the siege. We wept, copiously. I told her that the thought of her had sustained me through Hellish times, although I had been extremely anxious about her, knowing that she was trapped in a city under duress, where people were rumored to have been reduced to eating rats. She told me that she had been terrified for my safety, simply knowing that I was with Chazny's forces, who were rumored to have been virtually annihilated, and that when the news arrived that I was alive she had been unable to obtain much relief from it, because the news also arrived that I had been badly wounded. We delighted mutually in finding one another alive and, if not exactly well, with every hope of recovery.

"Our reunion did not last long, and was largely spoiled by my continuing fever and its associated fits of delirium. She spent as much time with me as she could, but she was in constant demand to help with other patients. There were very few doctors, almost no medical supplies, and all the nurses were volunteers, ranging from grisettes and prostitutes to marquises and vicomtesses. In a matter of days, though, I was able to stand up and get out of bed. The workers and National Guard had already declared the Commune, and I had not taken a dozen tentative steps before I was arrested.

"I do not know why the Communards put me in prison. I'm not sure that the men who locked me up knew themselves where the order had come from, let alone what the pretext was. Perhaps it was simply a reflex action, because I was a colonel in the regular army, or perhaps because I was an aristocrat, or both, or perhaps some denunciation had been made against me because of the manner in which my steward, Ignatz Fell, had administered my estate during my long absence. Fell was not an evil man, but I gathered that his administration had been stern, in difficult—not to say desperate—conditions. He was not arrested, however and he was even allowed to visit me in prison in order to confer with me regarding his administration, although I was hardly in a fit condition to make rational plans with him.

"I had made determined attempts to stay on my feet, but it was too soon and I suffered a relapse. The medical care given to me in the prison was very elementary, and my daughter was not allowed to resume nursing me. I gathered that the Communards had allocated her other duties, to which she had put up no resistance, probably in the hope that if she cooperated fully for a while, she would be allowed to see me again, and might even be able to secure my release.

"It might seem incredible to you that I had not observed, while I saw her immediately after my return, that my daughter was pregnant, but it is true. I saw her in March, when she was less than five months pregnant, and the condition was not yet so obvious that it was blatant to the distracted eyes of an invalid. She did not say anything to me about it, perhaps waiting to find a good moment that she never contrived to identify. It was not until Ignatz Fell told me that I found out, and my immediate reaction was one of violent anger. Most of you have doubtless heard that I ordered Fell to find the man responsible and to castrate him. That is true. Our meetings were observed, not unnaturally, and the report was widely distributed. The order was not carried out. Fell was not a good man, but he was a sane man; he knew perfectly well that such an order given in the heat of the moment by a sick man not in full possession of his faculties was not an order that ought to be executed.

"The fact that the order had been given, however, might well have reinforced the decision of the men then in charge of the prison not to allow my daughter to see me again. I know that she tried, but was not granted admittance. That was still the situation in the last few weeks of May, when the Regular Army, only partially disarmed under the conditions of the treaty with the Prussians, stormed the city and the so-called Bloody Week began.

"If Le Mans had been a massacre, it might be necessary to invent a new word to what happened during that week, when the Regular Army slaughtered the National Guardsmen and the workers who had been condemned as rebels and insurgents. Their psychology might be understandable, I suppose. They had just suffered the most absolute and the most humiliating of defeats. Many of them, in the course of the farcical war, had deserted their positions and their units and had only been reintegrated into the forces outside Paris because they had no alternative. Suddenly, they were launched against a new enemy—an enemy that was in the same position they had been in a matter of weeks before, unable to mount any significant defense, ripe for slaughter. What the Germans had done to the comrades they had failed or deserted, they came into Paris determined to do to the auxiliaries of the Communards, irrespective of the fact that they were their compatriots, their cousins if not their brothers. And they did it, savagely, in a fit of rage.

"I do not know whether my daughter had had any contact with the Prussians when they occupied the city briefly, but if she did, no harm came to her as a result. The Prussians were a disciplined army, not a pack of mad dogs. In the same way, the Communards and their auxiliaries did her no harm whatsoever. Perhaps they did not treat her entirely as one of their own, given that she was the daughter of a colonel and an aristocrat, but they knew perfectly well what she had done for ordinary Parisians during the siege and had continued to do during their interregnum. They would have defended and protected her, if they could, stoutly and perhaps heroically.

197

"The invading troops did not have the same attitude. The young man who was in love with her, I believe, did try to defend her, and he died trying. He was taking her back to her apartment on the Île Saint-Louis, to a quarter that should have been safe, but the island had been invaded by a considerable number of armed looters who had broken through the feeble defenses on the bridges. There were thousands of people on the island but they were mostly women and children, barricaded in their apartments, in hiding. No one went to help Yvaine when the soldiers killed the young man and dragged her away.

"She was taken into an empty ground-floor by four soldiers of the regular army, and raped repeatedly, in spite of being seven months pregnant. Then—I have absolutely no idea why—the four men struck her repeatedly in the abdomen with the butts of their rifles, in order to kill the child in her womb, which they succeeded in doing. As they left her, lying on the floor, unable to stand up, one of them handed her a bayonet and suggested that she finish the job by disemboweling herself—which she apparently attempted to do, presumably in a fit of utter despair, but she failed, because she was too weak, although she did manage to gash herself in the lower abdomen, badly.

"I was released from prison a few hours later, by which time Yvaine had been found by other soldiers, treated as a casualty, and taken to a hospital. The surgeons did what they could, but it was hopeless; she was bleeding internally and her placenta was ruptured. The hospital had run out of laudanum and there was no accessible supply. She was in terrible pain. I was beside her bed during the final hours of her life, but I don't know that either of us was fully conscious for much of that time.

"She was still able to speak in the beginning, and to tell me what had happened. She apologized repeatedly, for having been pregnant, and for not having has the courage to confess it to me; she seemed to think that what had happened to her was some kind of judgment, that she had betrayed me and had been punished. I tried to convince her, obviously, that it was not true and that she had nothing for which to feel remorse, but I suspect that what I had said to Ignatz in the heat of the moment had been reported to her. I remember as well, all too clearly, that when she could no longer speak but was still alive, I spent the time begging her ardently for forgiveness, without her being able to respond vocally, by the slightest flicker of her eyelids or the faintest pressure of her hand.

"It might seem odd to you that I felt the need so urgently to obtain that forgiveness, but you need to understand that I had been in the army even before the fall of the Second Republic, and throughout the duration of the Second Empire. The army had been my life, and my marriage and my daughter, although extremely precious to me, had been an adjunct to that life. I saw myself as a kind of personification and an encapsulation of the army—and I saw the four men who had raped and murdered my daughter, in the cruelest fashion imaginable, as personifications and encapsulations of that same army. Two of them, I believe, had been with Chazny before Le Mans, although I did not know them and they did not know me. That had nothing to do with what they had done to my daughter; she had told them who she was, she said, but they did not listen; they were incapable of listening, let alone understanding. She could have been anyone, she said; they did not even seem to see her as a human being.

"No official record of the incident was filled. The army, mindful of history and its image, finds it convenient to turn a blind eye to certain events, and certain personifications.

"It was easy enough for me to make enquiries that enabled me, eventually, to identify the four men responsible. It was easy enough for me to obtain information regarding their assignments, and even to influence those assignments covertly. One by one, I murdered all four of them. I could have had them arrested, court-martialed and shot, but I didn't. I murdered them, one at a time, without witnesses. I gagged them in order to prevent them from screaming, and I disemboweled each of them with a bayonet. I wasn't furious; I did it methodically, and consciencelessly, like the disciplined man that I was.

"As I said, there were no eye-witnesses to any of the murders, but there were abundant grounds for suspicion, and circumstantial evidence would not have been difficult to assemble. Those suspicions were never voiced and the evidence remained uncollected. I was never questioned, let alone charged. The army, as I also observed, ever mindful of history, uses its blind eye with great determination when circumstances seem to warrant it. When I had completed my schedule of assassinations, I applied for a discharge on medical grounds, and had no difficulty obtaining it.

"Ironically, the only murder about which I was ever interrogated, some time later, by the civilian authorities, was that of Ignatz Fell. I am not sure whether suspicion fell upon me because of the order I was known to have given him, or, if so, whether I was supposed to have been motivated by the fact that he had not executed the order, or because he had done so covertly—because there was no official report of the young man's identity, there was some speculation that he really might have been castrated. In any case, I had no difficulty proving my innocence of Fell's murder, but I did not denounce the real murderer to the police when I discovered who it was; nor did I take any reprisals.

"At about that time, I was informed that I had been awarded a medal for bravery shown at Le Mans. I never collected it; I had already thrown the medals I had been awarded after the Crimean campaign and Solferino into the Seine. I did not want any further contact with the army, and I never touched the pension to which I was entitled, of which I had no need. My heirs will doubtless appreciate my prudence. I was not equipped for any other kind of employment, and it seemed quite natural to me that I should devote my time and effort to study and scholarship, that vocation seeming to me to be the antithesis of an army career.

"I devoted myself, in particular, to occult philosophy, because conventional philosophy did not seem to offer any useful advice on how I might navigate a path through life after what I had done and what had happened to me. In addition, I was haunted, by what seemed to me, although I could not see her ghost, to be the spirit of my daughter. I often felt her presence, and always with the sensation that, seen in its totality, the relationship that had been forced upon us by circumstance had been direly unsatisfactory and woefully incomplete, through no fault of hers.

"I never wanted to marry again, even though I was not insensitive to the lack of an heir. I did not think that I was any longer capable of love, and I did not want to contract a marriage of convenience for the sake of a principle that I no longer held—which seemed to me, in fact, to have become absurd. In fact, the idea that I might have another child horrified me; it seemed like a sacrilegious possibility, a matter of trying to replace the irreplaceable, of dishonoring Yvaine's memory.

"I lived for a while in the apartment on the Île Saint-Louis that had been my home since my marriage, and Yvaine's home since birth, but after Fell's death I had to return to the estate in order to assume control of its administration. Both my parents had died before the war and my younger brother had been killed during the siege. I sold almost all of the immovable property and invested the money in stocks and bonds. Eventually, I had this villa constructed, and moved here with a small staff, all of whom have since been replaced except Madame Louvot and Fabien, who was still a child at the time.

"When Madame Louvot had come to me and asked me for permission to adopt Fabien, an orphaned nephew, I had agreed without hesitation, and had taken no notice of the child for some time although I was not sorry to have him in the house when we moved here. I never thought of him as a son, but I did take a certain pride in his growth and physical vigor, and have always thought that if I had had a son, I would have liked him to resemble Fabien. I have not loved him, nor has he loved me, but I have treated him well and he has always been loyal. In the same way, I have not loved Madame Louvot, but

I have treated her with generosity, and she has reciprocated that generosity. I have not been entirely solitary, or entirely lonely.

"I began to attend spiritist séances, initially more out of curiosity than hope, but inevitably entertaining the possibility that a medium might enable me to make a more explicit contact with my daughter. Several claimed to have summoned her spirit and received messages from her, but it was all too obvious that they were faking communications based on the garbled rumors they had heard about the circumstances of her death. Some evidently suspected that I had driven her to suicide, and tied themselves in knots trying to hint at such a possibility without giving explicit offense, but none could relay any supposed message that shed an atom of awareness of the actual circumstances of her death or the true nature of my guilt. I was angry with them at first, but that passed. Some of them, I think, sincerely thought they had received such messages, and even those who wanted money seemed to want to give reasonable value in exchange.

"The one exception to the general failure, I thought, was Talia Cadelan, but her honest refusal to work with me was initially relayed via Zosima, confusing my perception somewhat. When it was eventually reported to me that Talia had glimpsed 'a darkness in my soul,' I did not credit her with any particular acumen on that account, and that continued to be my attitude until I was leafing through the portfolio of sketches that Fabien had removed from under Monsieur Furneret's arm and had given to me as a kind of hostage, in order that he would have no alternative but to climb into my carriage and hear me out.

"I thought, at that time, that Monsieur Furneret was deliberately avoiding me, as he had four years ago, and my patience was exhausted, although I was trying my utmost to be calm and polite, and to maintain an iron self-discipline in spite of the fact that I was in some physical distress, because, as I believe you are all aware by now, I have developed tumors in my thigh, hip and lower abdomen, which, I am assured by the physicians I have consulted, will soon kill me. Their estimates of the time that it will take vary, but the consensus is that in the absence of a miraculous remission, I would not need the fingers of both hands to count the months. They prescribed laudanum for the pain, but I was fortunate to have an acquaintance who had some expertise in poisons of that general kind, who was able to make other suggestions as to experiments that might be worth trying. In the carriage with Monsieur Furneret, therefore, I was under the influence of hashish, to which I have become habituated, numbed but not somnolent, and capable of what I took to be rational and disciplined thinking.

"I had two revelations in the course of the bizarre interval when I was confronted by Monsieur Furneret's sketches. The first was when I saw the drawing of my daughter. I had been told, and had accepted, that Monsieur Furneret had been able to draw her during Madame Pommerat's séance because we were in the same room, and Monsieur Lemastur's hypnotism had established a momentary link between his mind and mine. When I saw that he had made a second sketch while he was in Toulouse, I realized that she was still haunting him. Then I saw the fetus. Immediately, of course, I jumped to the conclusion that it was an aspect of the same haunting, that it was the fetus that Yvaine had been carrying when she was murdered. Without hesitation, I invited Monsieur Furneret to dinner, in order that I might have a longer conversation with him, in more comfortable circumstances.

"Later, however, when I had had time to think about it in a calmer frame of mind, it occurred to me that Talia Cadelan might—in fact must—have had a similar vision when Madame Zosima had first established a connection between us at one of her séances, and that Talia might have identified the fetus as her own, just as Monsieur Furneret had identified it as that of his sister. The reason why Talia would not countenance the possibility of a more intimate linkage, I realized, was not because she had sensed that I was a multiple murderer, but because she feared the renewal of the vision of the fetus—and

203

rightly so, because if she had identified mentally with my daughter and had some inkling what she had gone though, it would, at the very least, have been extremely distressing.

"I had already brought and hung the portrait you can see above my head, because it had reminded me strangely of my daughter, even though the physical resemblance was slight. Suddenly, that feeling of association seemed to make sense, as I realized that Talia might, in fact, have made a more meaningful contact with her than any other medium had contrived, with the exception of Monsieur Furneret. My eagerness to obtain Paul's help, as you can perhaps understand, became extreme. My original intention in inviting him here had only been to negotiate a further association, but the new sense of urgency led me to change my strategy. He had already insisted on bringing Madame de La Vaudère with him, presumably for what conventional parlance calls moral support, so it seemed perfectly reasonable to invite others who might be able to lend assistance in holding a séance here.

"I have now had a chance to have a brief discussion with Paul about the nature of his abilities, and that has helped to convince me that he would not be running the same danger as Talia if he were to establish a more intimate connection with my daughter's spirit, partly because he is a man who does not have the same relationship with his sister's fetus that Talia might have had with the fetus that I believe that she lost, one way or another. Even if the psychic linkage were to enable Paul to associate himself, as a surrogate, the horrific experience that Yvaine underwent, I think he would be able to tolerate it, although my hope, based on his two sketches, is that he will actually be able to make contact with her spirit at an earlier moment in her existence, as it were. He does not believe that the spirits of the dead are vengeful.

"In that connection, perhaps I ought to say that I have only ever been conscious of being haunted by the one spirit: that of my daughter. I have never experienced an instant's remorse with regard to the murders I have committed, which I have always regarded as a matter of duty, and I have always been prepared to assume that the spirits of the men I killed are utterly impotent to pursue me. Even if such pursuits are theoretically possible, I hope that they would feel far too much shame themselves to think of pursuing the administrator of their justice, but perhaps that is merely my personification of the army rather than theirs. I cannot form any judgment as to whether their spirits might be roasting in some covert of Hell for all eternity, or whether they might have been reincarnated as dung beetles in order to begin an arduous upward path through the chain of creation in quest of redemption, but I cannot believe for an instant that they have been lurking in this house for decades waiting for a psychic door to be opened that might allow them to wreak a vengeance to which they have no moral entitlement. In all fairness, though, I cannot exclude the possibility absolutely.

"At any rate, that is my explanation of why we are all here. It is a story that I have not told before, but Gabriel had warned me, when he begin dosing me with hashish, that it has a tendency to make people talkative and indiscreet, and it might be partly the influence of the drug that has occasioned this very long discourse. As he has recently published an account of its effects, to which he has attached his signature, there is no indiscretion in my saying that. Similarly, his published account acknowledges that the drug's mental effects vary according to the personality of the user. He is a poet and a humorist, whereas I still have, even in my assiduous scholarship in philosophy, art and literature, the mentality of a soldier, a man of discipline. I do not believe that it gives me delusions or undermines the rationality of my thought. Doubtless, having heard me out politely, you will make your own judgments as to that. At any rate, I have discussed the matter with Paul, and he is willing to make the experiment of attempting a further contact with Yvaine's spirit. Are you, Madame Zosima, willing to hypnotize him in order to attempt to achieve that end."

"Absolutely," said Zosima.

"As am I," Henri Lemastur put in, without bothering to glance across the table at Madame Pommerat. "Tonight, or at any time in the future, I am at your disposal—and I swear on my mother's grave that I will not attempt any fakery with Monsieur Furneret or any other medium."

The baron looked at Jane de La Vaudère, as if seeking her consent. She immediately looked at Paul, who nodded his head. She did not seem at all enthused by ht encouragement. "For what it may be worth," she said, with evident reluctance, "Paul naturally has my blessing do to as he thinks best. But perhaps we ought to ask Monsieur Flammarion, given that he is the expert, whether he thinks that there might be any risk in the experiment...to anyone?"

Flammarion must have expected that his opinion would be requested, and presumably had one ready to offer, but he too looked at Paul, although their relative positions at the table made any understanding difficult. Paul suspected that the astronomer might be remembering what he had said, scrupulously, about not wanting to be cast as his protector, so he nodded again.

"Given that I was present the last time Paul was magnetized," the astronomer said, carefully, "and saw what happened to him and Talia then, I would hesitate to declare the venture safe, for him or for anyone else. But I am not the only scholar here. You are probably aware, Baron, of the fact that Madame Zosima and I disagree as to the fundamental nature of the spirits evoked, and sometimes manifested, by mediums. Might I ask you exactly what, in your scholarly opinion, is involved in your supposed haunting?"

"If you are asking whether I have considered the hypothesis that I am simply deluded in sensing my daughter's presence," Rochemure replied, a trifle testily, "of course I have, and at great length; I admit that Paul's sketches are flimsy evidence, as best, of the contrary. But I can certainly indulge in metaphysical speculation, if you wish. Philosophically, I am an idealist rather than a materialist. Like George Berkeley, and many artists, I believe that the true objects of sight are light and color rather than objects in themselves, and that what we mean by matter is the possibility of perception.

"Our powers of perception are limited, and they are also variable. Some people can see more or fewer colors than are discernible by others, and some are blind to all the sensations of sight that they experience. The same applies to the senses of hearing, smell and taste—which are similarly varieties of touch, responses to material stimuli. Some people, in some circumstances, can see and hear phantoms; some can sense phantom touches. Those who cannot inevitably dismiss those sensations as hallucinations and delusions, referring to objects that are not 'really there'—but that evades the question of what we can mean by 'really there.' If matter is merely the possibility of sensation, than perception is an adequate criterion of materiality. It might seem counter-intuitive to suggest that matter might not be the same for some people as it is for others, but it is not necessarily false, and from the idealist viewpoint, might even be reckoned necessarily true.

"From that viewpoint, in fact, I believe that there is no contradiction between your assertion and Zosima's. You have concluded, after long study, that the phenomena of mediumistic perception originate in the mind of the medium, often resurfacing from unconscious memory by a process that recent jargon sometimes terms cryptomnesia. Madame Zosima believes that the spirits of the dead are all around us, but only occasionally perceived, and only liminally. From the idealist viewpoint, however, even if they really are all around us, our perception of them is still located in the mind, and is still subject to the puzzling effects of cryptomnesia."

"But that's just wordplay," objected Madame Pommerat. "The question is: do the spirits of the dead have minds of their own and purposes of their own? Madame Zosima says yes, Monsieur Flammarion says no. Which is it?"

"An excellent question," said the baron equally, "very succinctly put—perhaps a little too succinctly to do justice to its complexity. If I were to say yes and no, however, or to ask you how certain you can be that the spirits of living people, apart from your own, exist and have purposes of their own, you would accuse me again of wordplay, and perhaps thought itself is nothing else.

"For myself, with regard to my own haunting, I will declare without hesitation that Yvaine's spirit exists, since I have the possibility of perceiving her. I can feel her presence, sometimes literally. I cannot see or hear her, but I suspect that to be a limitation in me rather than in her. No one else would have good grounds for believing me, without endorsement from another observer, but we have that. Monsieur Furneret, it is manifestly obvious, has been able to perceive her well enough to draw her face and to glimpse something of her distress. As to whether she has a purpose of her own, I am not certain. I suspect not, in the sense she has some demand to make or ambition to fulfill. So far as I am concerned, however, that is not a vital issue. The need that I feel, which has urged me to ask for Paul's help, is not a mere matter of hearing a phantom voice say: 'I forgive you.' Indeed, it is a need that it is difficult, and perhaps impossible to put into words, but which might be possible of expression in some kind of visual repression, symbolically if not crudely.

"If I were a religious man, I would probably call it grace, as symbolized by the Holy Spirit, but I am as incapable of faith as I am of love. Perverse as it may seem, although I do not believe in God, or in Heaven, I do believe that some kind of redemption is both possible and necessary, and for me, that redemption can only come from my daughter, because, of all the multitudinous failures I have had in my life, that is the one that matters, the pivot on which my entire life has turned. It is ludicrous, of course, to expect that a sketch made in a hypnotic trance might be able to provide that...but what it might achieve, I hope and believe, is that a psychic link that might permit Paul to make another sketch of my daughter might also permit, if only for moment, a fusion of thought, of inner vision, a fundamental and quintessential sympathy in which he can provide the means of connecting me with my daughter in a manner impossible of achievement in any other way."

Madame Pommerat's mouth actually opened in order to raise an objection, but then she winced, and Paul deduced that Henri Lemastur had caught her eye from the other side of the table and commanded her, by the force of his hypnotic gaze and he psychic link the two of them had, to shut up. He was sure that that was not the usual direction of command established between the two of them, but the lady obeyed nevertheless.

The baron, seemingly still possessed by the loquacity of the drug, continued: "As to whether my daughter's spirit has a similar need and desire, I cannot be sure, but I am sure that she is aware of my need and desire. I believe that she is capable, at least under certain circumstances, of hearing what I say and seeing what I do. As she can touch me, I can touch her, and because there is no action without reaction, I believe that I do touch her, that she can feel my touch, and that it is welcome to her, perhaps vital to her posthumous wellbeing.

"I have been magnetized myself, of course, in the attempt to enhance my communication with Yvaine, with some success. Entrancement has enabled me to see her more clearly, and even to hear her voice, but that communication is confined and imprisoned. Perhaps it ought to be sufficient, and perhaps for some people it would be—but it is only human to require what common parlance calls moral support. I need Paul to draw my daughter again, if she is present, and I need more than that. At the very least, I need more detail in the drawing he makes, if only symbolic detail. But most of all, if it is humanly possible, I need a link to be established between his mind and mine, in order that I might see, feel, hear and caress, even if he cannot, the spirit that he is drawing, in order that my communication with the spirit is no longer self-contained, no longer self-imprisoned. And I believe that to be possible, because I believe that Talia Cadelan once achieved it, liminally, and could have achieved much more if she had had more courage."

"It might not be irrelevant to remark," Zosima observed, with more than a hint of acidity, "that Talia often said to me that she could not choose what she saw, and more often saw things that she and our clients did not want to see. She was convinced that the universe is inherently perverse."

"Perhaps it is," said the baron, mildly—avoiding, Paul noted, the easy answer of suggesting that the perversity in that instance might have been Talia's rather than the universe's—"but if it is, it is still the universe in which we live, and must accept. For myself, I have hopes for Paul's enhanced vision, but no fears."

"I have fears," Jane put in. "Since Paul apparently has none, I feel obliged, speaking as he second in this strange duel, to have them for him. I dare say that your daughter had fears for you while you were alive, and she probably still has, if the dead are capable of feeling fear, but has never, in either instance, felt entitled to raise objections to your actions—but nevertheless, I have fears. Rightly or wrongly, I feel a certain responsibility toward Paul, and...well, Baron, I have fears."

"I have fears too," said Flammarion. "Perhaps we all do—but none of us, I think, would like to be thought the kind of person who would allow fear to deter them from performing a good deed. Am I right, Paul, in assuming that that is what you want to do?"

"Yes," said Paul, wondering, privately, whether it was, and looking at Jane—who lowered her eyes, refusing to meet his gaze. It was probably a gesture that spoke volumes, Paul thought, but what those volumes might say, he had no idea. So far as he was concerned, they might as well have been written in Hebrew.

"It's getting late," Zosima observed. "Have we said everything that we need to say, given that our decision is already made? Our cups and glasses are empty. I think."

Have we said everything that we need to say? Paul thought. *We've hardly scratched the surface—but if the baron were to continue explaining himself until dawn, we would get no further, and we must hope, I suppose, that this will be one of those proverbial instances where a picture is worth a thousand words.*

"I have pills, if anyone would like one," Gabriel de Lautrec put in laconically. "Although it seems to me that this is one occasion when the individual and collective imagination might not need or benefit from further stimulation."

"I'll take another, please, Gabriel," said the baron. "Purely for medicinal purposes. If the rest of you would care to return to the drawing room, where drawing apparatus has already been set up, Fabien will give me the assistance necessary to enable me to join you. Do you need anything further, Madame Zosima?"

"One request," said the hypnotist. "Could you possibly have the picture of Talia hung in the drawing room, where the Knopff painting is presently positioned? It might be easier to put Paul into a productive trance if he can fix his attention on that rather than on the blank sheet, as he did last time."

Paul had a strong suspicion that Zosima had other motives for wanting to put him to a somnambulistic state while gazing at a portrait of Talia than the one she had stated, but if the baron had the same suspicion, it did not cause him to raise any objection, and Madame Louvot opened the door in order to escort the company back to the drawing room.

CHAPTER XII

Talia seemed different again in the candlelight of the drawing room, once Fabien had hung her portrait in place of the Knopff. She seemed to be looking directly at Paul, not into his eyes but into his soul. Her unsmiling expression now seemed pitying, but not fearful. She did not remind him of Yvaine de Rochemure—how could she? But she did remind him, more than a little, of Juliette, who had tried so hard to disguise the love that she had gradually come to feel for him, in response to his kindness, because she was so firmly convinced that she was no longer capable of loving, and because she did not feel entitled to be loved. The baron, Paul thought, would have understood that perfectly, but not Yvaine. How could she, given that she had always felt loved, and fully entitled to love, and had presumably continued to feel it, and to make every effort to focus on it, even while she was being brutally violated, humiliated and battered to death by creatures robbed of their humanity by the burden of circumstance and the essential perversity of the universe?

He did not pay any heed to the order in which the baron and his other guests arranged themselves in armchairs behind him. He assumed that the geometry would have been designed strategically. The baron he knew, was only slightly behind him, displaced to his left, while Zosima took up a parallel position to his right.

Zosima instructed him to focus his attention and Talia's portrait, and he tried, sincerely, but the imp of the perverse was ever-present, and he could not help imagining the rapt fascination with which Camille Flammarion and Henri Lemastur must be observing an experiment unique even in their vast experience, and the fear that Jane de la Vaudère must still be feeling on his behalf, perhaps unreasonably.

But why was Jane so fearful on his behalf? he could not help asking himself. What was it, exactly, that bound the two of them together so mysteriously? It was not carnal desire, he knew. There had been a possibility of that, four years ago, but even then, it had been displaced by something more intense, in its way, than lust. He had considered the hypothesis that just as Talia had glimpsed Martine while the *Palatine*'s unfortunate lifeboat was sinking and had become psychically entangled with her, Jane had become similarly entangled with the living phantasm of Amélie Lambrunet, but on careful analysis that made no sense. Amélie Lambrunet had been kind to him, but she had never loved him, and at the moment when she was confronting horrid death, her thoughts must have been entirely focused on Gaston and Martine, the children that she did love. What Jane felt for him was neither the emotion of a lover nor the emotion of a mother, nor could it be a commonalty of feeling based on mutual confidences, because, in truth, they had never really confided in one another.

He hardly heard Zosima begin her verbal routine. It was four years since he had heard it, but it was so familiar to his memory that he did not have to hear it consciously, and it was, in any case, incomprehensible as a stream of words. It was a rhythmic sequence of sounds that evaded the grasp of any consciousness that might have searched them reflexively for meaning; they insinuated themselves directly and smoothly into the galvanic activity of his brain, which surrendered to their subtle influence and control voluntarily, even eagerly, as if it were impatient with its guiding spirit, which had kept it in a virtual person for far too long. His brain, the brute substance of his being, the antagonist as well as the foundation of his soul, had never been rebellious; when it heard the siren song of Zosima's charm, it was perfectly ready to respond, and he felt his consciousness draining away, swirling in a strange vortex as it circled the plughole of oblivion, and then...

Much later, he was certain that there had been a long absence of any vestige of conscious thought, but he was also certain, unusually, that he had had a dream. He had not had the dream, he was sure, while his hand had actually been drawing; that rule had not been broken—but when he had finished drawing, when the hand had returned to its brute state of paralysis, there had been an interim. During that interregnum of ordinary sleep, he must have had had an ordinary dream, a dream graspable, if only in fragments , by memory, and thus capable of being transported back into wakefulness, provided that his consciousness had the skill and the incentive to seize it.

For that reason, in a further phase of sleep, even closer to wakefulness, he had tried hard to cling to the flotsam of the dream, to commit the pieces of that floating wreckage to consciously-recoverable memory, and to make sense of them, if any sense could be made, even though he knew from long experience that such salvage from dreams rarely did make sense when it was remembered, because the kind of coherency that dreams possessed was not subject to the dominion and discipline of rationality.

He was certain that he had dreamed that he was in a carriage, which bore some resemblance to Baron de Rochemure's carriage, but was also reminiscent of a fiacre, at least in the sense that it seemed crowded, because that it was carrying at least three passengers, and he knew that popular wisdom held that three in a fiacre was a crowd, because, although fiacres had four wheels, unlike cabriolets, they only had one internal seat, which was not wide enough to accommodate three people without a squeeze that posed a severe challenge to comfort and decency.

In his dream, Paul was being squeezed by contacts from both sides, which did indeed seem to be posing a severe challenge to comfort and decency, but he was not at all certain whose thighs and other body parts it was that were making contact with his own, in a manner that seemed intimate even through several layers of fabric.

He had wanted to turn his head in order to see who was there, but he could not do it, perhaps because he was petrified, but also because he did not know which way to turn, and was afraid of offending someone by turning one way rather than the other. Instead, he remembered, he had leaned forward slightly, not simply to relieve the pressure slightly, but also to enable him to look out of the portière of the carriage, form the corners of his eyes, in order to distract himself by means of the fleeting surroundings.

That had been a mistake, he realized. He had somehow assumed that the carriage would be traveling through the streets of Paris, probably one or other of the boulevards, in company with other carriages of various shapes and sizes, trams, omnibuses and—was it really 1905?—the occasional automobile. But no; such was the inherent perversity of the universe that the carriage was actually traveling over a battle-field strewn with corpses: a battlefield in which the guns had fallen silent, and whatever action was still continuing, as in-fantrymen "mopped up" by killing the wounded, was now distant, but a battlefield nevertheless, on which gruesome wounds were still bleeding and danger was palpable in the air. And on the horizon, there was an infinite line of crosses, which were not the crosses of tombs but anachronistic crosses of crucifixion, at which he dared not look, even though they were too far away for him to identify anyone who might be hanging thereon.

He tried to close his eyes, but he was either petrified or fascinated, and his eyelids would not respond. All he could do was shift his attention, still peering sideways, at the nearer regions of the battlefield...but that was worse, because he knew that the dead and dying, many of whom were women who had somehow been caught up in the battle even though they were unarmed and helpless, would be a horrible sight, which would tear at his heart even if he did not know them.

He had had no refuge but the distraction of thought, so he had tried to think. He had tried to speak too, but could not.

Am I dead, then? he remembered having thought, be-cause he knew that the dead were silent—but he knew too, that there was an elementary logical error in arguing that be-cause the dead we silent, and because he was silent, he must

215

be dead. That did not follow. It was a false syllogism...but a common psychological trap.

Where are we going? he thought, not expecting an answer; but he was in an abnormal state of semiconsciousness, and his thoughts were evidently transmissible, because the answer came into his mind: *In search of the holy grail.*

What's that supposed to mean? he had retorted, knowing in advance what the answer would be, because he had heard the legends of the holy grail that still circulated in Toulouse, and had heard Clémence Sancerre's theories regarding the symbolic "truth" of those legends.

That all depends, said the inner voice, *on who is doing the supposing.*

In any case, he tried to say—and would have said, had he not been temporarily dead and silent—*I'm not looking for the grail—not yet, and probably not ever. I'm looking for Yvaine de Rochemure. I need to make a portrait of her for the baron. I need to make it hypnotic, so that when he sees it, he'll know, just by looking at it, that his daughter has forgiven him for being a bad father, for being a personification of the army, and so that she can tell him, via that gaze, that she still has the kind of spontaneous and wholehearted love for him that she had when she was a little girl, and never lost even though she had to learn to mask its expression. He needs to be redeemed, even though he doesn't know what the word means.*

You did that four years ago, the voice told him. *And he saw it again, on Monday night. He could have been content, if only he had read her eyes accurately. But how many of us can recognize redemption when we see it? How many of us can even believe in it, let alone grasp it?*

Is that you, Talia? the dreamer had wondered. *Are you sitting to my left or my right?*

No, said the voice.

Juliette? Martine? Jane? Yvaine? Clémence?

Why not Madame Pommerat? One way or another, it's a crowd, and you're in the middle. But that's the human condition. Life's a crowd, and you're always in the middle. Life's a battlefield, and sitting in a carriage going hell for leather for the distant horizon can't get you out of it. You can turn a blind eye, but that only works if you don't know that you're doing it. This is a mistake, my love—the dreaming, I mean. Better to draw and draw and draw, and let your hand do the talking.

But what should I draw? the dreamer wondered.

Water from a well. What else is there to draw?

Oil?

There you go again, always joking, always ducking, even though you've stopped smiling. Do you want some advice?

Yes, said the dreamer, remembering that he was not actually dead, and that he would need to know which way to go when he was no longer wedged into the fiacre.

Go home. You might have to wait a long time for Clémence or someone else to be able to love you, but it doesn't matter. In the meantime, you can paint. There's no better prison than paint. Believe me, I know. Paint, and hope. It's the best you can do. And if you want to call it redemption, do so. It's only wordplay, but there's no other game in time. Believe me, I know. The odds are against you, because the universe cheats, but there isn't any alternative. Go home, my love

It isn't safe, the dreamer retorted. *Yvaine was going home, with someone who loved her to watch over her, and look what happened to her.*

That was a foolish and reckless thing to say, because when he told himself to do it, he did look at what had happened to Yvaine, not with his eyes, which were blind in spite of being able to see the battlefield flying past at a supernatural trot, but with his imagination. He *felt* the rape, anatomically impossible as that might be. He *felt* the rifle-butts hammering the womb that he had once shared with his ill-fated sister, and he *felt* the bayonet pressed into his hand, and—the worse thing of all—he understood exactly why Yvaine had tried to obey the suggestion that had been given to her, and the tragedy of her weakness in only scoring her flesh.

With a steadier hand, he knew, she would have succeeded, and like her, he regretted that she hadn't. She regretted that her father had found her, and had wept over her again, not tears of joy but tears of utter despair, because she knew that those tears would never dry, and that he would always remember her the way she was now instead of the way she wanted to be remembered: he way that she had made Paul draw her, thirty years after the event: the way she wanted to haunt him instead of the way, now, that she always would, as long as his memory lasted.

The horror was too much, as he should have known that it would be, having been warned, and he woke up with start.

He looked around for Jane, sure that she would be by his bedside, again.

She was not. The person who reacted to his muffled scream was Madame Louvot, who leaned forward to take his hand. He looked into her face uncomprehendingly; her expression seemed full of affection and concern.

"Why aren't you with the baron?" he asked. "Is he dead?"

"He's asleep," the housekeeper replied. "It's the drug—it always puts him to sleep eventually. It's a mercy, in a way. He'll sleep for hours. It's impossible to wake him. Gabriel is with him. He's used to it."

"Did the baron drug the food?" Paul asked, suddenly suspicious.

"No, of course not," the housekeeper replied, as if deeply offended. "He would never do such a thing. It wouldn't be right."

Paul chided himself for the unjust suspicion. "Where's Jane?" he demanded, rather abruptly.

"She's in the next room. Monsieur Flammarion is with her. She...fainted, I suppose...the vapors, they call it, although I've never been sure what that's supposed to mean. The other lady had a bad turn as well, but her young man took her home in the carriage. It's not the first time, he said. She's lucky to have him. He really cares for her, I think."

"Jane fainted, you say?" Paul repeated.

"That's right. Fabien had to carry her upstairs. "But Monsieur Flammarion said that he'd seen it before, and that she'd come round in time. He was more worried about you, I think. He told me to stay with you, and to call him if necessary. Is it necessary?"

"No," Paul told her. "I had a bad dream, that's all. I'm fine. Did I draw while I was hypnotized?"

"Yes, indeed. I wouldn't have believed it possible that a human hand could move so rapidly and so precisely, if I hadn't seen it. You made four drawings in the space of five or six minutes. Strange drawings...very strange."

"Where are they?"

"Still downstairs."

"Did I draw Yvaine?"

"I don't know, although the baron certainly seemed to think so. The baron's daughter died long before I joined the household, so I couldn't recognize her if I saw her...but I'm not sure that the drawings were of real people, although the lady with wings did look a little like the portrait on the wall. I thought she might be an angel, even though angels are supposed to be men, but Madame Zosima said that she wasn't, and that Talia was no angel?"

"I didn't just draw faces, then?" Paul said, grasping at the first of several questions that sprang to mind

"No, Monsieur. The lady with wings, the sphinx and the mermaid all had human faces, but the other...Monsieur Flammarion said that it isn't a Martian, and I suppose he would know, but what it is, I wouldn't care to say."

"Is Zosima still here as well?"

"Yes, Monsieur. She didn't faint. She's downstairs. Don't worry about it being a squeeze if Fabien has to take you all home in the carriage—Gabriel can ride on the seat with Fabien. He's done it before."

That had been the least of Paul's worries. He lifted the coverlet that had been laid over him to make sure that he was still wearing his trousers, and swung his legs off the bed. "Do you have my coat and shoes?" he asked.

"They're just here, Monsieur," she replied, indicating another armchair, on which the coat had been neatly laid, while the shoes were underneath. Paul's gaze flicked around the room. There was a clock on the wall; the hands indicated half past midnight. It was not as late as he had imagined, or feared. There were paintings on three of the walls. He did not recognize any of the artists by their styles, but it was easy enough to imagine that they might have been exhibited a decade ago at the Salon de la Rose+Croix.

"I need to see Jane," he said, by way of explanation for his hurry. "I need to make sure that she's all right. Then I need to see the drawings. You're sure that your master is sleeping normally?"

"As to normally, I wouldn't like to say," said Madame Louvot, "but Monsieur Gabriel said that there was no need to call a physician. Monsieur Gabriel always says that." She reached a furtive hand up to her face to brush away a tear.

"Perhaps you ought to relieve Gabriel," Paul suggested, thinking that it might be a welcome suggestion. "I'm fine—I'll go to join Monsieur Flammarion, if you'll show me the way. Thank you for sitting with me, though. That was kind of you."

The housekeeper's expression suggested that kindness had had nothing to do with it, but she said nothing, and simply watched him as he reached for his shoes. When he had put on his coat, Madame Louvot stood up, and wasted no time in leading him along the corridor to the next room.

Flammarion stood up as Paul came in. "That's a relief," he said. "I wasn't entirely sure that I could rely on precedent, and Antoine isn't here this time to add the weight of his professional opinion. How do you feel?"

"Fine," said Paul, his eyes going directly to the bed.

"Jane seems to me to be simply asleep, now," Flammarion hastened to add, "although it definitely began with what common parlance calls an attack of the vapors."

"It's my fault," Paul murmured. "I insisted on bringing her, to provide me with moral support. It didn't occur to me that I might be exposing her to any risk, but that should have been my first concern. I knew perfectly well that what happened before had affected others more severely than myself, and that it had affected her more than she would admit. She wanted to protect me, but I ought to have been protecting her. I'm an idiot."

Flammarion smiled wryly. "Can you imagine what her reaction would have been if you had deliberately excluded her?" he asked.

"She would never have forgiven me," Paul muttered, still speaking quietly lest he wake the sleeper. "But there are circumstances in which in which it might be best to be unforgiven."

"This isn't one of them," Flammarion assured him. "The attack was brief, and she's sleeping peacefully now. Some of the others were affected, I think, but only slightly. No one sustained any damage, so far as I can tell."

"Have you looked in on the baron?"

"Not recently, but Fabien has made repeated checks, and has reported that he seems no worse than usual—usual, that is, as an after-effect of Gabriel's pills. He has been taking them for some time, in the belief that they're a more satisfactory remedy for his pain than laudanum. I have my doubts, but it's not my place to interfere."

"Did he see the drawings I made before he fell unconscious?"

"Yes, briefly—but he was in a state of near-delirium by then...or perhaps near-ecstasy. We won't know for sure until he wakes up, and perhaps not even then, but he seemed to think that the experiment had been a success, from his viewpoint. Even if that's pure wishful thinking, it surely counts as success."

"Did I draw Yvaine's face? Madame Louvot didn't know?"

"Nor do I. Madame Zosima half-recognized a image of a winged female as Talia, although she was quick to deny it, but there might have been a element of wishful thinking in both the recognition and the denial. There are two other chimerical creatures with human faces, which I didn't recognize. If the baron recognized Yvaine's face, it must have been in the entity that resembles a mermaid. The sphinx seemed entirely enigmatic to me, but that's expectable, I presume,"

"And the inevitable fetus?"

"If that's what it is. You'd better go down and take a look for yourself."

"You're not coming?"

"I'll stay with Jane for the moment, in case she wakes up. Zosima's down there, and you can come back when you've studied the sketches. We'll have plenty of time to discuss them, although I expect that the baron will want to keep them. Take the lamp from the sideboard. The one on the mantelpiece is quite adequate for me."

Paul glanced at Jane again, but she did seem to be sleeping peacefully. He picked up the small lamp that he had been invited to take, and left the room. The lamp was little more than a night-light, but its glow was sufficient to guide him safely down the stairs, and he found the drawing-room without difficulty. Zosima and Fabien were inside, engaged in conversation. Fabien came to meet him.

"Are you all right, Monsieur?" he asked, solicitously. "I wanted to call a doctor, but Monsieur de Lautrec told me not to do it, and he has authority here when the master is...indisposed."

"I'm fine," Paul assured him.

"How is Madame de La Vaudère?" Zosima asked.

"Sleeping peacefully," Paul said, and headed for the table where he had made the drawings. They were arranged in a neat square, not quite overlapping the edges of the table-top.

His attention was drawn first to the entity that was probably a fetus. As usual, the body was somewhat blurred, although it was possible to make out arms and clenched hands.

The head, large in proportion, was only unusual in that the eyes were open, and seemingly staring at the beholder, thus giving the face an expression that none of its predecessors had had. Exactly what that expression was, Paul was not sure, but it did not seem hostile.

None of the other expressions on the human faces of the three chimeras seemed hostile either. The mermaid, like mermaids he had previously drawn, seemed rather nostalgic, or wistful. Paul compared the face mentally with the sketch that the baron had identified in the carriage as his daughter. There did, in fact, seem to be a significant resemblance. But why a mermaid? In fact, why a body at all, given that he had previously only drawn the faces of the dead, save for the fetus?

If the mermaid's face really was Yvaine's however, it was Yvaine as he had drawn her before, not Yvaine as he had glimpsed her momentarily in his dream, agonized and suicidal; it was Yvaine as she would have wanted to be remembered by her traumatized father.

"The sphinx—which did seem to be a sphinx and not a sphinge—gave the impression of being pensive and slightly anxious, as if philosophizing about a difficult problem. Its face was not precisely reminiscent of the portrait he had previously made of Charles Cros, but it did have a vague family resemblance to it—and thus, by the same token, to Antoine Cros.

The winged female, whose face, so far as Paul could judge, similarly had no more than a family resemblance to Talia's, but similarly no less, seemed calm and serene—which further diminished the resemblance, Paul never having seen Talia in such a mood.

"How do you interpret them?" Paul asked Zosima.

"Me?" the magnetizer queried. "Aren't you the one who's supposed to be interpreting? I can understand why you might have drawn Antoine Cros as a sphinx, if that really is supposed to be him—not a very good likeness, if so—but why you might have given Talia wings or Yvaine de Rochemure a tail, I can't imagine; again, if that's who they're supposed to be. You were much more precise in your semblances four years ago, as I remember, and the sketch of Talia you gave me suggests that you've retained that precision in Toulouse. As for the fetus, one looks pretty much like another, although it doesn't take too much imagination to concoct a story as to why the eyes might be open. The baron appreciated that one, I think, before the hashish caught up with him and he folded up, but why chimeras at all, though? It seems a strange departure. It's because the images are polluted, I think—it's because you couldn't let yourself go completely. I was right, last time, when I wanted to exclude disturbing presences, and they made themselves felt to a much greater extent this time. Next time, no baron, no Flammarion, and above all, no La Vaudère. Just you and me—that way, we might be able to make some real progress."

"Next time?" Paul queried.

"Absolutely. You must see that you can't give up now—and you can see, too, that you were in no danger. It's just a matter of obtaining the right conditions."

Paul was still staring at the four drawings, trying to make sense of them. "But is it a departure?" he wondered, aloud. "In the past, I've always drawn the recognizable dead as disembodied faces. Who can tell what kind of bodies they might have had, if I'd been able to represent them in full?"

"You think the spirits of the dead are all mythological hybrids?" said Zosima, incredulously, with more than a hint of mockery in her tone.

"No," he said, "but I've always had a penchant toward mythological imagery of that kind. Perhaps that's the way I imagine the dead, symbolically...but I'm not at all sure that the sphinx is Antoine Cros, or that the winged woman is Talia, let alone that the mermaid is really Yvaine. I can draw better than that, even in my sleep. I might have borrowed features from real faces in order to compose imaginary ones, but I suspect those four faces are all imaginary, not the faces of people who exist, or once existed."

"You think you failed then?" she challenged. "Given that your specific purpose in allowing the magnetization was to make contact with the dead."

"Evidently," Paul conceded.

"I you'll pardon me saying so, Monsieur," said Fabien, who was still listening, patiently, "that didn't seem to be what the master thought. He seemed to think, in the few minutes before he allowed himself to fall asleep, that your attempt to make contact with his daughter had succeeded. I don't pretend to understand strange pictures the way he does, and perhaps it wasn't the just pictures that pleased him, but I don't think you need to feel that you failed, Monsieur—quite the reverse."

Paul looked at the coachman, more inquisitively than gratefully. "That speech he made after dinner," he said, "was all new to you, wasn't it?"

"Entirely new, Monsieur," Fabien confirmed. "So far as I know, Madame Louvot had never heard it before either."

"Not entirely surprising," Zosima observed. "A man is not likely to admit to have carried out four cold-blooded murders, even to his servants—perhaps especially to his servants—until he's absolutely sure that he has nothing to lose by it."

"Murders, Madame?" said the coachman, mildly. "I didn't hear any such admission—and nor, I'm certain, did Madame Louvot. The baron is not a man who would ever commit murder. He's a man with a very strong sense of justice, who has always done his duty very scrupulously."

Zosima laughed. "Good for you, lad," she said. "I apologize for speaking carelessly, and you won't encounter any contradiction from me if you insist on that story. Madame Pommerat might not be so accommodating, though.

"Have no fear, Fabien," Paul said. "I believe that I can speak for everyone who was present, even Madame Pommerat, in saying that although we were not asked to swear any formal oath of secrecy, no one will breathe a word of what was said in the dining room tonight to anyone who was not also present. And when one bears in mind the nature of the rumors that have been circulating for years about the death of the baron's daughter, even if anyone did repeat what was said tonight to indiscreet ears, it would simply seem to be one more fanciful story. There is, after all, no official record of any of it."

"Thank you for that, Monsieur," said Fabien. "Excuse me, please, while I go to check with Monsieur Gabriel that there has been no change."

"If La Pommerat does decide to spread the story," Zosima observed, when the door had closed, "Lemastur will have to back her up—and no one who believes that Madame Louvot has been the baron's mistress for twenty years and more is going to believe denials issued by her and her adoptive son."

"It doesn't matter," said Paul. "As you said, he no longer has anything to lose—and in any case, most people, on hearing the story, would simply think, as you presumably do, that the baron should have collected the medal to which he was fully entitled."

"They would think that in Naples or Cairo," Zosima said. "Paris in 1905...well, as you say, it doesn't matter. Flammarion, I assume, only had his usual cosmic vision, if I had any effect on him at all, but Madame de La Vaudère's vapors suggest that she might have experienced something a little more surprising. I don't suppose she'll tell me, but you ought to ask her about it. Whatever Fabien says, though, it seems to me that there was an element of anticlimax in it. Perhaps that's not a bad thing; no one jumped off the Pont Neuf—although, given the frequency with which it happens, perhaps I shouldn't tempt fate.—but even so, you can do better...much better...if we can only exclude the psychic interference..."

The door of the room opened then, and Jane de La Vaudère came in, a trifle pale but quite steady on her feet, followed by Camille Flammarion.

Jane went to the table, and Paul moved side in order to allow her to study the pictures at her leisure, which she did for some three minutes before turning to Paul and saying, abruptly: "Will you take me home now, please, Paul."

"Of course," said Paul. "I'll ask Madame Louvot to telephone for a fiacre."

Madame Louvot was already standing in the doorway, having left Gabriel to keep vigil with the baron for a while longer and followed Flammarion downstairs. "There's no need for that, Monsieur," she said "Fabien will take you both back to Paris, and Madame Zosima too. Monsieur Flammarion will have to stay here for the night before returning to Juvisy, it seems, and Monsieur Gabriel says that he'll stay too, but the carriage is already harnessed."

Paul looked at Jane, who simply nodded, evidently eager to accept the offer. The road from Passy into the center of Paris was, Paul knew, sufficiently brightly lit for there to be no difficulty steering the vehicle, even at one o'clock in the morning, and the boulevards would still be busy even if the residential quarters had largely gone to sleep.

While Madame Louvot went to fetch the coachman, Paul asked Flammarion to make their apologies to the baron, and to say that he would be at his disposal again, at least for the next few days, should he be needed. Flammarion assured him that he would make sure that the message got through to the baron.

Gabriel de Lautrec came downstairs briefly to bid Paul, Jane and Zosima *au revoir*, and after various confused interchanges of politeness, Fabien helped Jane to climb into the carriage, followed a few moments later by Zosima, and then by Paul.

"Not exactly the evening I was expecting when the invitation reached me," Zosima said, as the carriage made its exit through the coaching entrance, "but quite fascinating, in spite of the disappointing nature of the art-work. Don't you think so, Madame de La Vaudère?"

"We seem to have survived," Jane replied, colorlessly.

"And the baron seems to feel that he obtained satisfaction," Zosima said, "Although, to be honest, I can't quite see how."

"He's a collector of symbolist art," Paul said, slowly, sensing that Jane was still feeling some indisposition and that it was up to him to carry the burden of conversation. "He would have been disappointed if I'd simply drawn faces. He needed the communication from the other world to be wrapped in mystery. Perhaps it was purely a matter of his unconscious mind playing tricks, but I strongly suspect that he made the contact he desired with his daughter, and that he saw his unborn grandchild gazing at him with what he doubtless took to be sympathy. He won't die happy, or in peace, because fate has nothing left for him now but a ration of anguish and pain, but I think he'll be able to die feeling vindicated, for having done his duty, and having been seen to have done it. He's an old soldier, when all said and done, with the soul of a true army man. His life wasn't completely blighted by tragedy. He had some good memories, and several loving relationships. Weren't you able to sense, then, the reaction he had to the psychic contact you established between us?"

"No," said Zosima. "Even in the old days, with Talia, I couldn't share her experience. I only knew what she reported to me...and toward the end she became increasingly secretive about that, especially with regard to you...as we discussed yesterday."

"You ought to forgive her for that," Paul said. "Reportage isn't as simple a matter as you imagine...especially if, like me, your own memory refuses to register the experience. I can't tell you anything about the detail of my contact with the baron—or, for that matter, with any other minds and spirits present. I suspect, as you've suggested yourself, that it was inherently confused, because rather than in spite of the fact that some psychic links had been previously established."

"With the dead as well as the living—with Talia, for example?"

"For one, yes. I can't give you any account of that contact, if it was, in fact made...unless the drawing of the winged woman really was influenced by her. I'm sorry if that's disappointing...after you went to so much effort. But that's the way my ability, or my disease, seems to function. It's frustrating—far more for me than for you, I assure you—but it does function. If we can believe Fabien, the baron certainly felt that he had achieved something. When he wakes up, he'll probably be able to give some account of what it was, and whether Talia was involved in some way. The link you forged between the two of them four years ago seems to have been enhanced since her death, thanks to the painting."

"So it has," Zosima said, pensively. She was silent for a few minutes.

Paul looked at Jane, but she shook her head. The light of the lamp suspended from the ceiling of the carriage was poor, and Paul gauged from her expression that she did not want to engage in conversation, so he allowed the silence to endure until Zosima broke it—which she did, eventually..

"If I hadn't seen into your soul," the magnetizer said, "I might suspect you of having faked those drawings, tailoring them to your client."

Paul's immediate reaction was to object that Zosima had just admitted that she hadn't seen into his soul, and couldn't, but he knew that she was referring to the confidences they had exchanged the day before, in an ironically metaphorical fashion. "Having been unable to see into my own soul," he remarked, instead, "I can't help but suspect it of having done exactly that."

"That is one possibility," Zosima admitted, thoughtfully. "Let's see what happens the next time, then, without the baron's needy presence. At the very least, I assume, you're still intending to hold the séance at Juvisy? With me and not Lemastur? You can always try him out at La Pommerat's, if you want to."

Paul hesitated momentarily—long enough for Jane to cut in and say: "No, Madame Zosima, that's out of the question. Paul will not be carrying out any further experiments in somnifabrication while he's in Paris."

Zosima stared at Jane, more surprised than annoyed, but soon turned to Paul without saying anything, clearly expecting that Paul would not allow Jane to speak for him in that manner.

Paul said nothing.

Zosima reflected for a moment, and then said. "Am I right, Monsieur Furneret, is suspecting that you have not taken a great leap forward tonight is your own quest to understand your ability, and are still in further need of enlightenment?"

"I'm not entirely sure," Paul said, carefully. "It will take me some time to weigh up all the implications of the experiment. But in the meantime, Madame de La Vaudère is surely acting in my best interests in forbidding me to make any further arrangements for the moment."

"Forbidding you?" Zosima queried, evidently astonished that Paul might concede to anyone the right to forbid him to do something that was entirely a matter for his own decision.

"Yes," said Paul. "Sometimes, even if they have not seen into our souls, other people can see our interests more clearly than we can ourselves. It would be foolish, I think, not to listen to someone whose judgment I trust."

Zosima's gaze alternated between the two people sitting on the opposite cushion. Paul suspected that she was having difficulty restraining herself from making an acidic comment about Paul trusting Jane de la Vaudère at all, let alone in preference to her—but she had always known when the right tactical move was to yield with good grace, temporarily.

"You're right, of course," she said. "It's fortunate, nowadays, especially in a hypocritical city like Paris, so full of conventional artifice, to find someone that one can trust, and such friends are very precious. But if you change your mind, tomorrow or at any time in the future, I will always be prepared to make an exception to my Order's rule for you. I can understand your wariness in dealing with phenomena of which you retain no memory—but might I suggest that if I were to hypnotize you, in private, and enable to you remember one or more of your past incarnations, that might be a more fruitful route to self-discovery than the kinds of séance we have so far attempted? If Madame de La Vaudère has no objections, of course."

"In fact," said Jane, bluntly, "I have."

"May I know what they are?"

"If Paul thinks it desirable to communicate them to you—but in the first instance, I need to discuss it with him in private."

"I see," said Zosima. After a pause, she went on: "I apologize, Madame. I should have realized, should I not, that your fit of the vapors was a symptom of something more serious? Obviously, I will not ask you what your vision was, since you are inclined to confidentiality, but my offer is open to you too, and I would not even have to bend my own rule to accommodate you. If you would like me to enable you to remember one or more of your previous incarnations, I would be very glad to help, and I believe that you might find it...therapeutic."

"Thank you, Madame," Jane said, "but I'm not ill."

For a moment, Paul thought that Zosima might challenge that assertion, but instead, she said: "Of course not. Even so, would you like me to ask the coachman to drive directly to your house, Madame de La Vaudère, before going to the convent and then to Monsieur Furneret's hotel?"

"That's not necessary," said Jane. "I've already instructed Fabien to drive to the convent first—as you can see if you look out of the portière."

Zosima obeyed the suggestion, and saw that the carriage really was approaching the convent. "That was very thoughtful of you," she said, in a tone full of conventional artifice. "I appreciate the consideration." She hesitated, and then added: "You do realize, do you not, Madame de La Vaudère, that I am not your enemy? I can understand why you might have formed a certain resentment against me four years ago, when I asked you to sit at the back of the room as I hypnotized Paul for the second time, but..."

"You did not ask me," Jane reminded her. "You stated the condition, and when I challenged it, you simply said that it

231

was not negotiable. You will forgive me, I'm sure, for following the precedent. Good night, Madame Zosima, and *adieu*."

The magnetizer shook her head, as if in bewilderment. "*Au revoir*, Monsieur Furneret," she said, as Fabien came to open the carriage door. Paul half-expected her to add one last barbed comment, but she did not. Fabien helped her down, and she disappeared into the darkness.

Fabien closed the door and climbed back on to the seat without asking for further instructions, but that was unsurprising. Etiquette demanded that he take the lady home first.

As the vehicle pulled away, Paul said: "That was...surprising."

"Yes, it was," she admitted, breathing out as if giving relief to a tension that she had been maintaining for some time. "I surprised myself, but I was afraid that if I didn't intervene, she would worm a commitment out of you, and I know that you're loyal to your promises. Paul, you must not let Zosima magnetize you again. I don't know whether you said that you trust me simply as a conversational ploy, but I would like it to be true, because I believe that what you said was accurate: in this instance, I believe that I do know what your best interests are far better than you do. Perhaps the vision I had tonight, when it seemed that my mind was linked with yours by way of Zosima's psychic force, was merely a dream, a fantasy confected by strange imagination, but I'm not prepared to take the risk. I believe that you were in danger, tonight Paul, and I believe that any further dealings you have with Zosima will increase that danger considerably. I'm not saying that she's malevolent, or that she has any hostility toward you, but if you don't avoid her, I honestly believe that she might cause you great harm."

Paul was perplexed. "But I feel fine," he said. "I didn't sleep this time for as long as I did at Antoine's house, and I certainly didn't draw anything as disturbing tonight as I did then. In fact, the drawings I made tonight are very similar to drawings I've been making in Toulouse for some time, some of them since the very beginning of my career. You have two paintings that could easily have originated from similar sketches. The only strange thing that happened is that Baron de Rochemure seems to believe that I had achieved what he wanted of me...and that, I suspect, is largely a matter of self-delusion on his part."

"No," said Jane, "it isn't. I know that you can't remember, but you must trust me. Something did happen—and yes, you feel fine, thanks to the stern censorship of your conscious mind; but you're not. If you submit to Zosima's magnetism again, or even Henri Lemastur's, the consequences could be drastic. Do you really trust me? Do you believe what I'm saying?"

"Yes," Paul said not at all sure whether it was anything more than a conversational play, "I trust you. But you'll have to explain why you're saying what you're saying."

"I will," she promised. "You might think that I'm mad, but I will explain. You and Flammarion had a brief conversation in the baron's house before we left didn't you? Did he tell you whether he had a vision during the séance?

"He didn't mention having had one tonight," Paul said, "but he did tell me yesterday about the one he had during Zosima's last séance, and he explained it. If he had one, it's likely to have been of the same sort. These things do seem to have a definitive consistency about them. Does it matter?"

"Perhaps not—but I thought that there was a possibility that Flammarion might have seen or sensed something that might lend some support to what I have to tell you. If not...I have no great hopes of La Pommerat, but Lemastur or Lautrec might, although they might not have realized the significance of anything they glimpsed. Lautrec will come to see us tomorrow, I dare say, with news of the baron. We can ask him then. Here we are."

The carriage had pulled up outside Madame de La Vaudère's house. Fabien came, as usual, to open the door and to help the lady down.

Before she had even set foot on the ground, she said: "You can take the carriage home now, Fabien. Monsieur Furneret will be staying the night here."

Paul was astonished, but when Fabien offered him a hand in his turn, he took it and dismounted meekly. He waited until the carriage was in motion again before saying: "You do realize that you've just practically told a *coachman* that we'll be spending the night together? You're a married woman! I know you want to talk to me urgently, but you could have told him that I'll take a cab back to the hotel...as I'm perfectly capable of doing. What if he repeats what you said?"

"Do you think it would have made the slightest difference to what he might think or say if I'd told him that you'd take a cab?" she said. "You can't be that naïve. In any case, I don't care about gossip, false or true. And I do need to talk to you, urgently. Would you really rather have let him take you to back to the hotel, just for the sake of appearances? I apologize for any prejudice I've caused to your reputation; I can quite understand why you might not want to be compromised with a woman my age, but you must realize that when you went out of your way this evening to tell Madame Pommerat that you'd never been in my boudoir, she seized upon the opposite inference? This is Paris, and she doesn't know that you're as innocent as Candide."

"You heard what I said to her?" Paul queried.

"Of course I heard it. I was watching her like a hawk—and listening. Not that it made any difference. She'd already made up her mind. The fact that you called on me on Monday before calling on anyone else might just have passed for conventional politeness, but as soon as you came back for dinner, it was only a matter of time before All Paris had us inscribed in the rumor register for a second time as lovers. That's my fault, obviously, and if it offends you, I'm sorry—but, justly or unjustly, my reputation has been in the gutter for a long time, and you and I have more serious things to worry about than what might be whispered in the salons for the three nights that is the nowadays the average lifespan for rumors of that sort."

While she was speaking she led the way upstairs and opened the apartment door with a key. She lit the gas as soon as they were inside.

Paul was still trying to catch up. "For a second time?" he queried.

"Of course. You painted my portrait, remember? I went upstairs to your studio half a dozen times on my own."

"But nothing happened."

"You and I know that. Even Juliette knew that, although it didn't stop her biting her knuckles. But slander doesn't care about realities, only about appearances...and as regards appearances, we were doomed long before we first met. I live in Paris on my own, with a husband and son in the provinces. You're a painter. We could be as pure as the driven snow, with our haloes polished till they shine, and it wouldn't make any difference. So to hell with them all. I'll write my books any way the whim takes me, without worrying about what some prim bourgeois moralist might think of them, and I'll live my life the same way. Now, for God's sake come into the boudoir, take that absurd frock-coat off, and have a glass of port. Then I'll explain why your sanity might be in dire danger if you don't keep away from Zosima."

CHAPTER XIII

Having acquired the habit of obedience in regard to Jane de La Vaudère, Paul did exactly as he was told, although he paused before sitting down to inspect the portrait of his hostess that he had done four years before. It was, he thought, one of his finest works, painted with idolatry. It was easy to see, meeting the oblique gaze of the eyes, why she had the power of command over the artist.

For the first time, he wondered what the effect on Juliette might have been of seeing the painting take shape on the canvas day by day, before she and he had even slept together, although she had made her intention of "hooking him" perfectly clear, and he had expressed the opinion that she would surely succeed.

He was still convinced that Juliette had not loved him at that point in their curious relationship, but though that he could understand, now, why she might have been, as Jane had put it, biting her knuckles even then. She had felt that she had a proprietary right, at least to his kindness, and in watching him paint the idolatrous portrait, she might well have felt that she was paying a price for that kindness.

Then, for some reason, he thought about Baron de Rochemure and Madame Louvot. He was quite convinced that the baron had never loved Madame Louvot, and had never been able to love Madame Louvot—but that did not mean that Madame Louvot had not loved him, whatever she had or had not said to him. Now, she would have to watch him die, doubtless maintaining long vigils by his bedside, just as he had watched Juliette die and Zosima had watched Talia die.

He could not help feeling sorry for Madame Louvot—and, for that matter, for Zosima—because he could not help placing himself, imaginatively, in their shoes. But how much worse it must have been, he thought, for Baron de Rochemure during Yvaine's last hours. How could a man survive a trauma like that?

The answer to that question, he knew was that the baron had only survived it in the physical sense that his lungs had continued drawing in oxygen, and his heart had continued pumping the blood that ferried the oxygen to his brain. Materially, he had been alive for thirty-four years since that horrid day, but spiritually? Had he not already had much in common with the dead throughout that time, existing only as a memory of what he had previously been, within a new incarnation, still an echo of a soldier, a professional murderer, at least until he had completed his final mission of butchery, but then reconfiguring himself as a student of the occult, a seeker of the beyond, a collector of arcane books and symbolist art.

How easy it is, Paul thought, *to believe in the serial reincarnation of our souls, given that it is something we experience within our own lifetimes, sometimes smoothly and sometimes abruptly. How easy it is to believe in a life after death, when it is so easy to die spiritually while our bodies remain obstinately alive, leaving our consciousness to recreate itself, or to be recreated, by means of a new spontaneous blossoming of whatever seeds might be lurking in our unconscious mind.*

"Admiring your own work?" Jane said, handing him a glass of ruby red fortified wine. She had let her hair down and put on a peignoir while his attention had been rapt.

"It is good, I think," Paul said. "Chazelle would love it, and Victor too. They'd want me to do more like it...but I couldn't. I could paint you with that kind of intense absorption and emotional involvement, and I could paint Talia. Perhaps I could paint others, too...but not just anyone, and not just for hire. That's a flaw, I think, which might not only prevent me from making a fortune, but might prevent me from making full use of what ability I have. There's a rich mythology, of course, of painters and writers who need muses to inspire them, who can only draw out the best of their ability if they'd steeped in lust...except that it isn't really lust, is it? It's a brutal and absurd distortion to construe what Dante might have felt for Beatrice or what Raphael might have felt for La Fornarina as simple carnal desire. But that complication makes it far more difficult to manage and exploit one's ability, far more difficult to understand what one is actually doing, how and why."

"I can understand why you'd rather stare at the image than the model," she said. "Age has withered me, and will continue to wither me, inexorably—but sit down now, and look at me, please."

Paul sat down in the armchair that was indicated to him, positioned for the convenience of intimate conversation near to its twin. She sat down too, and leaned forward, studying him.

"I'm sorry," she said. "I'm bullying you. I shouldn't have said what I said to Zosima and I shouldn't have said what I said to Fabien. I'm frightened. I'm telling myself that I'm frightened for you, and that's not a lie, but really, I'm frightened for myself, because if what I tell you harms you, it won't be easy to forgive myself. Popular wisdom says that there are some things it's better not to know, and perhaps that's true. Perhaps I ought to trust your own mind, which presumably could have allowed you to remember what happened to you while you were making those drawings, but didn't...but I think that was a kind of reflex action, the mechanical following of a rule, without any calculation of future consequences...possible consequences, at any rate, which I can see only too clearly."

She paused, apparently waiting for encouragement, or at least endorsement.

"Go on," he said. "I need to know."

She touched her forehead with the fingers of her right hand, very briefly. "What I saw," she said, "was only a dream—a nightmare. All that happened to me physically was a simple malaise, a fainting fit accompanied by a vague nausea. A physician might judge that it was the physical malaise that generated the delusion rather than vice versa, but I don't think so. I think that my mind really was linked with yours while yours was linked with the baron's, and it was intimately linked, because of the curious connection we have—which is indeed far more than and different from mere lust, although I certainly can't deny that there was a component of that to begin with—on both sides, I think. At any rate, I believe that the vision was real, expressed in symbolic terms, because such things have no other mode of expression, but nevertheless real.

"I was on a cross—not just any cross, but the one you drew. I don't suppose for a moment that you drew that in a moment of precognition; evidently, my seeing the sketch operated as a suggestion, but it connected with something within me, something deep. So, I was on the cross, in that peculiar position, naked and immobilized by nails. I was in agony, but I had contrived to detach myself mentally from the pain, so that I was seeing quite clearly.

"I was on the edge of a battlefield, a vast battlefield that extended as far as the eyes could see in all directions, although I was sure that it wasn't infinite. There were no troops involved in large-scale maneuvers, no cavalry, and no working artillery, but there were ragged groups of soldiers moving back and forth, and there were vast numbers of casualties, wounded and dying. There were no stretcher-bearers; the men moving among the wounded weren't helping them, but finishing them off. Perhaps they thought of it as a matter of kindness, of sparing them further pain.

"Traveling across the battlefield there was a carriage, not very large, drawn by two black horses at a rapid trot. You were inside the carriage, with the baron, but the two of you weren't alone, even though the carriage wasn't a vis-à-vis and wasn't designed to carry more than two people. I couldn't make out the other people—if they were people—who were in the carriage, but they seemed to be struggling to make room, pressing you from both sides so closely that you and the baron were fused into a single person. I don't think that was their intention, and I got the impression that some of the entities, at least, we trying to pull you apart again, even though there was no room to do that.

"Even though I couldn't move, and the cross was firmly planted in the ground, whereas the carriage was traveling rapidly, the distance between us didn't increase. If anything, it seemed to decrease, but that might have been an effect of my trying to lean forward, as if I might be able to help even though my arms were wrapped around the arms of the cross and my hands were nailed to it at the wrist. I wanted to scream a warning to you, but I had no voice, and I knew that you couldn't see me. I knew that even if you looked at me, you wouldn't see me.

"The idea occurred to me that the reason that the carriage wasn't getting any further away, even though it was raveling rapidly, was because it was moving through time rather than space, and when I realized that, I wanted to shout to the coachman that he was going the wrong way, but I couldn't. The coachman was wearing a bulky overcoat with a tightly-secured hood, of the kind that coachmen often wear in winter, but he wasn't a big man, if he was a man at all. I thought perhaps that he might be a monkey of some kind, perhaps a baboon, but I couldn't tell. The carriage was definitely heading in the wrong direction, however, not so much because it was heading into the past instead of the future, but because the past into which it was heading was as a strange, artificial past, compounded out of memory and legend rather than an objective sequence of events, and I knew that that kind of past was inherently treacherous, and dangerous.

"I knew that you were uncomfortable in the carriage, because of the lack of room, but I knew that you weren't frightened, because you didn't know that you were heading into danger; you had no idea of the kind of monsters that awaited you there. In addition, you were sharing the space with the baron, who was scared, but was also determined not to be put off by his fear. The baron knew that the carriage was heading into danger, but he was drawing energy from that fear, creating courage, telling himself that he needed the fear, and the courage, in order to do what he felt that he had to do. He didn't care about the risk, and he wasn't even thinking about the fact that he was taking you with him...or, more accurately hitching a ride in a carriage that, although it wasn't yours, you had hired, the direction of which you were able and entitled to govern, but weren't. Instead, the carriage was going where the baron wanted to go, not only back in time but back in *his* time, into the past compounded out of his memory, his somewhat faulty understanding, and his nightmares.

"I knew that the carriage was heading for disaster. It was steering there quite deliberately, but not because the baron wanted to prevent the disaster—that was impossible—or even because he wanted to help in some way, there being no effective help he could render, but simply because he wanted to share in it. He wanted to be with his daughter, he wanted to participate in her death, not because it would lessen her share of it, but because it would allow him to make a kind of sacrifice, to accept a fraction of the responsibility, to execute an imagined duty. But he couldn't do it without you, without the vehicle you had hired, and he couldn't get there, because the carriage was so crowded with contending passengers, without being fused with you. And you were allowing him to do it, partly out of kindness, and partly out of curiosity, but mostly because a kind of inertia, because that was the way that the direction of your life was flowing at that particular point in time, even though it was just an eddy in the flux, just a momentary turbulence, irrelevant to the desultory tide.

"I wanted to scream in your ear that you were going the wrong way, that you had to turn back, that if you stayed with the baron, you wouldn't be able to sustain the culmination of his quest. For him, what he was seeking was the holy grail, the symbolic cup of redemption, from which he needed to drink the mortal blood. He needed to take part in his daughter's immolation. For him, it would be a cleansing fire, something he needed to pass through in order to be purified, but for you, the blood in the grail would be pure poison, the fire nothing but agony, which would burn your soul irredeemably.

"You didn't know. You were inside the carriage, and you had no idea where you were going and why. You had no idea where you wanted to go, what kind of destination was possible. You could have communicated with the coachman. Even if you couldn't find a voice, you could have hammered on the wall to order him to stop. If necessary, you could have opened the door and leapt out—but that was the last thing you wanted to do while you were traveling through a killing field.

"I thought that there might be other ways that you could change direction and destination, purely bye mental effort, if I could just get the message through to you. I knew that you had far more power than you imagined, if you could only work out how to draw upon it and deploy it. I knew that you could even change the past into which the carriage was heading, which was, after all, an imaginative compound, imprisoned by the reality of elapsed events but still permitting movement and modification in all sorts of ways, if only you could master the trick of it.

"But even though you were so close, in spite of traveling so fast, I was pinned and helpless, naked and voiceless. I could only watch.

"The carriage reached its destination. It reached the point in that vast battlefield where four things in uniforms, monsters rather than solders—not even apes like the coachman, but hideous chimerical figures, part reptilian and part insectile, were crowding around a poor supine young woman, very obviously pregnant. The baron leapt down from the carriage without it even slowing down, and he took you with him, because you were fused with him and couldn't extricate yourself, even though you were finally beginning to panic.

"The baron threw himself over his daughter, as if to shield her, but he melted into her, as if he and she were both gaseous rather than solid, or some kind of shadow or virtual image on a screen. He took you with him, because you were in the same unsolid condition, and even though you were terrified now, you couldn't separate yourself from him, from her, and most of all from the fetus in her womb, which opened her eyes under the pressure of the rifle-butts that were raining down on her, one after another, although she had no comprehension of pain, not knowing that there was as any such thing, and hardly even being conscious that she existed, but nevertheless having mentality enough to be aware that something was happening. You tried to shield her, automatically; while the baron tried to shield his daughter, you tried to shield the unborn child. But it wasn't possible. All that could have happened is that you would have taken aboard all the pain, all the terror and all the harm that she, in her absolute innocence, was incapable of feeling.

"Time had become meaningless. If I said that you were seconds away from death, it wouldn't signify anything. There were no seconds, even though the event was unfolding. Nor, I think, would you have died, in the physical sense of the term. Your lungs wouldn't have stopped drawing in air, nor your heart pumping blood to your brain. All that would have happened to you physically, I think, is that you would have fallen into a more profound sleep than the somnifabricatory state that you were already in. Whether you would ever have got out of it again, or whether you would have been the same person if you had, I don't know. I suspect not; I think that you would have been damaged. You might not have been aware of having been damaged, but you would have been, irreparably.

"But it didn't come to that. Something, or someone, pulled you out: something, or someone, that had been in the carriage with you, crowding you, shoving and jostling you, and which had spilled out with several others—I couldn't count exactly. God, how I wished that it could have been me—but it couldn't; I was pinned, helpless. And God forgive me, I as jealous. I wanted, more than anything in the world, for you to escape, but I was jealous because it wasn't me that plucked you out and pulled you away. The person, or the creature, who did it had wings, but whether they were avian or insectile wings I couldn't say.

"Either way, it took off and rose above the battlefield with you in its arms...her arms, because I'm certain, although I don't know how I can be, that it was female. Except that the air above the battlefield wasn't really air, because the battlefield was time only symbolized by space, and not space itself. And when the winged creature rose up, there wasn't anywhere for it to go: no Heaven, and no other words floating in space like Mars of Saturn. I lost sight of it, but I knew that there was nowhere for it to go, in the distance, because the distance wasn't really distance, except in a symbolic sense.

But I followed you with my eyes. I lost sight of the battlefield, the carriage, the baron, his daughter...everything. I just watched you, moving further away and disappearing. And I wept, and felt lonely, and remembered that I was dreaming, and wanted to wake up.

And then, I suspect, I fainted...or evaporated. The cross could no longer hold me; it was vaporous...and I had a fit of the vapors. Physically, though, I was unharmed and unchanged. I was still alive, with no stigmata to remind me of how close I had been to a kind of death. But I honestly think that I might have died, in a sense similar to the sense in which the baron died in May 1871. And I think that you came extremely close to dying, in that sense, and that you would have done if something or someone—something already dead but nevertheless capable of heroism—hadn't saved you.

"I wished it had been me, but it wasn't. I was helpless to do anything...except to remember. I hadn't been able to help you when you were in danger, but I knew that I could warn you, and that I had to do my utmost to convince you of the danger you had been in, and the danger that you would be in again if you ever submitted again to that kind of hypnosis. Zosima isn't malevolent, and nor is the baron. Not only didn't they want to harm you but they wished you well...but even so, between the two of them, they came within a inch of destroying you last night, and next time, even your guardian angel might not be able to save you."

Jane fell silent. After a few seconds, in which she obtained no immediate response, she said: "So there it is. Now you can tell me that I'm insane."

"You're not insane," Paul told her. "I wasn't conscious of it while it was happening, but I remembered fragments of it subsequently, while I was in a shallower phase of sleep, and managed to cling on to the memory. I thought it was just a dream, but even so, I tried to hang on to it. There are aspects of it I couldn't see, but I saw enough, and remembered enough to be able to assure you that you're not crazy. If we dreamed it, we both dreamed it, and if we're deluded, then it was a *folie-à-deux*...or *trois*. *Trois*, I think, if we're only counting the living, although it's not improbable that Flammarion and one of two of the others had some marginal perception of it, without realizing what it was, and their minds probably let it go, like any ordinary dream. How many the total number of participants would be if we included the active dead, I don't know...possibly none, if the dread don't dream, but if they do...who can tell?"

Jane had no difficulty following that line of argument. "Do you think it was Talia, then, who pulled you out?"

""No. I don't. I think she would have, if she had been able to do so, but if she had any awareness at all, she would have been helpless. One thing that I could see but you couldn't was that there was a vast line of crosses. Maybe they were just for the spirits of the living, but I don't think so. I'm truly sorry."

"For what?"

"For nailing you to a cross, even in a dream."

"I don't believe you did. You wouldn't."

"It was my dream."

"Was it? I don't believe so. We were all in it—you, me, the baron, perhaps others—but I don't believe that any one of us was dreaming it. You were the instrument, or at least the catalyst, but you weren't the dreamer."

"Who, then? The dead? God?"

"No. I don't think that the dreamer was a person at all, but a process. It doesn't have a mind or a purpose. It just is. It wasn't the dreamer who saved you, Paul, it was a figment of the dream, alive, dead, mythical or hypothetical. Are you sure it wasn't Talia?"

"It wasn't her," Paul insisted. "It wasn't her voice."

"What voice?"

"You couldn't hear it, but there was a voice. At the end of the dream, there was a voice. I thought perhaps it might have been yours, although I'm sure that I'd have recognized it if it had been."

"What did it say?"

"It said: *Go home.* There was some elaboration, but that was the gist of it. *Go home.*"

"Perhaps it just meant that you should wake up."

"No, it meant more than that. It meant it literally. It was telling me to go back to Toulouse."

"It wasn't me, then. I was trying to scream all sorts of things to you, but not that. It's probably the best advice you could be given, but I couldn't give it to you. Consciously and rationally, now, I can agree with it, just as I agreed with it before, but not in a dream. I don't know why—we both know that it isn't mere lust—but when you go, it will hurt, just as it hurt before. You have no idea how I envied that worthless little whore the freedom she had to go with you, the opportunity she had to go with you, to exploit your kindness. But I had to be rational. I was trapped. Everybody in my social class has a home in Paris as well as a home in the provinces, and can move between them freely. You can be alone in Pars while your husband is in the provinces, no matter what scandalous gossip says...but you can't run away. If you run away, that transforms the situation completely, and ruins everyone concerned. So I bit my knuckles and let her hook you, because there was no rational alternative. But it hurt."

"She wasn't worthless," Paul said. "I never loved her, but she wasn't worthless. She was very valuable to me."

"Of course she wasn't worthless," Jane said. "That was just spite talking. But you're fooling yourself if you think you didn't love her, setting the qualifying bar way too high. And there's no need. As you say, she was far from worthless, entirely worthy of love. I hope you told her that, even if you thought you didn't feel it. But that's by the by. What matters, for the moment, is that you believe me. I was desperately afraid that you wouldn't. So you'll stay away from Zosima, won't you?"

"It isn't that simple," Paul said.

Jane sighed. "I had a nasty feeling that you were going to say that," she said.

"You know that it isn't that simple. You know that I don't need Zosima to slip into a somnambulistic state. It happens spontaneously at irregular intervals, and I've even got to the point where I can almost induce it at will. The psychic links might be much weaker than those created, or strengthened, by Zosima's psychic force, but they still operate. Returning to Toulouse can't free me entirely from the intrinsic hazards of my nature."

"Perhaps not—but there's a world of difference between those intrinsic hazards and arranging séances in which psychic force is deliberately deployed, and you lend yourself wholeheartedly to its effects."

"The danger on this occasion came from the link with the baron. Other links don't carry that danger...some might even be wholly beneficial. Tonight's adventure has surely proved—although I've never doubted it for an instant—that my link with you is something positive and valuable. A séance at Juvisy in which the only witnesses were you and Camille Flammarion..."

"Isn't going to happen," Jane said, positively. "I am not going to lend myself to any such adventure. If you want to take foolish risks, I can't stop you, but I won't participate again. I might have emerged unscathed, but last night's excursion to Hell, while it lasted, was the worst episode of my life, and don't try to put the entire blame for that on the baron. Remember Juliette...and Talia. The real danger is Zosima. She knows that—why do you think she's abandoned her old career and found a new vocation? Or had, until temptation came along, wearing your face. She's not my enemy, she says, or yours—and she means it. But she *is* my enemy, and yours, and if I have any authority over you whatsoever, I'll use it. I forbid you to arrange any further séances, and if you defy me, I'll

247

never speak to you again. And now, I think I'm too tired to continue this conversation. There's a spare bedroom, if you prefer to use it, but I'd rather you didn't. And I know, because you've made the point so emphatically, that you're perfectly capable of sleeping with women you don't love, so I can't see that you have any reasonable excuse."

"If there were a problem," Paul said, "it would be the inverse of that one."

"Flatterer. I'll have to turn the light off though, in case you expect me to look like that nude sketch you made in your dreams."

There were several replies that Paul might have made to that, but he ignored them all—all the verbal ones, at any rate.

CHAPTER XIV

"I'm delighted to find you both here," said Gabriel de Lautrec, the first of the morning visitors to arrive, once the ritual politeness was out of the way. "It saves me the trouble of a duplication of effort and a bothersome expenditure of time and distance. First of all, the baron is, as the conventional phraseology has it, as well as can be expected—which, in this case means little more than not yet dead. No, that's understating the case; mentally, he's a good deal better than might have been expected. He asked me to give both of you his warmest thanks for what you did last night. He says that he will treasure the drawings you made then, Paul, as a memento, but that you will both understand what he means when he says that they are a mere adjunct to what you enabled him to do and to see. He says that, although there has not been the slightest remission in his cancer, he feels, in himself like a renewed man...a redeemed man.

"I'm glad," said Paul, sincerely.

Lautrec continued: "The baron is sure that between now and the end, he and his daughter will never be apart, and that they can face the future together, reinforced by their communion. You are very welcome to call on him at any time, of course, and he hopes that you will, but he does not think that he will need your services as a medium again. He has asked me to finalize the details of a number of purchases that he expressed the intention of making, if you are willing to complete the transaction; he says that he has already given you a list. He has given me full authority to negotiate financial terms, with instructions not to be miserly. He will transmit the agreed fee to Auguste Chazelle, with a firm instruction that as Chazelle had absolutely nothing to do with the purchase, he is not too retain a commission of more than ten per cent You may transmit the sketches via Chazelle, deliver them to me or take them to Passy yourself, as you please. Is that agreeable?"

"Of course. I'll leave the drawings with Chazelle, it that's agreeable to you, and leave him to negotiate the price—he'd be terribly upset if I left him out entirely. I'll deliver them later today and tell him to expect you. May I enquire as to what you thought of the drawings yourself?"

"You may, if you're prepared to take the risk."

"That sound ominous, but go ahead."

"I was enormously impressed by the speed at which you completed them, but I fear that they show the evidence of that haste, and, with one exception, they seemed to me to be a trifle banal. I somehow got the impression, however, that your attention and ability were not fully invested in the work. In fairness, though, perhaps that was a matter of projection, as I was feeling the inevitable effects of the pills I had absorbed. The carriage we had shared in coming from Paris to Passy must have left a lingering impression, perhaps emphasized by the fact that I was sitting next to the redoubtable Madame Zosima. I sensed an unaccountable hostility in her that was a trifle uncomfortable. When she began her ritual of suggestion, it gave me the strange impression of being stuck in a fiacre with her, crowded by other presences, and heading for some fatal rendezvous. Hashish and I have had a long friendship, which is normally manifest in pleasant dreams, but there are no guarantees in such odd relationships, and one must never forget that poisons are, in fact, poisonous. There is a medical adage that the poison is the dose, and I make every attempt to be moderate, but last night, the green god was in a treacherous mood. So, in sum, don't take it too hard that I didn't like your drawings. The fault is probably entirely mine."

"Not at all," said Paul. "I have no consciousness of producing my somnifabricatory drawings, so I don't feel any particular responsibility for their quality, I'm always delighted to find, occasionally, that I have done good work, but more often than not, the results are a trifle painful to see. As long as the baron was not disappointed, however, the séance can be reckoned a success."

"It can. Henri Lemastur was a little put out, I think, that you chose Zosima as your magnetizer, but Madame Pommerat was not. I think she is looking forward to your attendance at her next soirée, when she will be in control, at least in her own opinion."

"As I explained to her," Paul said, "I doubt that I shall be able to attend. This is only a flying visit. Urgent matters will recall me to Toulouse very soon."

Lautrec glanced at Jane then. Once again, it was evident that he was endeavoring to evaluate the relationship between the two of them, which undoubtedly struck him as odd.

"We shall all be sorry to lose him, of course," Jane said, "but artists, like priests, must go where their vocation calls them. We can look forward to his next exhibition, however, which Auguste Chazelle will organize as soon as he can."

"It will be eagerly anticipated," Lautrec assured them. "I hope to see you again before you leave, Monsieur Furneret—you have my address—and I always look forward to encountering you in the course of my peregrinations, Madame de La Vaudère. *Au revoir* to you both."

Only half an hour went by between Lautrec's departure and Camille Flammarion's arrival. For him, Jane instructed the maidservant to make tea.

"I went to your hotel first," the astronomer said to Paul, "but when I was told that you were out, I hazarded a guess that I might find you here. Last night's events proved much food for discussion, did they not? Have you recovered from your indisposition, Madame de La Vaudère?"

"Yes, thank you," Jane said.

"I must confess that I was worried about you. I wanted Fabien to call a physician, but Monsieur de Lautrec overruled me. I'm not entirely unsympathetic to his cynicism regarding the medical profession, but there is a difference between refusing its assistance for oneself and denying it to others."

"In this instance," Jane assured him, "he was quite right. I fear that I'm not exempt from womanly weaknesses, and roast wild pig does tend to be a little heavy on my delicate stomach."

"I was not immune to a touch of nausea myself," Flammarion told her, "but I attributed that to the effect of Madame Zosima's suggestion. The effluvia that she claims to exert when exerting the force of her psychic radiation might be imaginary, but if so, I fear that I am vulnerable to the illusion. In spite of all my experience—or perhaps because of it—I often feel a disturbance in the presence of expert hypnotists. Then again, the brief discussion that we had at table when the baron had finished his confession, although it recycled the age-old enigmas, was conducive to launching trains of thought. To be honest, Madame de La Vaudère, I was glad of the opportunity to sit quietly beside you while you slept, under the pretext of serving as a *garde-malade*. In all decency, I should have stayed with Monsieur Furneret and asked Madame Louvot to sit with you, but the lady opposed the suggestion."

"Why was that?" Jane asked. "Had she something against me."

"Oh, no, I'm sure that she didn't—but she particularly wanted to sit with Paul, it seemed. She said that he might have come to harm, and that she had abundant experience of caring for the sick. I couldn't see any cause for alarm in his condition at the time—less in fact, than in yours, Jane, let alone the baron's—but there seemed to be no reason not to let her have her way. Monsieur de Lautrec has told you, I suppose, that the baron does not anticipate any further need or your services as a medium?"

"Yes, he has," Paul confirmed.

"We had a conversation after Monsieur de Lautrec had left that surprised me somewhat—although less, than I would have expected. He asked me to give you his sincere apologies for having exploited you, and to tell you that he had not anticipated that you might be exposed to such danger. He would not explain what he meant, saying that I should ask you, but he advised me, quite forcefully, not to hold a séance at Juvisy with you. He said that, even without his presence, he feared that you might be in peril. I recalled that Talia Cadelan had said the same thing, four years ago, but that Zosima had attributed it to her excessive sensitivity. That is not, I think, a judgment that could be rendered against the baron. Do you know what danger he meant?"

"Yes, I do," Paul said. "I had no memory of it last night—or, to be strictly accurate, I thought the memory I had was that of an ordinary dream, but it seems that it was a nightmare shared by several of the people present, in which I almost met a nasty fate, although I was snatched from the jaws of danger at the last moment by something resembling the winged creature that I drew. Do you have any memory yourself of having had a vision while you were slightly nauseated, akin to the one you described to me yesterday?"

"No," said Flammarion. "I fear that I was still under the influence of the baron's story, and the impressions induced by my malaise were of battlefields and blood. I had to fight quite hard to conquer the queasiness, but it did not last for long, and I was successful in its suppression. I had the unworthy suspicion for a moment that the food might have been dosed with hashish, but I rejected the hypothesis as absurd, and I felt perfectly well again by the time that you came into the bedroom where Madame de La Vaudère was asleep. However..."

He paused to rake a reflective sip of tea.

"Yes?" Paul prompted.

"I hope you will not be too disappointed, especially after we had come to a firm arrangement, but I would rather not hold a séance at Juvisy during your present visit to Paris. In my experience, it is unwise to overtax mediums, and last night's endeavor was unusually harrowing in more ways than one. I still feel a measure of guilt because of my part in the distress caused to Mademoiselle Cadelan, which probably hastened her demise, and the fashion in which her portrait seemed to be staring at me while Zosima was unleashing her hypnotism recalled it to mind quite sharply. I am minded to take the baron's anxieties into account, even though they might, as you say, be based on nothing but a nightmare. If anything were to go wrong at Juvisy, after I had received and ignored such a warning, I would have difficulty forgiving myself. I shall write to Madame Zosima to inform her, when I get back to the Observatory."

"There's no need," Jane put in. "I told her last night that I had forbidden Paul to lend himself to any further experiments in hypnotism, with her or anyone else."

Flammarion raised his eyebrows. "Indeed?" he said. "How did she react, if I might ask?"

"As you would expect. She was astonished by my presumption, but it allows her to blame me, rather than Paul or anyone else, for her disappointment. As she didn't like me anyway, I'm happy to make that sacrifice."

Flammarion was still puzzled, but infallibly diplomatic. "You share the baron's anxieties, then?" he said, carefully.

"I suspect that the baron's anxieties are mild compared with mine," she said. "You doubtless remember that I realized immediately, during the first séance at Juvisy, that Paul's unconsciousness of what was happening to him while he was entranced was a danger in itself, from which he needed protection. As there was no one else present on that occasion immediately ready to lend that protection, I assumed the responsibility. The other two séances that I have witnessed have only served to intensify that anxiety—with the result that the responsibility now seems to be a matter of duty. Paul has been kind enough to humor me. If he regards it as the mere whim of an eccentric old woman, he is far too polite ever to say so."

"Having seen his sketches," Flammarion said, "I find it impossible to believe that he thinks of you as a eccentric old woman, and I can understand why he is willing to trust your judgment, as I would myself, especially in view of the baron's endorsement. I'm glad to find, in fact, that my withdrawal from our arrangement has not caused any offense. I really ought to make my way to the Gare du Nord now, but I would welcome a further opportunity to continue our theoretical discussions before you return to Toulouse, Paul. Perhaps you could telephone me tonight or tomorrow, if that would be possible."

"Of course," said Paul. "I'll walk with you to the boulevard, if I may. I need to return to the hotel, in order to write a few telegrams and letters, and then to deliver some sketches to Chazelle." He took Jane aside momentarily to say: "I'll come back later."

"Of course," she replied.

Almost as soon as they were out in the street—sunlit, for once—Flammarion said: "You had the impression of being snatched from the jaws of death by the angel with Talia's face? You do realize, I suppose, that that would be meat and drink to the psychoanalysts.

"And perhaps rightly so," Paul said, "but I'm not at all convinced that the creature was really an angel, even less that its face was really Talia's. As you saw yesterday, in addition to recognizable faces, I draw a great many that are merely generic. Given that the three chimeras I drew cannot be imagined as spirits of the dead, unless the dead go in for masked balls and carnival parades, I'm hesitant to associate any of them with anyone I know or knew. As for the fetus, that is surely generic, even though different observers inevitable associate it with particular examples. Perhaps the fact that its eyes were open is a good augury for the future."

"Perhaps," the astronomer agreed, dubiously. "Will you return to see the baron before you return to Toulouse?"

"Certainly—but not this afternoon. I need to send my apologies to Madame Pommerat and Henri Lemastur, address a polite letter to Zosima, telephone Victor Marvaud and answer any other correspondence that might have accumulated at the hotel, as well as taking the sketches to Chazelle. But be sure that I'll make time during the next few days to visit Juvisy again."

"Thank you. Might I make an indiscreet request?"

"What is it?"

"Please be kind to Jane. She is, I fear, as fragile as she seems. I don't doubt that she is absolutely sincere in wanting to protect you, even from yourself, but she might well be the one in greater need of protection. I'm aware of the folly of judging authors by the products of their literary imagination, but her recent writings give me some slight case for anxiety."

"I'll do my very best," Paul assured him, as they reached the boulevard and lingered for a moment, before each of them took a fiacre. "She is the last person in the world that I would want to harm, or allow to come to harm...and you may be sure that if I conclude that it is in her best interests for me to stay away from her, that is what I shall do, in the kindest way possible."

They shook hands. Before saying *au revoir*, however, Flammarion said. "In the fragments of the dream I had last might that I can still remember," the astronomer said, "I had the impression that there was a carriage making its way across the battlefield, and that you were in it. Did you, by any chance, have the same impression?"

"I did," said Paul

"Do you know, perchance, where that carriage was going?"

"For the baron, yes: it was taking him where he wanted to go, in order to achieve what he believed to be his redemption. As I told you, however, I was snatched away from that climax, to which I had no further contribution to make, and carried away by a creature with wings. Where to, I have no idea, and perhaps I never shall...even if Jane has her way and I never allow myself to be hypnotized again, this isn't over. I'm still a prisoner of my own strange nature...as are we all."

"Indeed," said Flammarion, thoughtfully. "Do telephone me, won't you, so that was can meet again and make what progress is possible in the investigation of that strange nature by means of rational thought alone?"

"I will," Paul promised, and helped the old man to board a cab.

Paul did exactly has he had said, in the order that he had specified, writing separately to Madame Pommerat and Lemastur to offer his apologies for being unable to attend their next séance, and an even more diplomatic letter to Zosima making vague promises about the possible renewal of their acquaintanceship when he was next in Paris. He had to write four more polite refusals to invitations that he had collected from the hotel reception desk. Then he tried, unsuccessfully, to telephone Victor at work before he set off with the sketches that the baron had asked to buy. He and Chazelle argued for a while over the price that it was feasible and reasonable to ask for them, but Paul was able to haggle Chazelle down from exorbitant figures on the grounds that if they sold the sketches to the baron for a modest fee, he might be tempted to commission an oil painting.

Chazelle, who appeared to be unaware of the baron's medical condition, in spite of having his finger on the pulse of Parisian rumor, quipped: "Perhaps he'll ask you to paint his mistress. It's about time she got something for twenty-some years of loyal service. But these old aristocrats take everything for granted. They don't know the meaning of the word gratitude."

"That wasn't my impression," Paul told the dealer, mildly. "He seemed to me to be a man with a very precise and accurate notion of the meaning of words."

"Good," said Chazelle. "If he made a good impression on you, you probably made a good one on him. Delville's gone off to Scotland now, so he's probably ripe for choosing a new favorite—no reason why it shouldn't be you, given your penchants. You say Lautrec will collect the merchandise and bring the cash? An odd friendship, that, although there's a definite similarity of taste. The baron was something of a dandy in his day, I gather, but that was a long time ago. Danced with the Empress Eugénie once, he says, but to be honest, who didn't, back in the day? Napoléon III had two left feet, it's said—twice as many as Loubet. Did you bring any more of these with you?"

"A few, but I've given some away and I might use one or two of the others as bases for oil paintings. The baron saw them all, and these are the only ones he wanted."

"Pity. No matter, though—just concentrate on the material for the exhibition. You're not going back to Toulouse until the middle of next week, did you say?"

"Probably sooner than that, so if you want to introduce me to anyone, make it soon."

"I will, if the opportunity comes up. I haven't had that much interest, to tell the truth. You've been away for too long, and your best paintings are hidden away. The exhibition will change things, though, if you can raise your game."

"I'll do my very best," Paul promised.

When he returned to the hotel he made another attempt to telephone Victor. This time he got through.

"Well," said Victor, "how did it go in Passy? Is the baron as mad as he's said to be? Did you get any details of his various murders?"

"The baron isn't a man to commit murder," Paul told his friend. "He's as sane as you or me and has a very strong sense of justice and duty."

"More likely to encourage murders than to prevent them, in my experience," said Victor, with an unusual acumen, in spite of the blatant lie regarding his experience. "Did you get him to commission a painting?"

"No, but I drew him four quick sketches and he bought four more. I'll go to see him again before I return to Toulouse."

"You're on friendly terms, then?"

"Absolutely. I won't say that were twin souls because that would be absurd, but we found some common ground."

"That's excellent news—and I have some more. I can do lunch tomorrow. How does the Café de la Paix sound?"

"The name sounds excellent. Is the food any good?"

"Oh, hark at the boorish provincial, Surely they've heard of the Café de la Paix even in the wilds of Provence, half way up that blessed mountain that you, Gaston and I once climbed as adolescents. Dress up—in fact, buy some new clothes if you haven't already. Twelve o'clock all right?"

"Perfect. Where is it?"

"Oh, you're incorrigible. There isn't a cab driver in Paris who doesn't know it, but if you insist on walking, it's at the intersection of the Boulevard des Capucines and the Place de l'Opéra. We can have a long talk about the past and the future, Toulouse and the world, and I'll make a serious attempt to persuade you to come back to Paris. I've almost had to give up on Gaston, who fancies himself as a cosmopolitan, but I haven't lost all hope of anchoring him by finding him a nice Parisian wife, and you've got no excuse at all for putting down roots down there...unless you're in love—but it can't be that."

"Why not?"

"Firstly, because it's you, and secondly because if you were in love, you'd merely have to mention the word Paris in her ear, and she'd be begging you to bring her with you. Must go—no time at all. Until tomorrow, then?"

"Until tomorrow," Paul confirmed.

By the time he returned to Jane's house, dusk was falling.

"Madame Pommerat called," she said. "She got your note and hurried round—to try to get me to change your mind, she said, and to look at the portrait of me that you'd painted, 'about which she'd heard so much.' She told me all about her troubled relationship with dear Henri and lamented the difficulties that women our age have in managing young lovers. I refrained from strangling her—although I doubt that I could have got my short slim fingers around her thick neck—and I explained that last night's séance had drained your strength so utterly that you couldn't possibly participate in another before you returned to the Midi. She expressed her sympathy. I haven't got any writing done. How was your day."

"A complete waste of time, but I appreciated the relief from intense thinking. Victor and Chazelle are right—there is such a thing as being too *trouvère* and insufficiently Parisian. I'm having lunch at the Café de la Paix tomorrow."

"Good. Every provincial visitor to Paris ought to have lunch at the Café de la Paix. Émile Zola, with whom I once collaborated, used to eat there at one time, as well as Guy de Maupassant, whom I was accused of plagiarizing. Naturally, I can't set foot in there. Don't be tempted by the absinthe, no matter what your friend Victor says. Remember what it did to Charles Cros."

"I won't."

The conversation continued in that deliberately light vein or some time, and it was not until dessert that Jane finally said: "You know, of course, what conclusion Flammarion drew when he found us together this morning."

"Yes."

"Did he say anything on the way to the cab stand?"

"He asked me to be kind to you—but I think he knew that the request was unnecessary. He just wanted to express his concern."

"Do you mind, that he knows?"

"Knows what? Why should I mind what he might think? You said last night that you didn't care what anyone might think."

"I don't...but Camille isn't exactly *anyone*. Did you get the impression that he disapproves?"

"No. I don't believe that anyone who isn't exactly any-one would."

"Antoine advised me against it four years ago He suggested that it would be bound to end in disaster."

"That was four years ago. And what he advised us against was falling in love. Haven't we agreed that whatever there is between us, it isn't a vulgar matter of falling in love. It wasn't then, and it isn't now."

"You do know, I suppose, that it's not me I'm worried about, but you? I'm past the stage when I could be devastated by that kind of catastrophe, but you haven't even reached it for the first time yet...and we know that you're too sensitive for your own good."

"I'm not as innocent as you seem to think, and you're not as guilty. For four years we've been conscientiously following Antoine's advice to be kind to one another, and there's no earthly reason why we shouldn't continue to follow it for another forty. We can both draw strength from it, even while I'm in Toulouse and you're in Paris. I'm convinced now that we can never be entirely separated, in fact, so we ought make the most of our connection."

"That's exactly what I thought last night. Tonight, the reaction has set in. I'm afraid."

"Of what?"

"Of myself. I'm sure of you, for exactly the same reason that Juliette gave you: I know that you'll always be kind, and that it won't ever matter how much or how little you love me, because no matter how your hormones are reacting at any point in time, you'll always be kind. I'd like to think that I could do the same, but I'm prone to excess, as you've doubtless observed. I asked you last night to trust me, which you naturally did—how could you refuse—but I don't know that I can trust myself. I'm prone to jealousy, you see. I ought to have been glad that you took Juliette to Toulouse, and that you and she had a relationship that you can still look back on with satisfaction, but it's difficult for me. And when you do fall in love, out there in the Midi, with some fresh-faced young milkmaid. I'll want to be glad for you, but I don't know whether I'll be able to do it. I'm sorry."

"There's nothing for which to apologize. We're not responsible for our hormonal reactions. I know that you'll always have my best interests at heart, and that's what I need, because sometimes it's not easy for me to see what my best interests are, and it's good—invaluable, even—to have someone that I can trust who can tell me, if the need arises."

She was silent for a moment or two, and then she said: "If I were what you needed, we wouldn't be having this conversation. If I were what you needed, when I had that lunatic dream last night, as soon as I saw that you were in danger, I'd have ripped my hands and feet right through those nails, and

I'd have flapped my wings—in the dream, I'd have had wings—and I'd have flown to your rescue and carried you away. But I didn't. I was pinned down, like a butterfly in a display case, and I was jealous: jealous of the woman with wings who did what I couldn't. I don't know who she was, but I ought to be grateful to her, to love her for what she did that I couldn't. But I don't. I know that I'm not her, and that hurts me."

"But with regard to the vision, you were exactly what I needed," Paul told, "and you did do what you could. Without you, I wouldn't have known that my dream wasn't a dream. I wouldn't have known that I was in danger. And before I knew it, you had already acted. Before I could make any reckless promises to Zosima, you had swooped down and swept me away. And then you explained to me what had nearly happened, and explained to me what the voice in my dream had meant, and why. Without you, it would have been so much empty noise. You, not the ambiguous figure in the dream that flew away, were my guardian angel...better than that, in fact, because while I had you, I didn't even need a guardian angel. If the angel had known that, imagine how jealous she'd have been. The jealousy that Madame Pommerat must have felt this afternoon, when she stood in your boudoir and looked at that portrait, and ground her teeth in the unjustified conviction that I'd lied to her when I said that I'd never been in that room, would be a teardrop on the ocean by comparison."

Jane laughed. "Your flattery is coming on by leaps and bounds," she said. "Heaven only knows what it will be like when you've had lunch in the Café de la Paix, soaking up the atmosphere of all that dandyism. But I'll still be jealous of the angel, until you can tell me who she was...and if you can, I'll probably be even more jealous afterwards.

"It was real," Paul said. "The danger you sensed was real...and it isn't over. It never will be, unless my ability fades away and I become psychically blind. But it was still a kind of dream, with the particular illogic of dreams. I don't think that the winged creature was a particular individual, any more than

I, at that point in time, was a particular individual. The creature, whatever she was, was what she was and no more. She was an idea—almost a cliché—but you're not. You're an individual, and unique. If she really is capable of thought—and given that she was capable of giving me some coherent and cogent advice, she must be—she can only be jealous of you, and with reason. The reverse does not apply."

"It's a nice story," Jane said. "It would probably work on someone who hadn't spent the recent part of her catastrophic life making up stories, most of them not nice at all. But I'm being stupid. I should be glad. I am glad. If I asked you to stay in Paris, would you?"

"Of course," he said. "But precisely for that reason, you're not going to ask me, are you? You have my best interests at heart, and you have to protect me, because you know that I sometimes don't. That's one of the reasons why what we have is far better than mere lust."

"You'll never get rid of me, you know, whether you're in Toulouse and I'm in Paris, or you're in Heaven and I'm in Hell. You might think that Juliette is clinging, and that little minx Talia, but believe me, you won't know what haunting is until you've been haunted by me."

"I believe you," he said. "And you can be sure that if I ever paint an angel, it will have your face."

"I forbid it," she said. "Unless your artist's imagination can take thirty-five years off me, and show my soul they way it really was, when it was almost innocent."

He didn't challenge the use of the word *almost*. He had read her books.

"Thirty-five years ago," he said, "I wasn't even a fetus. I didn't exist even in embryo."

"If you were anyone else," she said, "it would be unkind of you to remind me of that, but I forgive you. I always will. You'll remember that, won't you? No matter how long you live, you'll never need forgiveness from me. If I haunt you, my presence will be entirely benign."

"That won't be necessary for a long time yet...and in the meantime, wherever I am, however far from Paris, I'll always be aware of your living, loving presence, and it will help me to stay sane and to make progress."

"Better and better," she said. "The flattery, that is. Will you swear to me, then, that for as long as I live, you won't allow yourself to be hypnotized again? I know that you can't help slipping into a somnifabricatory state spontaneously, and that it isn't without its dangers but promise me that you won't seek peril deliberately. Because it's not just you that it endangers is it? And you wouldn't want to endanger anyone else, would you?"

"No, I wouldn't," he said, "and for precisely that reason, you have my word. I can't stop trying to understand, but no more experiments like last night's. From now on, I'll leave Zosima in her convent, undisturbed. But there is one favor I'd like to ask, if I may."

"What's that?" she asked, suspiciously.

"When I return to Toulouse, I'd like to paint Juliette...and I'd like to paint Yvaine de Rochemure, as she is in the sketches I made, happy and unviolated."

"You don't need my permission for that," she told him, "but for what it's with, you have my blessing. You're a painter; you need to follow your inspiration. I don't say that I won't feel a twinge of jealousy, but that's irrelevant. You have my blessing, now and forever."

"Thank you," he said.

READ THE FIRST VOLUME IN THIS TRILOGY:

THE PAINTER OF SPIRITS

US$ 20.95/GBP 16.99
5x8 tpb, 248 pages
ISBN-13: 978-1-61227-900-8

Paul Furneret, a young artist working in Paris in 1901, is invited to attend a séance at Camille Flammarion's observatory after having participated in an experiment in "automatic drawing" at another séance a week earlier, in which he drew a picture, while unconscious under hypnosis, of a young woman recognized by one of the participants as his dead daughter.

Paul's friend, Victor Marvaud, is unable to accompany him, as arranged, because a ship carrying another of their friends, Gaston Lambrunet, has struck a rock in the Channel, and although all the passengers have been put into lifeboats, the one containing Gaston's mother and sister has not yet reached land. Victor insists however, that Flammarion's séance is too important for him to miss, and, in order to make sure that he gets there, has asked his physician, Antoine Cros, to take Paul to the observatory in his stead.

The skeptical Cros is also escorting the writer Jane de La Vaudère, who has previously taken part in Flammarion's experiments, and the two of them provide Paul with a great deal of food for thought on the journey. Their contrasted perspectives become all the more significant when Paul, hypnotized by a "magnetizer" named Madame Zosima, produces four images, including one of Gaston's sister, whose lifeboat still has not landed yet, Dr. Cros's late brother Charles, and a woman tentatively identified as Jane's long-dead mother.

Cros tries hard to provide a naturalistic explanations of what Paul has done, but the uncertainty as to the fate of the lifeboat turns Paul's artwork and its apparent supernatural nature into headline news, spurring the participants in the séance to meet up again in Dr. Cros's house the following night in order to discuss the implications of Paul's seeming ability to draw the dead, albeit unconsciously.

A second experiment produces even more challenging results, which throw Paul's life into dire confusion, nearly cost a young model her life, and also affect the lives of his new acquaintances, leaving Paul with difficult dilemmas to address and an intriguing metaphysical mystery to resolve...